Born and raised in Stockport, Jo has always loved reading, puzzles and music. After graduating in Chemistry from Oxford she was employed in various marketing management roles, but after having children, has focused on raising her family, caring for her parents and writing.

Dear Fellow Reader,

Thank you so much for choosing this book. I do hope you enjoy it. If you too love puzzles, perhaps you will try to beat Ben, Jess and Freddie in cracking the codes. But you don't have to. Read and relax, if you're not in the mood.

Should you feel inclined to follow part of, or all of their trail, you will find that one dark and unsettling venue is now much brighter, whilst the ghostly apparitions in another have vanished (for now) to make room for a restaurant.

An appetite for science has also got to cater for its stomach, I suppose, as Aunt Miriam maintains. (But Freddie and Uncle Henry are still loudly complaining.)

Warmest wishes,

Jo Welch March 2016

*To my darling daughters, husband, mother and fondly
remembered father.*

J.D. Welch

The Einstein Code

AUSTIN MACAULEY
PUBLISHERS LTD.

A CIP catalogue record for this title is available from the British Library.

ISBN 9781786129871 (Paperback)
ISBN 9781786129888 (Hardback)
ISBN 9781786129895 (E-Book)

www.austinmacauley.com

First Published (2016)
Austin Macauley Publishers Ltd.
25 Canada Square
Canary Wharf
London
E14 5LQ

Acknowledgements

My warmest thanks to those whose encouragement and feedback was so helpful to an aspiring author, especially Almira, Charlotte and all my friends at Commonword, Verna Wilkins and also Malorie Blackman, Melvin Burgess and all others who made Arvon so valuable; and to Neil who made it possible.

Many thanks also to the kind readers who encouraged me to persist with this book, after sampling important sections as it evolved, or reading the entire draft: Catherine, Jonny, Elinor, Lydia, Katie, David and Louis, plus school groups from Tithe Barn, Priestnall, St John's and Colmers (special thanks there to Jo and Kelly).

My heartfelt thanks to Mum for inspiring the love of reading that has so enriched my life and my love for whom gave me the initial idea for this book.

Particular thanks to Emma and Laura, my final draft checkers and intrepid code crackers. Emma has read every version of this (and every story I've written) with unflagging enthusiasm; and Laura's artistic insights have been invaluable. Thank you, my darlings.

And finally, to Tom, Lynne and all at Austin Macauley who have transformed my dream into reality, thank you so much.

Prologue

The woman waited, hidden, listening, in the dusty, cramped enclosure. Two men entered the room talking, an American and an Asian. She recognised neither. She frowned. Had she made a stupid mistake?

But then *he* entered, and she knew the long drive had been worthwhile. He was discussing *her* product with these strangers. How *dare* he? And what was he talking about? Making it for them? Why? It was far too toxic to apply to crops.

She listened carefully, amassing evidence. Four of them, no five would buy it. The Chief would retain the lion's share. But use it for *what*? And who was this Chief they kept mentioning? Not present, but obviously the kingpin of the operation. John Knox? But no one referred to Sir John as the Chief.

'Sorry I'm late, everyone,' said a light, pleasant voice.

She gasped. *No!* Not *him*? Surely *he* couldn't be involved in this sordid scheme? Now their discussion became more intense, their voices quieter, their plans murkier, but she could hear every word they said from her perfect vantage point. Knowing him so well, she couldn't believe he was flogging off her star product as mere rat poison. And how irresponsible! It was far too dangerous to be sold as a rat poison. Burning to march out and stop the meeting, she instead forced herself to wait, amassing evidence.

Poison *people*? Horrified, her hand flew to her mouth but knocked against the tight wooden enclosure.

'Thought I heard a noise. Out there,' the American said.

'I'll check.' Shoes clacked across the wooden floor towards her hidey-hole. She daren't breathe. They were ruthless killers, they wouldn't hesitate.

Ben, I'm so sorry. I love you.

She waited, taut as a trampoline, as his footsteps approached – and then passed, going on to the main door. Listening to him pulling it open, she exhaled slowly.

'No one there.'

'Better not be.'

As he returned to the group she felt sick with relief, and even sicker as she heard of their plans. *Millions* would die, men, women – and *children*. They would mainly target *children*. They were *monsters*.

Desperate for them to finish, longing to be away from these disgustingly depraved men and at home with her beloved Ben, she waited in the darkness, determined to stop them.

She knew two of the men outside, she would start with them. She would have to cancel her holiday and move fast. They were on the brink of mass production – a week, maybe two, was all she had.

But she must be very careful indeed. As the only witness against such murderous men she would be in terrible danger – and so would Ben, she realised, her stomach contracting in fear.

She couldn't bear exposing Ben to such monsters. Maybe Miriam would have him? He'd hate being there, away from home and from her, but she must insist. They wouldn't be truly safe until she'd found the Chief – bound to be a man, Pete would never take orders from a woman.

And then she sneezed …

Chapter 1

Prey

As they left school Ben turned his phone on and noticed Mum's text. Trouble?

V late night cld even be midnight sorry. Go to M's. Love, Mum xxf

'Oh… shoot!' he cursed, mindful of the Deputy Head looming ahead.

'Wassup?' Naz asked.

'Mum's stuck at work, so that stuffs the takeaway.' He'd been looking forward to it all afternoon, having missed lunch for Chess Club with Naz.

'Bummer,' sympathised Jonno.

'Yeah.'

'Takeaway? Why?' asked Naz.

'Holidays. Mum's off too. Both weeks.'

'Cool. No HHoH then?' Jonno asked, shorthand for Henry's House of Horror, his name for Aunt Miriam's (on account of the man she had unaccountably married).

'Except Easter Sunday lunch, and that's with Mum so that'll be okay,' Ben said absently, re-reading the unbelievable text. 'But tonight will be pants. She wants me to go there now.'

'What? For two or three hours?'

'She won't be back till midnight, she reckons. Weird. She's never that late.'

'What does xxf mean?' Naz asked.

'She's mistyped,' Ben said briefly, exiting the text to stop Naz prying. But she was a stickler for accuracy and it should read xfe, meaning love you forever. Something was wrong, he knew it. 'I'll call her.'

'I wouldn't do that if I were you,' Dan warned, smirking.

'Why not?' he asked, hesitating.

'You're not gonna go to your mad uncle's are you?'

'No way. Not even if she paid me.'

'She'd never do that.'

'She should. I spend half my life there. It's so not fair.'

'Yeah. Like she gets paid for working, so why don't you get paid for going there?' Jonno agreed.

It was a frequent argument at home.

'It's Miriam I should be paying, not you,' Mum would say. 'She pays for all your treats herself, you know. Well, Henry wouldn't.'

'No. He hates spending money even more than he hates me,' Ben would reply.

'He doesn't hate you.'

'Yeah he does. And Freddie and Robert, they hate me too.'

'Miriam and Jess love you. You know they do.'

'But it's not my home. This is.'

'Sorry, Ben. I really am. I wish my job didn't force me to travel so much.'

'Get another job.'

'I can't. Not without retraining.'

'Retrain then. You're smart.'

'But you don't get *paid* to retrain. Often you have to pay them. I can't afford a year without wages. Sorry, Ben.

I'm stuck in agrochemicals, which means stuck in SPC. Unless we move?'

'No! No way.' Ben loved home life. He just wished he had much more of it and much less of Henry's House of Horror.

'If you phone her she's gonna make you go there,' Dan warned.

'I'm not! No way on earth.'

'She won't like it.'

'I don't care. I'm not going.'

'Why should you? You're fourteen next week.'

'The week after,' Ben corrected him. 'But it's next Saturday we're celebrating, remember? Two-fifteen at the cinema. Then we're going for a meal,' he added as casually as he could manage. Dining out without adults was a new and exciting step for him, but not for Naz or Jonno with their elder siblings, he realised, so he wasn't stupid enough to say so. The three of them confirmed they'd be there as they reached the shops. Dan and Jonno called in for snacks, but Ben, penniless, continued home, hoping there would be something to scavenge there.

But there wasn't. Not in the bread bin, the cupboard or the fridge, apart from milk and Parmesan and a few unpromising jars. But then he tried the freezer, and there saw the pizza, pepperoni and peppers, his favourite – and started to see what a fun night it could be.

There was no one to tell him not to eat at the computer desk, so he did.

There was no one to tell him to hang up his blazer, so he didn't.

And there was no one to tell him he'd spent too long on the computer, so he played and played and played. It wasn't until long after nightfall that he remembered the strangeness of Mum's meeting. He checked the time and, shocked it was eleven-thirty already, called her. There was no answer either from her work phone or her mobile, so she was presumably driving home.

He resumed the game but kept looking left, checking the road for cars. As midnight approached he walked to the window and peered into the darkness. The gleam of approaching headlights gave him hope, but the car continued along the main road rather than turning up theirs. There was no traffic for a long time after that. The chill of the still wintry night bit at him. He shivered.

She should be home by now. He returned to the desk to call her, but her mobile was turned off. He checked her text but there was no hint as to where she was or what she was doing. He resumed his post at the window, impatient to see her car, but the road remained stubbornly silent whilst he became increasingly anxious.

Suddenly he thought, what if she's gone to Aunt Miriam's to pick me up? Oh no! He'd be in so much trouble. Turning, he realised he'd be in even deeper trouble if she saw the state of the lounge. He snapped into action, carrying the dirty pots through to the kitchen and putting them into the dishwasher along with the pizza slice. Returning to the lounge, he shut down the computer, then flicked off the light and went through to the hall. He hung up his blazer and checked he'd locked the front door before hurrying upstairs to the sanctuary of his bedroom. He was in bed feigning sleep in under a minute. In a couple of minutes he was dead to the world.

BANG! Ben woke, panicking at the noise downstairs, until he realised it would just be Mum getting in. He got up to find out why she was home so late, but as he reached the doorway, he heard a man speaking downstairs. He froze, hardly daring to breathe, listening.

'She just says there was a meetin', not wharrit was about.'

'Yeah but he can't know there *was* a meetin',' another Mancunian man replied.

The phone downstairs bleeped and announced, 'Message erased. You have no new messages.'

'Check around, don't just stand there gawpin'.'

Hearing them move about downstairs Ben opened his bedroom door wider to see if Mum had heard them too. Her door was shut. She must be asleep in there, when he needed her so much. He waited, willing her to appear, but she didn't.

'*Mum*!' he breathed, desperate for a response, but of course there was none. He would have to shout to wake her up and with them downstairs, he daren't.

He pulled his door wider and ventured out into the darkness, heart hammering, breath ragged, mouth dry. If they left the lounge they'd see him at the top of the stairs, but there was no other way to reach her. As he carefully placed his foot down, a treacherous floorboard creaked beneath him.

He froze.

'What was tha'?'

'Could it be the kid upstairs?'

Me?

''E'll be at 'er sister's, Pete said.'

'Sweet. So 'e won't know she's missin' till mornin'.'

'NO!' The cry was wrenched from deep within him, a howl of horror and shock and despair. The agony doubled him over, but as he straightened and saw her door still shut, he knew for sure she wasn't home. So where was she?

He charged downstairs. The lounge door opened and a man emerged, tall, bald and bulky. Ben shouldered him off and kept going, through the open door, onto the empty drive that should have contained her car and out into the cold, dark night.

'GERRIM!'

A white Mercedes saloon with tinted windows was parked outside, presumably theirs. It faced the top of the road, so Ben ran down it, desperate to escape, desperate to find help, desperate to find her. Heavy footsteps pounded down the drive as he turned the corner, so he veered left towards the main road, just as an engine flared into life.

He raced towards the shops, usually bustling with helpful staff and friendly shoppers, but now, in the dead of night, deserted – yet still brightly lit. In his white T-shirt and pants he'd stand out like a peacock in a penguin parade.

He turned left towards the park then left again towards the library, where there were lots of dark side streets to duck down. He needed a phone, fast. His friends' parents might help, but might not hear him, or choose not to answer the door in the middle of the night. In the absence of Mum the only person he could truly count on was Aunt Miriam, but she lived two miles away in Didsbury. Twenty minutes, twenty-five tops, he reckoned, wishing he had running shoes on and not bare feet.

Turning down Thornfield Road he heard a car approaching, so decided to cut through the park. The gates were shut and secured by a single internal bolt. With the engine getting ominously louder Ben curled his fingers through the ornate ironwork and pushed, but the bolt was stiff and resisted.

'*Come on*!' he urged, pushing with all his might. As he spotted the car rounding the corner, a white Mercedes heading towards him, the surge of fear gave him the impetus to beat the bolt. He yanked open the gate and raced through into the dark park, diving behind the screening trees as the car purred past. He got up and ran, but only managed a few paces before the car stopped. At the traffic lights? Or was someone getting out to grab him?

He headed for the nearest exit, past the play area onto Mauldeth Road, but to get to Didsbury Road he'd have to turn left towards them. Unless he tried the track by the allotments? It led towards Didsbury, maybe not all the way, but at least the first part of the journey would be pedestrianized, so Mercedes-proof. It was a dark, narrow footpath, which he'd never consider on a normal night, but this was the weirdest night ever – and getting weirder, and scarier, by the minute.

The park exit was open so he went straight through, but a few paces on he heard the car start up. It turned towards him, only seconds away. He plunged into the nearest garden, hurdled a flowerbed onto the lawn and crouched behind some giant rhododendrons, just beating the car, which was travelling unnervingly slowly. He found a gap between the waxy leaves and peered out.

A face, bald, bearded and angry, was staring back at him, leaning out of an open window, as if searching for something. Or someone.

Me, Ben thought, sick with fear. He's searching for me. He should never have stopped. He shouldn't have hidden. He should have kept running. He'd been so stupid. He crouched, shivering, awaiting the inevitable.

But slowly, unnervingly slowly, the car continued on. Had the man not seen him? Ben forced himself to wait, pressed into the leaves, with cold dew trickling down his neck, until he finally heard the car round the bend towards the tennis club.

He left the soft damp grass and ran down the hard path and across the painfully stuccoed road. He sprinted the last few feet of pavement then swung onto the soothing mud of the allotment track, which quickly became painfully stony, but he didn't falter. He had to find help fast.

He was safely shrouded in darkness by the time they returned, but as he passed the brambles where every September he and Mum picked blackberries, his mind was spinning with questions.

Who are they? How do they know about us? Where is she?

But the only people that could tell him were out to get him.

Chapter 2

Henry's House of Horror

St James's church meant he'd reached Didsbury at last, but birds were chirping so it would soon be light. Watching for their car, he ran as fast as his tired legs could manage past the spookily silent bars, bistros and prohibitively expensive shops of Didsbury Village (as residents ridiculously termed the bustling Manchester suburb). Exhausted, both physically and emotionally, the terror gripping his guts drove him on. Left by the cheese shop, right, left, right and at last he turned onto the tree-lined road of enormous Victorian houses, redbrick, detached and daunting, where Aunt Miriam lived.

Their house was halfway down on the left, with three incongruously modest cars parked outside, now that Robert had passed his driving test. He mounted the steps to the oversized door and banged on it, carefully avoiding the valuable but ugly stained glass (featuring hideous sea monsters) and kept his finger on the doorbell until Uncle Henry appeared.

'What a racket! You'll have woken half the neighbours!' he complained, grappling with their numerous locks. At last he opened the door. 'What on earth?' His jaw gaped and his eyes looked Ben up and down with disbelief and even more disgust than usual. Tall, thin and angular, he had long, slim hands, stick-thin legs and a large hooked nose. His black hair was currently tousled and he was wrapped in a burgundy dressing gown, but Ben was bare-armed, bare-legged and cold in the chilly morning air. Uncle Henry was barring the doorway, blocking him.

'Mum's missing. I need to call the police,' Ben said. His long face screwed into a ball of disbelief. '*Please*. She's been gone all night.'

Uncle Henry retreated into the hall, allowing Ben to edge inside, but then he gawped at Ben's feet. Ben looked down. They were in a bad way, muddy and bleeding, but that didn't matter, nothing mattered except finding Mum.

'I need a phone.'

'Stay there!' Uncle Henry barked. 'MIRIAM!' he roared towards the stairs, then turned back to Ben. 'Don't move a step off that mat. You'll get blood on the tiles!' Multi-coloured Victorian monstrosities but, like everything in the Winterburn home, prohibitively expensive. 'MIRIAM!'

Mum's elder and only sister emerged from the stairs. Dark-haired, short and plump, she was as physically different from Mum as possible, but so similar in temperament that Ben and she had always got on.

'Ben! What's wrong?'

He stepped towards her.

'Wait there!' Uncle Henry again commanded, glaring at his feet.

'Oh Ben! What's happened?' Aunt Miriam exclaimed looking horrified at Ben's appearance. 'The poor boy's shivering, Henry, he needs some clothes. Get some of Robert's. You won't wake him.'

'A brass band wouldn't wake him,' he grumped, but he went upstairs, giving Ben a chance to speak.

'We need to get the police. Mum's missing.'

'*What*?'

He quickly summarised the events of the night, watching his fear, confusion and horror mirrored on her face. He hated upsetting her so.

'Come on, Ben.' She led him briskly down the hall towards their kitchen. He followed her gingerly, more for fear of damaging the tiles than of hurting his feet. The kitchen was huge, with a central oak table at which she told him to sit. 'Let me get you a drink,' she added.

'Mum first, *please*,' he entreated, dropping onto a chair. 'Phone the police.'

'I can do both,' she said, and did, getting him water, orange juice and a bowl of granola, whilst omitting no detail of the harrowing night – except about Pete, which was Ben's fault since he'd forgotten to mention him. She was still talking as she filled a bowl with water and, supporting the handset between her shoulder and her chin, used both hands to pour in two capfuls of disinfectant. She placed it by him, nodding at his feet.

He caught his breath as his feet hit the water. The pain was as sharp as knives, but diminished quickly.

Was Mum in pain? Was she cold, too? He had never felt so frightened. Where was she?

As Jess bounced in, Aunt Miriam said, 'I've just phoned the police.'

'Why?' she asked excitedly. Fair-haired like him, she was small, slight and already dressed (in a green jumper and purple trousers, her favourite colour combination). Conscious of his underpants, Ben shuffled his chair further under the table.

'Aunt Sue's missing,' Aunt Miriam explained, giving him a towel and a box of plasters. Jess's face fell.

'Oh no. Why?'

'Can you explain, Ben? I can't let the police see me like this.' Clutching her coffee, she hurried towards the door.

'I don't know why, Jess. I wish I did,' Ben replied, applying plasters to the worst cuts.

'Why are your feet so bad? Why aren't you dressed?'

Ben was saved from responding, and Aunt Miriam prevented from leaving, by the return of a grumbling Uncle Henry with an armful of clothes.

'The mess on his floor! It's worse than a pigsty! And in here! Look!' he added, pointing to Ben's blood-and-mud footsteps.

He hadn't seen the hall yet.

'Sorry.'

'Ben's feet are washed now. Give him those clothes, he's freezing.'

'He's filthy! He needs a shower first.'

'He was running for his life, Henry, he hardly had time to dress. Put them on, Ben. They'll soon wash. Which is where I'm going, Henry. The police are on their way.'

'Running for your life?' Jess queried, eyes wide with fascination. She sat under their Museums of Manchester poster, depicting Manchester Museum, the Science and Industry Museum, the People's History Museum and many, many more fascinating (to them) venues. 'Why?'

'Tell you in a minute.'

Glaring at him, Uncle Henry dumped the clothes on the table; a navy jumper, grey sweat pants and sports socks. In their draughty house with his stingy eye on the thermostat it often felt colder inside than out, so Ben reached for them gratefully. They smelled clean and the jumper was gratifyingly thick. Even more gratifyingly, Uncle Henry left, but whilst Ben attempted to eat his cereal he was

bombarded by Jess's questions. Why, what, where, who –
but she raised an interesting point.

'If they'd kicked the door in, you'd have noticed.'

'I didn't have time to notice.'

'You don't notice what's expected. You notice the
unexpected. Every detective knows that,' said Jess, a keen
fan of mystery stories. 'So the door was undamaged. They
must have had a key.'

'They can't have,' Ben maintained, but it made him
wonder.

Uncle Henry returned, now dressed in trousers, shirt
and jumper.

'Why didn't you call the police from home instead of
bothering us?' he grumbled, restarting the coffee machine.

'Burglars chased him through the night,' Jess said.

'*Burglars*?' He couldn't have looked more incredulous
if Ben had claimed to see fairies flitting about the worktops.

'Yes, Ben was burgled, well we think he was, but
maybe they just came to wipe the answer machine and
capture you,' Jess finished, turning towards Ben.

'*Capture* him? *Why*?'

'Dunno,' Ben replied, as baffled as Uncle Henry.

'It's not as if you could have identified them, is it? If
they hadn't come searching for you, you wouldn't have
posed a risk to them,' said Jess, her sharp brain working
faster than Ben's, as was usually the case with the
Winterburns – apart from Robert, who had never been as
clever as his dad would like.

As Uncle Henry left, clutching his drink, Freddie
entered, wearing jeans, a jumper and zebra slippers more
suited to a boy of five than fifteen. Though small and dark-
haired like his mum, he was more like his father in every
other way, looking down on fashion and sport and modern

music (by which he meant anything produced in the last 150 years) and many other things. He was yawning.

'What are you doing waking us all up?'

'Can you tell him whilst I finish my breakfast?' Ben asked Jess, who animatedly did, giving him a chance to think. If they had used a key, they must have got it from someone. The men said Pete knew that Ben was supposed to be at Aunt Miriam's. To have such intimate knowledge of their family life, Pete must surely work at SPC with Mum, but Ben couldn't think of her mentioning anyone with that name. Debs, Mum's closest colleague and friend, would doubtless know him, but her number was on his mobile at home. Unless those burglars had pinched it?

'Then Mum phoned the police,' Jess concluded.

'The police? But she's probably just having a dirty weekend with some boyfriend,' Freddie said.

'She doesn't have boyfriends!' Ben protested.

'She wouldn't tell you if she had, would she? You'd be the last person to know,' Freddie said, grinning in such an infuriatingly superior way that Ben swore at him, just as Uncle Henry returned for a refill.

'We don't allow language like that in this house,' he said.

Tempted to swear at him as well, Ben instead swallowed his anger down and muttered an apology. He'd promised Mum to follow Uncle Henry's rules in his house, but what a lot of rules he made, and they were constantly changing, which added to the tension in Henry's House of Horror.

The doorbell rang.

'More visitors.' Uncle Henry glared balefully at the kitchen clock.

'It'll be the police,' said Ben, hopeful at last.

Inspector Bill Davies and Sergeant Shazia Khan were soon seated in the sitting room (as Uncle Henry insisted on calling their bookshelf-lined and TV-void lounge). The room contained three large sofas and Uncle Henry's imposing leather chair, which no one else was allowed to occupy. The police chose the sofa under the stained-glass window, whilst Ben sat alongside Aunt Miriam and Jess on the largest sofa, opposite the ornate marble fireplace. Freddie sat on the small two-seater beside his dad's chair.

Once again Ben had to run through the terrifying events of the night but he struggled to make a point before Uncle Henry rubbished it. He claimed Ben couldn't have heard everything they said, couldn't be sure the Mercedes was theirs and was scathing about the fact he hadn't got the number-plate of either the car containing Goatee Man (as Ben now called the scary bearded man) or the one parked outside his house – which would be identical, Ben believed.

'The roads were empty. There can't have been two white Mercs with tinted windows driving round the Heatons at that time.'

'Of course there could. How many Mercedes are there in Manchester?' Uncle Henry asked the police, as if they'd know.

'I don't know, sir, but it's true we can't be sure it's the same car,' Inspector Davies replied, disconcertingly.

Uncle Henry was so incredulous about Pete and the Chief that he practically accused Ben of lying.

'What you're saying implies that a gang, the Chief and Pete and those thugs you say broke in, have kidnapped her. And who would want to kidnap *her*? Or *you*?'

'I don't know. But that's what I heard and that's what happened,' Ben insisted, feeling his jaw tighten with anger.

'There's nothing to suggest she's been kidnapped. Kidnapping's a very rare crime,' said Inspector Davies.

'Much more likely she's staying the night with a colleague.'

'She wouldn't leave Ben. He's only thirteen,' Aunt Miriam said. Sergeant Khan goggled, as people often did when learning Ben's age, because he was already taller than most adults. 'And she's a good mother. An excellent mother.' Ben noticed Uncle Henry rolling his eyes as Aunt Miriam said this. It made him so angry, the way Uncle Henry assumed single mum meant bad mum. His mum was a great mum. But where was she?

'She thought she'd be late,' he revealed. 'So she said I should come here.'

'Why didn't you?' Aunt Miriam looked so hurt that he felt a pang of guilt.

'Because I wanted to see Mum come home. And to play on the computer,' he added, guiltily.

'You've always been too truthful for your own good,' Aunt Miriam said, causing Uncle Henry to roll his eyes again, with Inspector Davies watching him.

Oh great. Now he'd think Ben was a liar.

Sergeant Khan suggested he call Mum. Appalled he hadn't already done so, he asked for permission to use their phone – well, one of them. There were so many handsets in so many rooms that the house was practically a call centre, Mum had joked (horrifying Uncle Henry, which made it funnier than it would otherwise have been).

With everyone watching, he dialled her mobile. He had never wanted to speak to her more, but her mobile was still switched off. She didn't pick up at home either, though he held on for a long time, hoping.

'Ring off, Ben darling, so that she can get through if she calls us,' Aunt Miriam said.

'Oh yeah, sorry.' Ringing home had made Ben long to be there, so he asked the police for a lift, but they insisted they had to check it was safe first. They requested Aunt Miriam's spare key and whilst she went to get it, asked about other spares.

'Only me, Mum and Aunt Miriam have keys – and Helen next door,' Ben added. 'She wouldn't give them our key.'

'You're sure the door was locked?' Freddie said.

'Positive. I locked it myself.'

'They probably kicked it in then.'

'No they didn't. They must have had a key,' Jess maintained.

'We'll go and check,' said Inspector Davies. They took the address, plus details of Mum's workplace and then left.

'What can I do now?' he asked Aunt Miriam.

'Take a shower,' Freddie replied. 'You stink.'

'Freddie! You don't,' said Aunt Miriam. 'But a shower will make you feel better. You'll need some clean underwear, won't you?'

'He can't have mine!' Freddie cried, looking horrified.

'Yours wouldn't fit him. I'll get you some of Henry's,' Aunt Miriam said. Ben didn't have the energy to be as appalled as he would normally be; he felt emotionally numb to everything apart from the loss of Mum, which was overwhelmingly painful and terrifying and mystifying.

He followed Aunt Miriam upstairs, wishing he'd given a better account of himself against Uncle Henry. The police had hardly believed him about the men. He was glad they were going to check the house, so they would see he'd been telling the truth.

The shower was warm and it felt better to be clean. The boxers were disgusting, but better than no pants, he told himself as he pulled them up. He quickly finished dressing and hurried downstairs.

Aunt Miriam was in the kitchen, glugging coffee. Jess was in full flow, fizzing with theories.

'Any news?' Ben asked, cutting in.

'Not yet I'm afraid. Do you want another drink?' Aunt Miriam asked.

'No thanks. I just want Mum.'

'Of course you do, darling. We all do. But the police will find her for us. She'll be back with us soon.'

But she wasn't. All around the house were family photos of the five Winterburns but without Mum, Ben had no family. Suddenly he felt so alone.

'Can I phone her again?'

'Of course. Jess, get the phone book please. We should try the local hospitals, in case she's had an accident.'

There was again no answer from either her mobile or home.

'She'll phone just as soon as she can. We'll leave the landline free for her to get in touch. We'll use my mobile to call the hospitals,' Aunt Miriam said, thoughtfully.

Jess returned with the phone book and gave her mum the first number. Ben waited by the kitchen handset, willing it to ring, whilst listening to Aunt Miriam describe Mum to various A and E departments, once Jess had given her the number from the phone book. (There were no mobile internet-enabled devices in the house, apart from Uncle Henry's phone, so the only computer downstairs was a desktop in Uncle Henry's study, where he was doubtless working and it would be easier to access the Crown Jewels than that.)

But Mum wasn't in Stepping Hill, Macclesfield Hospital, Manchester Royal, Wythenshawe Hospital or even Salford Royal.

'But why she'd be that far north I don't know,' said Aunt Miriam. 'Where might she have had the meeting?'

'Usually on-site, when in the UK,' Ben said, meaning in Wilmslow, where SPC's headquarters were based.

'Didn't you ask?'

'I phoned her but she didn't answer,' said Ben, wishing he'd phoned her earlier in the evening rather than wasting so much time on the computer.

The doorbell rang. He and Jess raced to answer it, Aunt Miriam and Freddie following in their wake. He hoped it would be Mum, but it was just Sergeant Khan.

She handed the key back to Aunt Miriam and said there was no sign of burglars.

'What? None at all?' asked Jess, looking as astounded as Ben.

'None. Maybe they saw her having an accident and pinched her bag. That would explain how they got her keys.'

'But not what they did,' said Freddie. 'If what Ben said happened actually happened.' He made it sound as unlikely as mermaids in the Mersey.

'It did! Did no one else see the Merc?'

'I don't know. We didn't get as far as door-to-door enquiries. They didn't appear to have stolen anything either,' she added, before Ben could ask *why* they hadn't got as far as door-to-door enquiries.

'You frightened them off,' Aunt Miriam said to Ben.

'*If* they existed,' Freddie murmured.

'They did!'

Sergeant Khan asked for a recent photo to put on the Police National Computer.

'You take lots when they're little but I haven't taken photos for a while,' Aunt Miriam replied.

'I did! Last Christmas!' Jess exclaimed, her blond ponytail bobbing and her blue eyes shining in her enthusiasm to help. Her physical similarities to him and her pleasant manner made her much more of a Baxter than a Winterburn, Ben had always felt.

'Thank goodness we got you a camera,' her mother responded, smiling at her.

'Yes. They're in my bedroom.' She scampered upstairs whilst the sergeant asked Aunt Miriam about any financial pressures or health worries Mum had.

'None that I know of. And I'm sure she'd have told me, or Ben, or both of us.'

'Yeah. There's nothing,' Ben confirmed.

'There's been no accidents reported involving your mum's car overnight. I've checked.'

'Thank you,' Ben said, the unease in his guts growing. What other explanation could there be for Mum's continued silence?

'It might be worth double-checking if there were any financial pressures she'd tried to conceal. Often that's why adults disappear. Or relationship problems.'

'She didn't have any relationship problems. Sue and Ben get on wonderfully well.'

'With boyfriends I meant.'

'She doesn't have any boyfriends! She's devoted to Ben. He's devoted to her.'

Jess returned, brandishing the photo like a trophy.

'Here it is. Sorry, I had to take it out of my album.'

Ben looked at it. Mum was giving Jess the bright smile he so loved, a smile he would love to be seeing now. He handed it to Sergeant Khan.

'Thank you. It's a good clear image,' she congratulated Jess. She stood up. 'I'll get it on the national database back at the station. I'll be your designated contact. Here's my number.'

'Thank you. But you won't find her back in the station,' Aunt Miriam said.

'We do a lot online now. And there's a lot you can do. I recognise it's a very difficult time for you, but you know her best, so any enquiries you can make will be a great help.'

Grim-faced, Aunt Miriam ushered her to the door and showed her out. She turned back to Ben, looking disgusted.

'So it's down to us, not them, in other words. So much for our fabulous police force.'

She was drifting away from him like smoke from a bonfire. He was terrified she too would vanish into the sky.

Chapter 3

The Einstein Code

The key to finding Mum was finding where she'd last been seen, they agreed. Which meant finding out where the meeting had been.

'I need to get home. I need to talk to Debs,' Ben said.

'I'll take you and help with the investigations there,' offered Aunt Miriam. 'Jess, could you continue ringing hospitals here?'

'If they're not local I'll need to get the numbers online. I could check out missing persons' sites too.'

'Good idea. Come on then. You too, Ben, please. We need to get something on your poor feet.'

'I'm not bothered about them, I'm bothered about Mum.'

'I know, darling. We all are. Come on, let's get Jess set up, then we can go.'

They started to climb the stairs behind Aunt Miriam. Her study was on the second floor, Uncle Henry having nabbed the larger, grander room downstairs for himself, of course.

'You'll need to log me in,' Jess told Aunt Miriam. 'We only get an hour now Dad's changed the settings.'

'How do you get your homework done?' Ben responded, surprised. Jess looked confused. 'Most of ours is online,' he added.

'We still use text books.'

'I must tell your father,' said Aunt Miriam drily. 'All the money he's saving on energy bills will make him feel better about the fortune we lavish on school fees.' All his cousins were privately educated. Jess attended Manchester's leading girls' independent, whilst her brothers attended the male counterpart.

Freddie was on the landing, approaching the stairs.

'Where are you going?' he asked.

'To Mum's computer,' Jess said.

'But she's not done her practice!' Freddie wailed, causing Aunt Miriam and Jess to stop and turn to him. Ben groaned inwardly, tapping his foot in frustration at the delay.

'I'm not *playing*, Freddie, I'm trying to find Aunt Sue.'

'Have you done your piano yet?' Aunt Miriam asked.

'Surely not today.'

'Yes, today. Else how will you pass your grade eight?'

'Genius, Mother, genius,' Freddie replied with his cocky grin.

'Go and do your practice.'

'Why not Jess?'

'Because we need her to find Aunt Sue.'

Freddie's eyes widened and mouth gaped. He couldn't have looked more aghast if she'd slapped him. But rather than engaging further with Freddie, as Ben feared she would, Aunt Miriam turned away and continued on to her study. Freddie gave Jess a filthy look, but she too ignored him. He went downstairs, muttering.

Despite the study being as huge as all the bedrooms, it was so full of bookshelves, boxes and tottering piles of books that there was hardly room for the three of them in there. Aunt Miriam taught history at Manchester University and Uncle Henry was a physics professor there. They were the brainiest parents Ben knew. Aunt Miriam sat down and switched on the computer whilst Jess and Ben stood behind her. It took an agonising age to come to life.

'There you are Jess, you're in,' said Aunt Miriam, rising from the chair. 'Ben, you'll need something on your feet.'

'It's okay. I'm fine,' he replied, desperate to get going.

'I'm not putting your no doubt extremely painful feet through yet more punishment. What size are you?'

'Nine.'

'Henry's will fit you then. He'll have an old pair of trainers you can borrow.'

She went into their bedroom. Ben waited, worrying, listening to Freddie's furious scales. Aunt Miriam soon emerged, carrying shoes old men wear on the beach.

'Will these do?'

'Great,' Ben said. They hurt, but he would have forced his feet into skinny stilettos if it would get him home.

Freddie came out of the music room whilst Aunt Miriam was finding her car keys and Ben was waiting by the front door.

'Where are you going?'

'Home.'

'Why?'

'To get my mobile and speak to Debs.'

'What about me? What should I do?' he whined to his mother, who had emerged from the kitchen carrying her handbag.

'Anything you can think of that we're not. Of which I'm sure there'll be plenty,' Aunt Miriam responded drily.

In the car they lapsed into silence, Aunt Miriam concentrating on driving whilst Ben gazed out of the window, worrying. What did those men mean by missing?

He should have asked, no, *demanded* to know what they knew about Mum. For the first time, a frightful possibility occurred to him, one that caused a sickly taste to enter his mouth and his stomach to constrict with fear. After her reaction earlier, he realised it might terrify Aunt Miriam too, so he waited till they stopped at Parrs Wood lights.

'What if Mum's dead?'

'She's not. I'm absolutely sure she's not,' she replied, smiling reassuringly.

'Why?'

'Those men said she was missing, didn't they?'

'If you're dead you're missing.'

'No, you're not. If you're dead you're departed. Missing is a present continuous state, Ben. She's alive somewhere and those men know it. I'll bet they stole her bag from the scene of an accident, as Sergeant Khan said.'

'But why come to our house?'

'To burgle you. But you scared them off.'

'So why did they come searching for me?'

'It might not have been them. It's not often I admit it, but your uncle might have a point. The police seemed to think so.'

'They definitely mentioned Pete and the Chief. They're from SPC, I know it.'

'Ask Debs. She'll know them too.'

'Yeah.'

Pulling up outside the house, knowing Mum wouldn't be inside was awful. It was so different from her being away on business. Not knowing where she was and when she'd come back was agonising – and the fear that she might not come back was gnawing at his insides, whatever Aunt Miriam said.

She unlocked the door. The hall proved he hadn't been dreaming.

'Look, my bag's tipped over. I didn't trip over it, they must have.'

'There you are! Ahead of the police already. I've a good mind to call Sergeant Khan.'

'Useless. We'll get more out of Debs.'

Ben had left his mobile on the computer desk, so he went into the lounge. The curtains were open, but otherwise it looked like it always did.

'Probably the police opened them to look round,' said Aunt Miriam. 'Everything looks in order, doesn't it?'

Ben agreed it did.

'They were here, with the answer phone,' he said, patting the desk. The new message light was blinking. He pressed it hopefully, but it was just him earlier, begging Mum to pick up.

'What was in the message they wiped?'

'Something about a meeting, I think.'

'It was a message for you presumably. Didn't you listen to it?'

'No, I wish I had,' Ben admitted, flooded with guilt. He was a useless son. He'd ignored her message, he'd played on the computer while she was having a terrible accident or something unimaginably awful, and he'd run away from the only men that might know where she was and what had happened to her.

'They didn't take the computer or TV. So they're not common or garden thieves,' said Aunt Miriam thoughtfully.

As Ben switched on his mobile a faint hope that she might have managed to text him was crushed. She hadn't.

'What's up, Ben?'

'Nothing. It's okay.' He remembered what he was meant to be doing, went into contacts and found Debs's number whilst Aunt Miriam went to check round the kitchen.

'Hello, Deborah Moore,' she said, uncharacteristically formally.

'Hi, Debs, it's Ben.'

'Oh hi Ben, how's it going?' she said in her friendly Yorkshire accent.

'Not good. Are you driving?'

'No, I'm standing outside a café in Aviemore. We've actually got snow! In April! What's up? Homework?'

'No,' said Ben, somehow embarrassed she didn't know. Surely the whole world should know? 'Debs, I'm sorry to tell you, Mum's disappeared.'

'*What*?'

'She went missing after a meeting last night.'

'Missing? Why?'

'We don't know. That's why I'm ringing you. Where was that meeting?' Aunt Miriam had returned and stood watching him.

'What meeting?'

'Oh no! Weren't you at it?'

'Sorry, Ben, no. Last night you say? We never have meetings on Friday nights.'

'It must have started really late. She didn't expect to get home till midnight.'

'We never start meetings after four on Fridays. Unless it was off-site. That's right, she left early, to take you to the dentist.'

'I didn't go to the dentist.'

38

'Maybe it was for Tricky's benefit.' To understand Debs you had to understand her nicknames, but having known her all his life, Ben understood most of them. Tricky Dicky was Mum's boss, Richard Ballantyne, about as trustworthy as a starving snake, Mum thought.

'Those burglars said she'd been to a meeting.'

'What burglars?'

'They broke in here last night.'

'And talked to you?'

'No I overheard them. They were talking about Mum going to a meeting so it must be a work meeting.'

'Well it wasn't anything I knew about. Which is really weird, because we're like Fred and George in work.' Ben knew she meant the Weasley twins from Harry Potter. Mum was the Fungicides Product Manager, managing SPC's portfolio of fungus-busting chemicals commercially, whereas Debs was the Development Manager, managing their development to market, so they worked very closely together.

'And they talked about the Chief.'

'Chief? Maybe John Knox our Chief Exec? Oh if JRK's involved it must be very important and perhaps so commercially sensitive that she couldn't tell me. But Tricky would have to know, as her line manager. Any meeting her and Knox were at, he'd be there too. But *he* didn't leave early. Hang on, how do you know they were connected with SPC?'

'Pete told them I'd be at my aunt's house.'

'*Really*? Oh heck. They knew your mum well then, didn't they? Or Pete did. Blimey, Ben.'

'Who could Pete be?'

'Probably Slimy Swarbreck, I'd guess.'

'Who?'

39

'Peter Swarbreck, he's Tricky's oppo in Regions. But it could be Pete Parker from Operations – he's one of the new grads, cold as cod, he is – and that's about it, as far as I can think, unless they meant Peter Nixon, one of the Stiffs.'

'Stiffs?'

'Stiff as a board – one of the Board. He's the Operations Director. He'd probably be at that meeting if JRK was. But not Parker. He'd be too junior. Look, I'll make a few calls, see what I can find out.'

'Great, Debs, thanks. I'll be at Aunt Miriam's. Have you got her number?'

'Course. I'm your standby if she's ill aren't I?' Debs reminded him. (It had never happened, so he'd forgotten.)

'Great. If we're out I've got my mobile now.'

'Someone will be in won't they? In case your mum calls?'

'At Aunt Miriam's. Not here. I've got to stay there whilst she's away.'

'Oh of course. Hard cheddar. Look, I'll get on to Judy right away.' She was one of the two secretaries shared between the Strategy Department where Mum and Debs worked. 'When you find her, you'll let me know, won't you Ben?'

'Of course I will.'

'Okay. Take care.'

'You too, Debs. Thanks.' He rang off and looked across at Aunt Miriam, who was raising enquiring eyebrows. 'I'll bet it's Peter Swarbreck! Peter Nixon maybe, but probably Swarbreck. Mum wouldn't have much to do with Nixon, he's a director.' At last he was getting somewhere.

'Good work, Ben.'

'I'll let Jess know. She can check him out online.'

The phone only rang twice before Jess answered.

'Have you found Mum? Has she called?'

'Sorry, Ben, not yet. Where was that meeting?'

'Debs didn't know.'

'Oh no! I've covered Cheshire and Manchester and I'm onto Staffordshire now.'

'She can't be there.'

'She must be somewhere.'

'True. Peter Swarbreck from SPC might be Pete.'

'Really? Number one suspect?' Jess sounded excited.

'Yeah. He's head of Regions.'

'What?'

Ben had heard his Mum answer this question so often that he could easily answer. 'The Product Managers like Mum manage *some* of SPC's products *all* round the world, and the Regional Managers sell *all* SPC's products, but only in *some* of the world. Debs reckons he could have been at that meeting. There's Peter Nixon too, the Operations Director.'

'Operations? Like in hospital?'

'No. Manufacturing and shipping and stuff.'

'Oh. Great work, Sherlock. I'm on the case.'

'Thanks, Watson.' Ben rang off. 'Jess hasn't found Mum yet. She's starting Staffordshire next.'

'Good for her. She's like a terrier when she gets her teeth into anything, she'll stick at it come what may. I want to double-check there's no financial pressures. Do you mind if I look through her bank statements and the like?'

'No, of course not. They're in the files in the bottom drawer.' There was nothing Mum would hide from Aunt Miriam or him.

'You should probably pack some clothes. We hope she'll be back this afternoon, but just in case, pack for a few days.' Ben winced. 'I know. Me too. But you'll feel better once you've changed into your own clothes.'

'True.'

He went to his bedroom and pulled the curtains shut (the police had opened them all) and gladly shed Uncle Henry's baggy boxers and Robert's clothes. He got his short stay bag (his case was reserved for those awful American or Far Eastern trips of a week or more) and packed a few sets of clothes, his toothbrush and comb almost automatically, he did it so often, all the time pondering how to find her. He put his watch on (his expensive Becoming A Teenager watch, inscribed *Darling Ben, love you always, Mum xfe*). He'd wear it until she was back home with him.

He was leaving the bedroom when he noticed he'd nearly forgotten his phone charger. He needed to stop being so slapdash! He was so grateful he had Aunt Miriam and Jess to help him in the search. Without Mum, his usual support in times of trouble, it would be overwhelmingly daunting to face it alone.

Had she left any clues anywhere about the meeting? He went to her bedroom. The turned-back duvet and the hollowed out pillow were just as she'd have left them on Friday morning. Her favourite photo stood on her dressing table, of them laughing together in the sunshine. It was a happy memory of last summer. One Sunday they had agreed to meet Debs for coffee at Dunham Massey, a former stately home in Altrincham, but as usual they were early and she was late. By the time she'd arrived Ben was starving but Mum had claimed lunch would be too expensive (although he knew she enjoyed their cooked food, so he could probably twist her arm). He'd offered her a bet: if he could spot ten deer, she had to buy him lunch.

She'd upped him to twenty-five but he wasn't worried. There were always plenty of deer.

Except on that gloriously sunny day, when for some reason the deer seemed to be in hiding. Ben's stomach was getting incredibly rumbly, and his mood decidedly grumpy, as they headed back towards the grand house well short of his target. But suddenly a young fawn had darted out from in front of them, performed a perfect arabesque (or so Debs had claimed – Ben wouldn't know an arabesque from an aardvark) and gracefully bounded across the path. Another fawn emerged from the trees, followed by another, and another, and another. By the time the ninety-third had passed they were helpless with laughter.

Debs had whipped out her phone and captured the moment, saying 'That'll be a cracker,' and it was. It radiated happiness, Mum said, happiness he could use right now. So he put the photo in his bag.

'Are you all right, Ben?' called Aunt Miriam from the lounge.

'Yeah,' he called, though he wasn't. He was so frightened for Mum. He carried his bag downstairs and went to see his aunt. She was sitting at the computer desk with a huge pile of papers in front of her.

'Got everything?' she asked

'Yeah. Found anything?'

'There's certainly no financial reason for her to disappear. She was on time with the mortgage and had enough to pay it for a few more months. So as we know, she's not done a runner.'

'She wouldn't have done.'

'I know that, you know that, but I'm just trying to get ammunition to convince the police. I can't *believe* they're not investigating more.'

'We need to find Pete. I'll bet he gave those men the key to our house.'

'Better check Helen's got hers. Whilst I put these back,' she patted the pile of papers, 'could you put your bag in the boot? Then we'll talk to Helen.' Aunt Miriam held out the car key. Ben took it, picked up his phone and returned to the hall. Lying on the mat was a cream envelope. In curly old-fashioned script was typed:

Mr B Baxter Private and Confidential.

Frowning slightly, Ben opened it.

To find your mum, solve the Einstein Code
Eight clues to get to her
But NO police and NO adults

The Einstein Code
Clue 1
A lowly patent clerk once dared
To prove I equalled mc^2

To find Clue 2:
One MoSI ghost struck gold,
Hear his atomic story told.
Saturday 1st April 3pm

Chapter 4

Ghosts

'All right Ben?' Aunt Miriam's voice brought him out of his stunned stupor.

'Yeah,' he lied, excitement tinged with trepidation surging through him. He knew how to find her! The solution was in his hand! But what did it mean? It couldn't really mean ghosts, could it? Ghosts didn't exist – did they?

He had to find Clue 2 fast, and then another six clues – and solve them, presumably. It was the most important test of his life – and of Mum's life too – but it depended on stupid, careless him, not clever, capable her.

He was terrified he'd mess it up.

What would she do now?

'Is there a problem with the key?' Aunt Miriam asked.

'What key? Oh, the car key. No. Sorry.' He hid the letter in his bag, which he carried out to her car, mind churning.

Helen emerged from next door.

'Is everything all right, Ben? I saw the police here earlier.'

'Mum's missing.'

'Oh no!'

No police and no adults. Suddenly, Ben felt he should explain as little as possible.

'We think she's had an accident maybe.' He must be somewhere unknown at 3pm, terrifyingly soon. 'Helen, have you still got our spare key?'

'Course. Why?'

'The police asked me to check,' Ben improvised, thinking. Someone had pushed that letter through the front door in the last few minutes. He looked up and down the road, but there was no sign of strangers, just a gaggle of elderly neighbours gossiping, as they so often did.

'Okay. I'll go and see,' Helen said. 'Are you staying with Miriam?'

'Yeah. She's inside now. Did you see a car pull up a few minutes ago? A white Mercedes or anything?'

'No, Ben, I was in the back. Why?'

'Doesn't matter.' Would the other neighbours have seen it? They looked so engrossed in their conversation that it was doubtful, but worth checking. As he walked down the path towards them, Helen turned and shouted into the hall.

'Pete, could you check the spare key box? Is Sue's still there?'

Ben stopped, shocked to his core.

'*Pete*?'

'He's my new man. We've been together for a while now – hasn't your mum said?'

'No.'

'Is this it?' A tall man with greying curly hair stood in the doorway, holding up a neatly labelled keyring with two keys.

'Yes, those are Sue's,' said Helen. 'Do you need them, Ben?'

'Please.' He took them from her and slipped them into his pocket, thinking. Sue had only the front door keys, unlike Aunt Miriam, who had a complete set like Mum. But the men had only needed front door keys – from Helen's Pete?

'Helen, I've got this project on Einstein, and with Mum away …'

'Couldn't your uncle help?'

'He's busy. I wondered if you could help – or Pete?'

'I know about as much about Einstein as I know about ice-skating. Do you know anything about Einstein, Pete?'

'What, Albert Einstein, the scientist? Are you kidding?'

'Ben needs to know.'

'I'd try the internet, mate. I'm clueless, sorry.'

Clueless? Was that a hint? The tanned face was utterly innocent as far as Ben could tell, but Mum saw things in people he missed. How he missed her now.

Pete went inside as Aunt Miriam came out, carrying his shoes and coat.

'You forgot these. You must wear shoes, Ben. Your feet must be agonisingly painful. You've got to protect them.'

'Yes, sorry.'

'Sorry about your sister,' Helen told her.

'Thank you. We'd better be getting back. Come on, Ben.'

'Helen, where does Pete work?' Ben asked, noticing Aunt Miriam's sharp look. But if he worked at SPC, he might know about the meeting.

'All over the place. He drives trucks. Why?'

'Just thought I'd recognised him from somewhere. Thanks, Helen.' He checked his watch. Two hours! Help! Hoping it was wrong, whilst he put his shoes on he asked Aunt Miriam for the time.

'It's almost one o'clock. Why? Hungry?'

'Yeah,' he agreed, but he was far too frantic for food. Two hours to find the next clue, which could be anywhere. So whilst agreeing with Aunt Miriam that it was strange finding a Pete next door and that he might have slipped the burglars the key, he was also frantically puzzling over what MoSI and ghosts and atomic story meant.

'I wonder what Jess has found out,' said Aunt Miriam.

Ben nodded, but it was down to him – not Jess, not Aunt Miriam, not even the police – to find Mum. It was a terrifying responsibility, and Ben felt sure any of them would be better at it than him.

But maybe he could solve the first clue. 'I equalled mc^2' reminded him of Einstein's famous equation $E = mc^2$. 'I' must therefore be E or energy, surely? But which? He wished he had his phone, but it was in his bag in the boot. He had only limited internet access on his contract but he could text his mates if he needed help.

Time ticked by on the dashboard clock and traffic through Didsbury was a nightmare. It was twenty-five past by the time they reached Aunt Miriam's.

Clutching his bag he raced upstairs. Seeing Jess emerging from the study, he feigned a desperate need for the toilet and locked himself in the bathroom. He retrieved his phone, clicked it on – and got a sickening lack of response. Out of charge again. *Useless*!

Ben reread the clue, pressing his clenched fist against his forehead, willing himself to think, but got nowhere. He needed help, fast.

Atomic story implied science. Uncle Henry was an expert scientist, but an adult. Freddie though, besides loving science, was also the cleverest (and by far the most annoying) teenager Ben knew. He checked the letter again, just to be sure. No police, no adults, but *not* no teenagers. He repeated the weird directions until he'd memorised them, then hid the letter in his bag and threw it inside the guest room as he passed. Freddie's room was next on the left. The door was shut, so he knocked.

'Come in,' Freddie called loftily.

Ben entered, shutting the door behind him. He was lying on the bed, reading.

'Hi, Freddie, I forgot about some homework.' Automatically Ben's eyes flicked to Freddie's poster of the apparent madman with the unkempt hair and tongue poking out. 'I have to get somewhere fast, but I don't know where. I just have a clue, a science clue.'

'Hand it over,' said Freddie, holding out a hand, still intent on his book.

'I've memorised it: One MoSI ghost struck gold, hear his atomic story told.'

'It's M-o-S-I not MoSI,' Freddie said, separating the letters.

'How do you know?'

'It's obvious. Eight syllables a line. It's from *school*?'

'They do teach us stuff in state schools, you know.'

'But clearly not enough to solve clues like this,' Freddie retorted triumphantly, sitting up. 'When do you have to be there?'

'Three o'clock today.'

Freddie looked at his watch. 'Then there's no time to waste. Come on. Lunch.'

'Why? Where are we going?'

'Manchester,' replied Freddie. 'Isn't it obvious?' He got up off the bed and put his babyish slippers on.

'Can't you just tell me where so I could go?' begged Ben. The last person he wanted around at a time of such nail-biting tension was Freddie.

'No. Come on. I thought this homework was important.'

'It is,' Ben assured him, following fast. 'Have we time for lunch?'

'Heaps. Breakfast was so early even *I'm* hungry. Aren't you?'

'I don't want to mess up this homework. We have to be there in time.'

'Why? What will happen if you don't?'

Ben shook his head. He didn't want to contemplate failure, he *couldn't* fail.

'Dunno. I just can't. I've got to get there, right?'

'I didn't know you cared so much about school,' Freddie said, smirking.

'I care about this science quiz, that's what I care about.'

They went into the kitchen. On the table Aunt Miriam had laid out ham, salami, chicken, cheese, bread, salad, olives, tomatoes, grapes and bananas. All the Winterburns were present, since Robert was now up. Almost eighteen, he was now as tall as his father, and had shed what Aunt Miriam called his puppy fat. His formerly blond hair had darkened to brown and was curly, like his mum's.

'Ran away again, did you?' he sneered. Nowadays his bullying was verbal, but it used to be physical and mainly directed at Ben. Under strict instructions never to retaliate, Ben had been forced to run away when he could, and suffer it when he couldn't; yet another reason for hating Henry's House of Horror.

'You wouldn't have tackled two thugs on your own,' Jess retorted.

'Ben did the right and proper thing, running here,' said Aunt Miriam. 'Jess has worked really hard on hospitals, Ben.'

'But no luck yet,' she said. 'With hospitals or Pete. Nixon's on a Meet the Board page, but nothing else and Swarbreck's completely invisible online. Unless you can think of anything?'

'I've got to go out soon. I've got a homework project on Einstein.'

'So I'm helping him,' said Freddie.

Though Uncle Henry looked pleased, Aunt Miriam looked astonished, understandably, since Freddie helped others about as often as City fans cheer on United. Though he felt no compunction over fooling the males, Ben felt deeply uncomfortable about lying to Aunt Miriam, but "No adults" meant he must keep it secret from her.

'It's a science project for the holidays. I have to get somewhere by three,' Ben said, checking his watch again, 'To find the next clue.'

'Oh, like a treasure hunt?' Jess enthused. 'Where?'

'I'm not sure yet. Freddie won't tell me,' he added, glaring at his tormentor.

'But surely your teacher would understand,' said Aunt Miriam.

'I have to get there!'

'No need to shout!' Uncle Henry snapped.

'Henry, he's bound to be emotional,' Aunt Miriam said.

'We should be going.' Freddie stood up. Ben stood too, still chewing.

'What about me?' Jess said.

'I think we should keep phoning round hospitals,' Aunt Miriam replied.

'How long will you be?' Jess looked hurt. Ben hated disappointing her, but he had no choice.

'Dunno,' he realised. He didn't know anything. Maybe he'd need Clue 1 with him to give to the 'ghost' (unsettlingly spooky, he wished he knew what that meant) but in his T-shirt and jeans he had nowhere to hide it. 'I need my jacket.' He ran upstairs to get the letter, hid it in the inside pocket of his jacket and then raced downstairs so fast that he nearly fell.

Freddie was making a point of looking at his watch.

'Come on, you don't want to mess up your homework.'

'I don't. Just tell me where I need to be, *please*. You don't want to waste an afternoon on my homework.'

'Surprised you haven't solved it yet. Do you know nothing about atomic physics?'

'Course not. Just tell me, please.'

'No. You've got to work it out.'

They left the house and walked to the Wilmslow Road, Ben boiling over with frustration and anxiety and the enormous pressure of solving the Einstein Code. It was only as they boarded the bus that he considered the fare.

'I'm not paying, it's your homework,' said Freddie, as tight-fisted as his dad, despite the huge allowance his rich grandma (Uncle Henry's mum) paid him.

Luckily Ben always kept a £20 note in the inner pocket of his jacket as an emergency fund. He remembered Mum giving it to him and entreating him not to waste it on sweets, but to keep it for emergencies. This was definitely an emergency. Whilst Freddie scuttled off to find a seat, he handed the note over.

'I shouldn't accept that. Got anything smaller?' the driver said.

'No. *Please*. It's really important. I've got to get there!'

'Where?'

Ben felt so stupid not knowing the answer.

'Where are we going, Freddie?' he yelled down the bus.

Freddie turned. 'Manchester centre.'

'Two juniors to Manchester centre please. We're under sixteen, honest,' Ben said, wishing he had proof.

'I'll believe you. Go on then,' the driver said, putting £15 in notes and some coins in the tray whilst printing out the tickets.

Ben went to sit by Freddie, hoping he'd relent and give Ben the help he needed, but he remained immersed in an e-book and didn't look up until they approached St Peter's Square.

'Get off here.'

Ben hurried to the front of the bus, and checked the time. Just twenty-five minutes to go.

'Is it far?'

'Not really.' Freddie smiled, obviously loving the power he had.

'Are you sure you know the answer? You're not just having me on?'

'Sure. It's simple.'

'It so isn't and you know it.'

'Your teacher wants to stretch you.'

Shaking his head, Ben decided to stop talking, because if Freddie carried on like this, it would drive him nuts.

Could he shake him off? They were heading for Central Library. Maybe the answer was in a reference book? Surely Uncle Henry had that reference book? (He had so many science books that it was hard to believe any more could possibly have been written.) But Freddie bypassed the entrance and led Ben down Peter Street, opposite the Midland Hotel. Was Midland the M of MoSI? What did the other letters stand for? But before Ben had got an answer,

Freddie continued over a crossing. They were now heading for the Opera House, the People's History Museum and the Museum of Science and Industry.

'I've got it!' Ben cried, so loudly that passers-by looked round at him.

'Got what?'

'The Museum of Science and Industry, that's MoSI,' Ben murmured, suddenly thinking they might be here now, Pete or the Chief or Goatee Man.

'Yes but it's a very big museum, isn't it?' Freddie taunted whilst Ben turned, scanning the shoppers. He couldn't see anyone he recognised. 'The air and space gallery, the textiles, the trains, it would take hours to get round if you didn't know where to go.'

Ben was very tempted to tell Freddie where to go, but he couldn't, he was in Freddie's power, and his know-it-all cousin was making the most of it.

'Come on, Freddie. It's really important and I haven't much time.'

'I'll help you solve it. How's that?'

'Okay,' Ben was forced to agree. 'How?' he asked, hurrying towards the museum. Freddie was right, it was enormous, he remembered from visits with Mum when he was younger.

'Have you ever heard of the plum pudding model?'

'No. Why would I?' Ben spotted a shaven head and his heart gave a jolt, but when he got closer he could see the man wasn't bearded.

'You know atoms consist of a tiny positive nucleus surrounded by mainly empty space, apart from the electrons zipping around it? On a very simple level. That's probably what you've been taught isn't it?'

'Yeah. The nucleus is the size of a football in the centre circle when the whole stadium is the atom,' Ben recited, one of the few things he remembered from science, because he could picture it.

'Probably. I'm not that familiar with football stadia and neither were Victorians with atoms. Their best stab at atomic structure was the plum pudding model – electrons being the currants in the positively charged pudding.'

'What use is that?' Ben asked testily.

'It's the key to *everything*, Ben! Life, the universe and everything!' Freddie declared, throwing his arms out and clouting a passer-by in the back. 'Oh, sorry.'

'I haven't time for life, the universe and everything, Freddie, I need to find the next clue!'

'That's where I'm taking you! Come on, in here,' Freddie said, striding towards the main entrance hall. 'Ernest Rutherford performed a world-famous experiment right here in Manchester. He fired alpha particles at a sheet of gold foil. Now *most* of the particles went straight through –'

'Where do we go now?' Ben cut in. 'Upstairs?'

'Up the ramp. *Most* went straight through, showing atoms are mainly space, but a few were deflected off the nuclei, showing that the centre of an atom is what?'

'Huh?' said Ben, looking around tensely, hardly listening.

'Alpha particles are positive, and like charges do what?'

'Like charges repel and opposite charges attract. Don't they?' Ben said. Like teachers, Freddie always made him unsure of his facts.

'Exactly! Showing there was a positively charged nucleus in the centre of an atom consisting mainly of space. Rutherford's hologram – his ghost – will tell you about the experience in the Manchester Science Gallery on the first floor,' Freddie declared triumphantly.

'It's *his* ghost? A hologram?'

'Yes.'

'Right.' Now he knew where he was heading he started to run, leaving Freddie behind. But a blockade of parents with pushchairs slowed him to a stroll, allowing Freddie to catch up.

They arrived at the gallery with only seconds to spare. It was dark and spooky and terrifying. Ben felt sick with worry. Four scientists were featured: Dalton, Joule, Lovell – and, as Freddie had said, Rutherford. Ben stopped by Rutherford's holodeck and looked around. No one was walking towards him. So if it wasn't a meeting point, presumably he was looking for another envelope? He pushed through a crush of giggling children to check the display case, but found nothing, so he crouched to check at floor level amidst a mass of fidgeting feet. This took longer in the gloom, but he was soon sure there was no envelope there.

Had he missed it? What if he was in the wrong place? Rutherford's hologram certainly looked ghostly, and Freddie had said he'd proved something about atoms – but so had other scientists, hadn't they? He straightened up to check, but there was no sign of Freddie.

Where was he? What if they'd got him? Ben hurried into the Rutherford room, which was brighter and crammed with display stands and charts. He spotted his annoying cousin's dark brown head bent over an exhibit, apparently engrossed. He marched over to him.

'There's nothing here! What if you're wrong?' Ben demanded (though he secretly considered that less likely than Freddie revealing a secret passion for cage fighting).

He turned and with a cocky smile held out a familiar cream envelope.

'Is this what you were looking for?'

Ben snatched it off him. It was identical to the one he'd found on the mat at home, once again addressed to him and marked private and confidential.

'Yeah, that's it. Where did you find it?'

'Over there.' Freddie pointed vaguely. 'But I don't get it. Where are the rest of your class?' Seeing Ben's confusion, he continued, 'If it's a school quiz, I assumed it would be a race against the rest of the class? Or did you each get different clues?'

'I dunno. Maybe we got different times. Maybe that's why we were told to leave as soon as we found the clue,' Ben improvised, because he was desperate to read the next clue. With Freddie's help he might find that too. The museum was so big that they could all be hidden within its many buildings. And then he'd get Mum back! 'Come on! Move it!'

'Must we?' Freddie asked regretfully.

'Yes we must! *Come on*, or you'll be buying your own ticket back.'

That got Freddie moving. Now Ben needed somewhere to read the clue in private. As they emerged from the ramps into the entrance hall he spotted the perfect sign.

'I need the gents'. Can you wait a minute?'

'I'll be fine,' said Freddie. 'Bet you're going to open that envelope.'

Ignoring the taunt Ben followed the signs towards the cloakrooms. In the gents' he found a vacant cubicle and with the door securely bolted, tore open the letter.

Clue 2

As far as man can ever go,

The biggest concept you will know,

It's wonderful and yet so strange

For when it's squared, it doesn't change

To find Clue 3:

In the beginning was the Word

Here ancient Mosleys will have heard,

But Hubble took the time and trouble

To burst the Mayor of London's bubble

Sunday April 2nd 12:00

Ben stared at it in dismay. Sunday was a whole day away. The Einstein Code might drag on for *ages*. Who would want to keep Mum away from him for so long? And *why*? He sagged back against the door, weighed down with despair.

Chapter 5

Jess Gets Mad

Ben had to fend off Freddie's nosiness all the way back to Aunt Miriam's. Finally, as they turned into the drive, he said, 'I'd like to try and work it out myself, okay? I don't have to be there until tomorrow, so if I'm stuck, I'll ask you tomorrow morning.'

'Fine,' said Freddie insouciantly, but Ben knew that he really did care, which made him determined to work it out without his infuriating cousin's help.

They were just taking off their shoes when Aunt Miriam came into the hall.

'Did you get there in time?' she said.

'Yes thanks,' said Ben.

'Thanks to me,' Freddie boasted but Ben had more important things on his mind.

'Any news?'

'Yes, Debs phoned. She thinks the meeting was in Oxford.'

'*Oxford*?' Mum never had work meetings in Oxford. She would definitely have mentioned it.

'Yes, I know, but it might explain her not coming back. It's a long way for her to drive on a Friday night. So we've phoned hospitals from here to Oxford, but we've not found her yet.'

'No,' Ben said in a low voice. They wouldn't, would they? Pete had her, or the Chief, or Goatee Man. He *hated* them having her. It made him so angry – but anger is counterproductive, Mum had told him. It stops you thinking clearly.

'Deep breaths, Ben. Cool it,' he suddenly heard, as clearly as if she was further down the hall. Was she thinking that somewhere? Was she closer than they'd suspected? Suddenly he had an idea. If all the clues were hidden in Manchester, Mum might be in Manchester too. He must check if the next one was also local.

'But what about Ben's intruders?' Freddie was saying. 'They knew she'd be missing, so they must know where she is. *If* they exist.'

'They do!'

'I think they saw her crash, stole her bag and planned to burgle your house. But you disturbed them,' said Aunt Miriam.

'Then why did they chase me?' asked Ben, desperate for someone else to spot something he'd missed.

'I think your uncle was right. Probably you mistook the two cars.'

'I didn't! I heard them running after me.'

'You heard them running out of the house. You heard them escaping, I think.'

'So you don't believe me?'

'It's not that I don't believe you. You thought they were chasing you, but they weren't.'

'But they *were*.'

'They can't have been. It doesn't make sense.'

Ben was deeply hurt to be abandoned by Aunt Miriam, usually one of his strongest supporters. Mum would have believed him. Without Mum he had no one to stand up for him. He stared to traipse upstairs, utterly miserable.

'Mum, if you're right, it doesn't explain the answer-phone,' Freddie said. 'It doesn't make sense.'

'Sue going missing doesn't make sense!' Aunt Miriam shouted, very unusually for her. 'We've got to find her, Freddie! Finding her is more important than science homework.' Oh no! Aunt Miriam thought he'd been messing around doing homework instead of finding Mum. As *if* he'd put homework before Mum. *As if.* But he couldn't tell her that, because breaking the conditions of the Einstein Code might mean he'd never get Mum back. He stopped and turned to her.

'I'm sorry I went out. I want her back more than anything. I was stupid as usual.' Freddie snorted, but Aunt Miriam still looked cross.

'Jess has been phoning hospital after hospital!'

'I know. She's been amazing. Has she finished?'

'Do you know how long it takes to find someone with time to talk to us?'

'No. Right. I'll go and help her,' Ben said, deeply embarrassed that he hadn't thought of that, and that he'd been putting Aunt Miriam and Jess through such a pointless task. If Mum was in hospital she'd get in touch. Nothing would stop her getting in touch.

Which is what Freddie said as Ben mounted the stairs, agreeing with Ben for once.

Aunt Miriam replied, 'If she's unconscious, maybe she can't.' Ben stopped, horrified.

'Unconscious?' He returned downstairs to join them.

'Temporarily so, Ben, don't look so frightened. Head injuries, are quite common after car accidents, but most people are fit to leave hospital after 48 hours.'

'I *am* frightened. I'm terrified.'

Aunt Miriam's kind face flooded with compassion. She came forward, arms outstretched. He stepped back fast. In front of Freddie? No way. She nodded her understanding and drew back from the cuddle she'd felt like giving him.

'It's terribly hard for us both. You'll feel better if you're doing something. Go and help Jess.'

'Okay.' As Ben walked upstairs, he reflected. The Einstein Code didn't say they *had* her, just that they'd lead him to her. If Aunt Miriam was right about the robbery, they might also know which hospital she'd been taken to. Maybe that was where the Einstein Code would lead him. There was no *way* he was going to wait around for that. He would find her. He didn't need their help.

He hurried to Aunt Miriam's study, where Jess was focused on the computer. She turned to look at him as he entered but didn't smile.

Right, he got it. Grovel time.

'Sorry I've been out, Jess. I want Mum back so badly I can't think straight. I hear you've been working really hard. Thanks so much. You're amazing.'

'It's okay. It's just so strange, you putting homework before your mum.'

'I haven't! Mum's all I've been thinking about whilst I've been out. So how far have you got?' he asked, sitting down in the chair beside her. As usual, she had a list.

'We've ten more to ring, that's all.'

'Okay I'll start with Solihull. You deserve a break.'

'Thanks. I'll go and get a drink. Want anything?' The choice in the Winterburn house was limited: water, milk or hot drinks, usually, with occasionally fruit juice for breakfast.

'A glass of water would be good.'

The next hour was spent in repetitive, fruitless calls.

'That's it,' Jess said, putting the phone down. 'We've spoken to every single one between here and Oxford. So where on earth is she?'

'No idea. I really wish I had.' Maybe there was no way to find her except through the Einstein Code, so when Jess said she'd log out, he was quick to react.

'Don't log out! I'd like to see if I can find anything on Parker.'

'Okay. Shut down when you've finished then, Ben. You know what Dad's like about wasting energy.'

He certainly did. Their house often felt more like a fridge than a home. He pulled Clue 2 out of his jacket pocket to check it.

<u>Clue 2</u>

As far as man can ever go,

The biggest concept you will know,

It's wonderful and yet so strange

For when it's squared, it doesn't change

To find Clue 3:

In the beginning was the Word

Here ancient Mosleys will have heard,

But Hubble took the time and trouble

To burst the Mayor of London's bubble

Sunday April 2nd 12:00

He opened one window to search for Hubble, opened another and looked up Mosley, and queried Mayor of London in another. In a fourth he typed *infinity*, because whilst he had been waiting for information from hospitals, he had been running the clue round the recesses of his mind and a phrase from an old film had struck a chord: "To infinity and beyond!" That was a joke, right? Suddenly he wished he'd paid more attention in maths.

He thought infinity squared was infinity, but wasn't sure. He checked it out and found a populist site saying that infinity squared *was* infinity. Mum had warned him not to treat the site as gospel for homework, so he felt he needed to double-check the fact with a Winterburn. Was infinity also a concept? Infinity *was* a concept, he soon learned from a maths site, but the rest, about Koch snowflakes and aleph numbers and Zermelo-Fraenkel set theory was way beyond Ben – and the clue author, hopefully.

Mosley led him first to Sir Oswald Mosley, a baronet who founded the British Union of Fascists. Ben scanned down the entry to see if he'd been Lord Mayor of London.

'What's that got to do with Parker?' Jess demanded, right behind him. 'What are you doing?' Ben started guiltily and quickly shut the window down, but it revealed his Hubble and Lord Mayor of London searches behind it. She slammed down a mug so violently that tea slopped over the desk. 'I can't believe you!' she spat out angrily. 'Your mum's missing, and everyone's looking for her, but you're just messing about!' Before Ben could think of anything to say in his defence, she stomped out of the room, slamming the door behind her.

'WHO DID THAT?' Uncle Henry bellowed from downstairs. 'WHO SLAMMED THE DOOR?'

Ben shot out of his seat. If Jess told Uncle Henry he'd have to explain his interest in Hubble and London mayors to all of them – and two of them were adults. Even worse they were adults who would instinctively tell the police. The consequences for Mum could be catastrophic.

He raced onto the landing just in time to see Jess's bedroom door slam. He hurried to the top of the stairs to check if Uncle Henry was on his way, but he wasn't. Remote parenting was his usual style, but not always. Jess was an angry loose cannon that needed calming, fast. Ben went to get the clues and, slipping them under his T-shirt, hurried to her room. He knocked on the door.

'Jess, I'm sorry. Can I come in?' No answer. 'Jess, I'm really sorry. Can I come in and explain?' Still no answer. 'Jess, *please*. It's for Mum.' He decided to go in, despite the Boys Keep Out sign on the door (totally understandable given her brothers). As he started to push Jess yanked the door open. He only just managed to stay upright.

'What do you want?' she demanded, arms folded truculently across her chest. Her face was pink and he suspected she'd been crying.

'Can I come in?'

'It's a boy-free zone,' she said, pointing to the sign.

'It's really important. I need your help to get Mum back.' She looked at him. He looked at her, knowing she could flip either way, and so hoping it would be onto his side. '*Please,* Jess. To get Mum back,' he repeated, knowing Jess loved her too. They sometimes went running together, and afterwards loved snuggling up on the sofa, sharing a big bar of chocolate and watching a detective show. (If it was modern Sherlock Ben watched it with them.)

She grudgingly stepped to one side, admitting him, so he sat on her guest bed, a single for sleepovers, whilst she sat on her double. The enormous bedroom also contained a desk, two huge wardrobes, a chest of drawers, a massive bookcase crammed with books (mainly Agatha Christie) and two bedside tables, yet still had plenty of floor-space.

He handed over the first letter, explaining where he'd found it and when. She scanned it, then looked up, eyes wide with horror.

'Oh Ben! How awful!'

'I know. But it's better than nothing. At least the writer says in eight clues I'll get her back.'

'*Writer*? It's not from a friend, Ben, it's from a kidnapper.' Ben stared at her, his stomach churning with anxiety. 'Sorry, Ben. She's been kidnapped.'

'They might just know which hospital she's in. When I've got the eight clues, they'll tell me. They haven't kidnapped her.'

'They have, Ben, that's what this means. I'm sorry, I know it would be nicer for you if she was in a hospital bed somewhere but she can't be. If this person can give her back after eight clues, it means he's got her. It's from Pete or the Chief and they've kidnapped her.'

Ben was silent for a minute, taking it in. It was bad news, awful. Kidnappers were dangerous, ruthless people.

'Ben, it's okay. Kidnappers look after their captives, they don't hurt them. They *value* them. They want something in exchange.'

'What?'

'They'll probably want a ransom. I've got nearly two thousand in the bank.'

'That's really kind. But that won't be enough, Jess.'

'You can have my trust fund too.' Uncle Henry's dad had died last year and Ben remembered Aunt Miriam telling Mum that he'd left each of his grandchildren *fifty thousand pounds* (he'd been incredibly rich) but that it was to be held in trust, so that they couldn't access it until they'd finished university.

'What if they don't go to university?' he'd asked.

'They daren't not. Henry would disown them,' Aunt Miriam had said – and how would he react to Jess spending it on getting Mum back? He'd go bonkers. It was supposed to be used to pay off student loans or towards their first house.

'You can't do that, Jess. It's so kind of you. I'll never forget it. But they don't want money, the kidnappers,' he forced himself to add, though he didn't want to, he *so* didn't want Mum to have been kidnapped, 'they want me to crack their code. Look. This is what we found this afternoon.' He handed over the second letter. Jess read it, then looked up.

'Does Freddie know?'

'No! I don't want him to know, Jess, or your mum and dad, or anyone. It's so important nobody goes to the police.'

'That's what kidnappers always say. But the police might help.'

'No they won't! You heard them this morning.'

'True.'

'And no adults, the kidnapper says, right? So you can't tell your mum or dad. I feel bad about your mum, but he says no police and no adults. I daren't tell her.'

'She'd tell Dad and they'd go to the police,' Jess agreed. 'So I'm the only person who knows apart from you?'

'Yes. It's down to us now. Can you work out what the clue means? And how to find Clue 3? If it's in Manchester, it might mean Mum's here too.'

She read it again.

'Oh, you think Mosley is Sir Oswald Mosley, do you?' Jess said, showing she'd noticed the window he'd shut down.

'Not sure,' Ben replied. 'What do you think?' She was super smart, but not patronising like her dad and Freddie. Her quick brain would be a big help solving obscure clues like these.

'Well the only Hubble I know is Edwin Hubble, who studied galaxies – in the 1930's I think. Is that when Oswald Mosley was alive?'

'I think so. So if we find out who was Lord Mayor of London then, maybe that will tell us where to go.'

Jess grimaced. 'What if it's *in* London?'

Ben stared at her in horror. This was a massive obstacle he hadn't envisaged.

'We can't get there without your mum knowing.'

'And where exactly? London's vast.'

'I know. I hope it's all local. And that Mum's local.'

'So do I. We need the computer. You didn't log out, did you?'

'No. But I left the other screens open!'

'Oh no!' They rushed out of the bedroom towards Aunt Miriam's study. Luckily the landing and study were deserted. The screen looked unchanged. Jess sat in Aunt Miriam's chair, scanning the information on it.

'What's infinity squared?' he asked.

'Oh that's easy, infinity,' she said, turning to him. 'That's the answer to the clue, isn't it?'

'I thought so, but I wasn't sure.'

'It definitely is, Ben. Infinity squared is infinity – only 1, 0 and infinity do that. It's amazing, isn't it? But it's not 1 or 0. As far as we can go and as big a concept that we know, that's definitely infinity. The clue's quite easy,' Jess babbled, prompting Ben to have an idea.

'Easy for you, but I wasn't sure. If the kidnapper knows that, does it mean he's a scientist?'

'Probably.'

'Nearly everyone at SPC has a science degree. Pete *must* be from SPC. He's the kidnapper I'll bet.'

'Or the Chief?' Jess speculated. 'And Pete works for him?'

'Could be. Or they could be the same man.'

'Or woman. The Chief could be a woman.'

'Most senior managers at SPC are men.'

'That's awful!'

'I know. Mum and Debs get really annoyed about it.'

'Maybe if we get there early enough tomorrow we'll see him or her plant the clue.'

'I thought that today,' Ben agreed. 'The Science Museum was busy. He couldn't have left the clue in the open else someone else would have found it.'

'Where was it?'

'I didn't see. Freddie got to it first.'

'Typical.'

'Yeah, typical.'

'We should get there early and spy.'

'*Where* though?'

'Right, let's take it from the top. "In the beginning was the word," comes from the Bible, St John's gospel, isn't it?'

'I dunno,' Ben replied, impressed that Jess did.

She grinned. 'Dad won't have a Bible in the house, but we get it all the time at school.' (Uncle Henry was an evangelical atheist.) 'So if ancient Mosleys listened to the gospel here, we're probably looking for a church,' she declared, brain buzzing in the way Winterburn brains so often did.

'But how does that link to Hubble?'

Jess considered for a minute then swung round towards him triumphantly. 'Got it! Edwin Hubble showed that everything started with the Big Bang – well he was the beginning of that proof – so he showed that in the beginning there *wasn't* the word, and in that way he proved those religious Mosleys wrong i.e. burst their bubble.'

'Why bubble?'

'It's just a rhyme, I think. Yes, why *are* all the clues rhyming? It's a bit corny isn't it?'

'It's hard to find rhymes,' said Ben, remembering a recent piece of English homework with which he'd struggled. 'But *which* religious Mosleys?'

Searching for Mosley, Lord Mayor of London, led to Nicholas Mosley, mayor. Reading down the thankfully brief entry on this gentleman, Ben was excited to see he was buried in the Church of St James, Didsbury.

'That's the church by Fletcher Moss, isn't it?'

'Yes,' Jess said, clicking on the link to it. Ben recognised the church by which Mum often parked when they visited Fletcher Moss. There, after a bracing walk by the River Mersey, Ben loved eating ice cream sitting on Rory's Bench (magically carved with bears and robots, mice and monsters and even some equations).

He was surprised to read that the church dated back to the thirteenth century, and even more convinced Jess was right when he read that there was a wall monument there featuring several of the family – including Sir Nicholas Mosley, Lord Mayor of London.

'Brilliant, Jess! You've cracked it,' cried Ben, delighted.

'Cracked what?' asked Freddie from behind them. Ben quickly folded his arms over the kidnapper's letters on the desk. 'Oh, St James's Church, is that where you've got to go for the next clue. When?' Ben didn't answer. 'Did you solve it for him, Jess?' he asked in his most patronising tone. 'I solved the first one for him. You're getting an awful lot of help with this homework, aren't you, Ben?'

'I've got a lot of other things on my mind at the moment. Like where Mum is.'

'Odd that you're so keen on homework, then. I've never known you this studious before.'

'It's only taken a couple of minutes. We've been ringing round hospitals for hours,' snapped Jess. 'With no help from you. Don't you care about your aunt?'

'Of course I do, but I can't see how ringing round hospitals is going to help.'

'Why not?' Ben demanded.

'Well, she's been kidnapped, hasn't she?' Freddie said. Ben stared at him. 'It's obvious. And it can't be money they're after, because you're poor,' he added insultingly and inaccurately. No they weren't. Mum had a good job and they had a nice home (tiny compared to his cousins' house admittedly) but they weren't kidnapper rich, it was true. As was so often the case, even when being insulting, Freddie had a valid point. 'So the answer must be in SPC. Once it's open on Monday we can investigate.'

'*We*?' said Ben, scathingly. He wanted Freddie around as much as he wanted measles.

'Well, you need Jess and me to help you with your homework. Catching a kidnapper is going to be a lot more difficult than solving a few science questions, Ben. You'll need us even more for that.'

And though he refused to admit it, Ben had the horrible feeling that his obnoxious cousin was right.

Chapter 6

Meeting Mr Wright

While Ben headed downstairs to get them some water, Uncle Henry and Robert were yelling at each other in Uncle Henry's study.

'IT'S MY MONEY!'

'NOT UNTIL YOU'RE TWENTY-ONE IT ISN'T!'

'I'LL BE AN ADULT SOON!'

'AN *AGE* DOESN'T MAKE YOU AN ADULT! YOUR *BEHAVIOUR* MAKES YOU AN ADULT!'

So it was about Robert's trust fund – again.

'It's caused more problems that it's solved,' Aunt Miriam often told Mum.

Ben continued to the kitchen, where he expected to find Aunt Miriam cooking, it being late afternoon, but it was deserted. He got the drinks and took them upstairs.

'The men who broke in were from Manchester. Does that mean she's here, do you think?' he asked.

'Even if she is, Ben, there's a million hiding places,' Jess said. 'There's no way we'll find her without the Einstein Code.'

'Suppose not.' Ben sighed. 'I'll go and get my mobile charged.' He went to the guest room, hid the clues in his bag and saw the Dunham Massey photo. He put it on the mantelpiece because the bedside table was now stacked with the paper, pencils and pens Aunt Miriam always supplied for him. She knew he enjoyed drawing to while away the many lonely hours he had spent here. But none had been lonelier than these.

He took his charger out of the bag, plugged it into the wall and, as he connected his mobile, the doorbell rang. Still with a faint hope that it would be Mum, he charged downstairs but Aunt Miriam was accepting plastic bags from a delivery man.

'I thought we'd have a takeaway,' she explained. Ben was astonished – Uncle Henry insisted on home cooking whenever possible (but never cooked, of course).

'Do you want a hand?'

'They're not heavy, thanks. Could you call the others?'

He knocked on Uncle Henry's study door, where he and Robert were still bickering, and went to the first floor to get Jess and Freddie.

'Dinner!' he called. 'It's a takeaway!'

They popped out of their rooms like excited meerkats.

'Takeaway? But it's not a birthday,' Jess said. 'Yet. Have you decided what you want for yours?'

'To get Mum back. That's all I want. It'd be the best present ever.'

'You wouldn't have said that last week,' Freddie said.

'You've no idea how much you'll miss someone until they've gone,' Ben said simply. It was pointless trying to explain. The yawning void in his life was astonishing even to him, who'd thought he was a loving son. It was like losing a limb, losing Mum. No, worse. He could cope without a leg, he reckoned, but not without her. So he mustn't risk doing anything to upset the kidnappers. He had to get her back safe, sound and soon. Very, very soon.

Ben and Jess helped Aunt Miriam unpack the containers onto the mats she'd laid down the middle of the table. There was plenty of food. Uncle Henry's eyes bulged in horror when he saw it.

'How much did this cost?'

'Not much. Surprisingly cheap.'

We should have been having a takeaway last night.

'Wouldn't it be lovely if she were here with us?' Aunt Miriam said, as if reading his mind. He nodded, too choked to speak. 'Get some food, Ben. You need to eat, darling. You need your strength.'

'It's true, Ben. And we're doing so well,' said Jess, proffering the spare ribs. Ben took one. 'We know the meeting was in Oxford, we've got the key suspects for Pete, and we're a quarter of the way there with the Einstein C– Quest,' she amended, far too late.

'Einstein Quest? What's that?' asked Uncle Henry.

No adults!

'Just that science homework,' Ben replied as casually as he could manage through the panic raging inside him.

'Is that what it's called? It's about Einstein?' asked Freddie.

'I guess so, I dunno,' said Ben, wanting to close the subject down before Jess gave any more away.

'You're such a mummy's boy I can't believe you're doing homework,' Robert scoffed. 'Stuff homework, you need to find your mum.'

'Stuff homework?' echoed Uncle Henry, scandalised.

'I'm *trying* to find her!'

'And why do you care so much about Ben's homework?' Freddie teased Jess, making her blush.

'Freddie, leave Jess alone,' Aunt Miriam said. 'How's the hospital ring-round going, Ben?' Ben silently thanked his wonderful aunt and quickly expanded on their hospital search.

'But it's hard to know where to look next.'

'You've covered everywhere? And no one's found her?' Aunt Miriam looked astonished.

'Yes. Weird, isn't it?'

'It's weird her car hasn't turned up,' said Robert, in a break from gnawing the last spare rib, which he'd grabbed before anyone else could. 'Cars are registered, the police can trace them in seconds.'

'You think,' said Freddie darkly.

'I do, yeah. They're watching us all the time, so how can something as solid as a car just disappear?'

'The police are doing all they can,' said Uncle Henry, showing how much he knew or cared about the search for Mum. 'Can we give it a rest over dinner? Let's talk about something else.'

Something else? Nothing else mattered. Ben looked down, burning with anger.

'I thought I heard you mention Hubble earlier, Jess,' said Freddie innocently. 'You were helping Ben with his homework, I think.' Robert snorted. Ben focused his anger on him and Freddie. They surely knew he wouldn't ask Jess to help him with his homework – it would be far too humiliating – but this was to find Mum, and he'd do anything to get her back. 'You said Hubble had started the proof of the Big Bang, but I'm not sure Ben knows why. Do you, Ben?' Freddie continued, as if Ben were a mentally challenged chimp.

'No.'

'Stars look still in the night sky but they're actually whizzing though space, which is lumpy and bumpy.'

'Space isn't bumpy!'

'According to relativity, it is. Space is deformed by all the stars and matter it contains. Like a sofa cushion is deformed by bulging bums.'

'Freddie! Usually they use a rubber sheet curving round the base of a cannonball or something similar,' said Aunt Miriam. 'But yes, relativity is easier when you think of space as curved.'

'Though light always travels in a straight line, going straight ahead on a curved path makes you go round a bend, like cyclists in a velodrome,' Freddie said. 'So light bends round heavy objects such as stars.'

'General Relativity was first proved in 1919 by Sir Arthur Eddington,' Uncle Henry said. 'Using stars whose light passes close to the sun,' (his fist apparently) 'in the day, but not at night, before reaching us.'

'Henry, please put your cutlery down,' Aunt Miriam said, only too aware of how much he used his hands to communicate science. He complied, but raised his eyebrows to show how ridiculous he thought this request.

'He used an eclipse to photograph their daytime positions, when the sun would usually mask their light. The difference between the actual and apparent position of the stars was much greater then,' (his hand shot out, just missing Freddie's face) 'proving that their light was bent by the sun, exactly as Einstein had predicted.'

'We only see them where we think they are,' said Freddie. 'And we're not really seeing them at all.'

'*What*?'

'Light takes time to travel to us, so we only see the star as it was years ago, when the light left it. It may since have died, and will certainly have moved from where it appears to us to be. You can only ever see stars in the past.'

'We can only see the sun as it was eight minutes ago. When it dies, we won't know for eight minutes,' Jess said.

'By then we'll be as dead as this duck,' said Uncle Henry, rapidly constructing a crispy duck pancake. 'There's about five billion years of hydrogen left,' he said, an expansive gesture projecting a spring onion towards Aunt Miriam, 'and then the helium will fuse to make heavier elements. Nothing bigger than iron though,' he added, dropping cucumber on the floor. 'Remember Sir Fred's seminal paper.'

'Henry, please eat that pancake rather than throwing it everywhere,' Aunt Miriam snapped, but it didn't deter him for long. He was soon boasting about having met Sir Fred Hoyle at Oxford (he made it sound like he'd talked him out of the Steady State Theory, but he'd just made Sir Fred a cup of tea after his lecture, Mum said). He then moved on to the speed of light.

'Which is how fast, Ben?' His mouth was too full to answer, so Ben simply shrugged. 'Even in a state school, I'd have thought they'd have taught you that.'

'Henry,' warned Aunt Miriam.

'Well I would.'

'Can we talk about something else? Poor Ben's going through enough, he doesn't need lecturing.'

'But if he doesn't even know about the speed of light, how will he pass science? That's what this science quiz is all about, getting him to understand science,' said Freddie.

'How do you know what it's about?' Ben said.

'Well it's not about sightseeing is it? Your teacher's doing it for a reason. And a treasure hunt is cool, it's exciting.'

'Excitement Ben could well do without,' Aunt Miriam said. 'If his teacher was talking about Hubble proving the Big Bang, surely she's referring to the red-shift?'

'What's the red-shift?' he asked her, refraining from pointing out that his teacher was male. He didn't mind learning from Aunt Miriam, especially now science might help him find Mum.

'Edwin Hubble was studying distant galaxies and found light from them *all* was red-shifted, which had a momentous implication. It's because of the Doppler Effect, have you covered that yet?' Aunt Miriam was always respectful of his school, unlike Uncle Henry and Freddie who seemed to view it as a daytime detention centre for delinquents.

'No.'

'Have you noticed that when a police car or ambulance is racing towards you the siren gets higher and higher in pitch, but as it moves away from you it gets lower again?'

'And quieter.'

'Well yeah, duh,' said Robert.

'Cars do it too, like when you're waiting to cross the road,' he said, to prove he wasn't as doltish as Robert had just implied.

'Exactly. That's because sound travels in waves. The waves get squashed up against your ear as they approach you, so that their frequency, and pitch, increases.'

'But they stretch out as they move away from you, getting lower in frequency and pitch,' Freddie just couldn't resist chipping in. 'And it's the same with light. Blue is at the high frequency, short wavelength end of the visible spectrum, whilst red is at the other end. So the fact that all the galaxies Hubble could see was red shifted means …'

'The light waves had stretched out – so the galaxies were moving away from us?' hazarded Ben, working hard.

'Quite right,' Aunt Miriam responded warmly. 'They were all moving away from us, as if they were dots on an expanding balloon.'

'So the universe was expanding everywhere,' said Freddie. 'So it must have started at a single point. Part one of the proof of the Big Bang.'

'And quite enough science for tonight, thank you,' said Aunt Miriam. 'Now, has everyone finished?' Robert took some more but everyone else had had enough.

As they were clearing up, Robert had another go at getting some money out of his parents.

'You have an allowance, Robert, and you have to learn to manage it, else you'll never cope at university,' Aunt Miriam said.

'But I'm broke!'

'We paid for your car and the road tax and the sky-high insurance, what more do you want?' retorted Aunt Miriam crossly.

'Petrol. And a social life,' Robert replied with heavy sarcasm.

'Then spend less money on going out and save up,' she snapped. 'That's the point about budgets. You can't have everything, you have to choose.'

Robert turned to his father. 'Dad, can I just borrow a hundred, just to fill the tank? I'll pay you back.'

'When the sands of time run out,' said Aunt Miriam.

'*What*?' He threw her a look loaded with scorn. He'd never dare do that to his dad. Ben felt sorry for Aunt Miriam. Robert was so unfair to her. 'Dad, can I? Please? Just a loan?'

'Don't give in to him, Henry. Your allowance will, as always, arrive on the fifteenth of the month, Robert.'

'But I'm already skint. And I'm seeing Bianca tomorrow night.'

'Then bring her here for dinner.'

'Oh great.'

'Beggars can't be choosers.'

Ben was trying to think of something useful to do. He needed to know more about the meeting and more about

SPC, but it was shut until Monday and he was so exhausted that he could hardly think straight.

The doorbell rang. Ben and Jess rushed to the door, with Aunt Miriam following at a more sedate pace. The tall blond man was somehow familiar.

'Ben, I'm so sorry your mum's missing. Debs said I'd find you here.'

'My word, is it Marcus?' exclaimed Aunt Miriam. 'Do come in.'

The only Marcus Ben had heard of was the high-flying Mr Wright Debs clearly fancied, but Mum called Old Marcus, giving Ben the impression he was over sixty. This man looked much younger. His toned physique was evident under his tight top. He was wearing trendy jeans like Ben. He stepped inside and hugged Aunt Miriam.

'It's so lovely to see you again, but I wish it were under happier circumstances.' He released her from the embrace, but held each of her hands lightly in his. 'When we've got Sue safely home, we'll have a proper catch up, shall we? Is this your daughter?'

'Yes, this is Jess. I've two boys, too.'

'Are they tucked up in bed?'

'Hardly, they're teenagers. Robert's nearly eighteen.'

'No! You're not old enough.'

'I am and so are you, though you haven't changed since university. You're still handsome and still full of flannel.'

Marcus took it well, smiling. 'And you're still sharp as butter.'

'But butter's not sharp – oh!' said Jess as she got it.

'I've come to help find Sue.'

'Wonderful! After the police walked away, that means so much,' gushed Aunt Miriam. Ben was delighted too. SPC had come to him! He started thinking of questions.

'Come and sit down,' Aunt Miriam said, leading the way down the hall. 'This is Freddie, my younger boy. And Henry, my husband, I can't remember if you've met?'

'Professor Henry Winterburn,' he announced, extending his hand.

'Of course I remember you, Henry,' said Marcus, shaking it. 'I attended your wedding, don't you remember? With Sue?'

'Oh yes,' Aunt Miriam recalled.

'Were you together then?' Ben asked, surprised.

'For a while, yes. But it was ages ago, Ben, at uni. We're still friends though. She's a wonderful woman, your mum,' Marcus said. Ben nodded fervently. He didn't need telling, but Uncle Henry did. 'When did she disappear?'

Ben went through his account yet again. Marcus's bright blue eyes were full of concern.

'How frightening. And strange.'

'Do you know who was at that meeting?'

'I don't, I'm sorry. I know nothing about it.'

'But Debs thought it involved senior people.'

'Not me, sorry.'

'I'm being very rude, Marcus, I'm sorry, we're so anxious about Sue, but that doesn't excuse me not offering you a drink,' Aunt Miriam said. 'What would you like?'

'I want to keep all my wits about me, plus I'm driving, so coffee would be ideal please.'

Aunt Miriam looked at Jess. 'Would you mind, darling?'

'I want to hear what Marcus has to say.'

'I won't say anything important until you're back. I'll just get up to speed with what you know. Promise.' Marcus smiled so warmly that Jess smiled back.

'Okay. How do you like it?'

'Milk, no sugar, please.'

'Darling, if you're making one, could I have one too please?' said Aunt Miriam.

'I will too,' said Uncle Henry.

'Anyone else?' asked Jess in a threatening tone.

'No thanks,' said Ben.

'Yes please,' said Freddie, grinning at her gloatingly.

'Right. You'll have to help me carry them then. Come on,' she said, rising from the sofa. '*Come on*!' she ordered when he didn't respond. Reluctantly, Freddie rose.

Ben knew this was a golden opportunity and wanted to make the best of it. As Mum's Director, Marcus was so well placed to help them.

'Are there any other Petes at SPC apart from Parker, Swarbreck and Nixon?' he asked. Jess hesitated in the doorway.

'Not that I can think of. If any spring to mind, I'll wait until you're back to tell them,' Marcus promised her. 'But I still don't understand why you think they're from SPC?'

'Because they wanted to wipe the message about the meeting from the answer phone.'

'More likely they were burglars. Maybe they pressed the delete button by accident when they were searching for valuables?' Marcus suggested. 'But you disturbed them, so they scarpered?'

'No. They mentioned Pete and the Chief.'

'Their fellow burglars?' Marcus suggested.

'Much more likely than some cock and bull story about SPC being involved in her disappearance,' Uncle Henry said. 'I mean she's always been flighty.'

'*What*?' Ben stared at his uncle, outraged.

'She's an unmarried mother!'

'That doesn't make her flighty!'

'Getting pregnant at –'

'Henry! Stop it! Now!' Aunt Miriam snapped. 'Sue is *not* flighty, would *not* have left Ben on his own and would *not* have given her key to intruders!'

'No, she wouldn't,' said Jess, wide-eyed at her mum's fury. She was carrying two mugs and handed one to Marcus.

'Thanks, Jess, lovely,' he said, smiling at her. 'I know Sue adores Ben. She'd never abandon him. Something's wrong.'

'Exactly. But we're running out of ideas. We've phoned round hospitals all day, but there's no trace of her. '

'Have you tried London?'

'Why?' Jess asked.

'We sometimes have meetings in a Heathrow hotel. It's worth a try.'

'Debs thought Oxford,' Ben said, calmer now Aunt Miriam and Marcus had refuted Uncle Henry's outrageous accusations.

'We never have meetings there. Cambridge, yes. At Haslingfield,' Marcus said, naming their research station just outside Cambridge. 'But not Oxford.'

He clearly knew nothing about the meeting then.

'Who could the Chief be?' Ben asked. 'If he or she is from SPC?'

'I really don't think they would be.'

'Sir John Knox?' suggested Jess.

'No. He's the Chief Executive, or the Chief Exec. Never just the Chief. It's such a generic name, it could apply to anyone. Henry would be the Chief in his lab, whereas Miriam would be the Chief in her department, is that right? You're both at Manchester Uni?'

'Yes, that's right. I'm the Professor of Astrophysics there and Miriam works in History.'

'Very impressive. What a clever family.' Freddie and Uncle Henry visibly preened. 'And Sue too, she's a very clever woman,' Marcus added, making Ben like him even more. 'The police aren't helping, you say?'

'I'm afraid not. She's a missing adult, you see, not a child,' said Aunt Miriam.

'Right. I'll see if I can push things along there. And as for ringing round hospitals …'

'We'll get onto it directly. London hospitals.'

'I doubt you'd get anywhere, frankly. They're so frantically busy that they get besieged. But if we use the clout of one the country's biggest employers, then we might get a bit more attention.'

'That would be wonderful, Marcus, truly,' said Aunt Miriam. 'Thank you. I don't suppose anything could be done tonight?'

'No chance, I'm afraid. It would have to have the SPC header to look the part, so it would have to be done from the office, and it's shut until Monday.'

'Then we'll have to wait till then. But it won't stop us searching.'

'I'm glad to hear it won't,' responded Marcus, setting down his mug on the ornate mantelpiece. 'Well thank you for the coffee – delicious,' he added, beaming at Jess, 'and if there's anything I can do to help, just let me know.'

When they had seen Marcus out, Jess said, 'That was nice of him wasn't it?'

'Yeah, really nice.'

'It's too late to phone institutions now. But I think tomorrow we'll focus on London and Cambridge,' Aunt Miriam said.

'I'll check with Debs about Oxford. It still could be there,' Ben said.

'I think you should get to bed, Ben. You're shattered.'

'But I need to find Mum!'

'I know darling, but where? You're too tired to think straight now. Sleep will do you the world of good.'

'Okay,' agreed Ben, determined to call Debs.

He went to the guest room to get his mobile – and saw the charger had been unplugged! He stared at it, outraged. He wasn't wasting energy! His phone needed charging! But his spurt of angry indignation changed to horror suddenly. Someone must have been in his room this evening. What if they'd found the Einstein Code?

He checked his bag where he'd left the clues. It hadn't been disturbed, as far as he could tell – but had they been read? He considered moving them to the bedside table, but quickly ruled it out. It was their furniture; they'd feel just as entitled to search it as they did to enter the bedroom. The only thing that was truly his own was his bag, so he decided to leave the clues hidden in its side compartment.

He reconnected the charger and called Debs. Once greetings were exchanged Debs said she was sure there *had* been a meeting in Oxford.

'Marcus said there wasn't.'

'Oh, that's interesting. Maybe it was more hush-hush than I thought. Did you tell him I'd told you?'

Ben was too tired to remember. 'Might have done. Sorry.'

'Whoops, me and my big mouth. But no! Why shouldn't we talk about it? We're trying to find your mum. She's far more important than SPC.'

'Yeah.'

'But if it's so hush-hush, that's as far as I'll get until I'm back on Monday and can talk to people face to face. I might worm a bit more out of them then.'

'Is there no one who could help before Monday?' Ben asked. 'I can't wait till then, Debs. I need to find her.'

'I know, but if Golden Boy doesn't know about it our best chance is Tricky and I'm hardly going to get him to come clean over the phone.' Golden Boy must be Marcus because of his golden hair, Ben supposed. Or maybe his rapid rise in SPC. Or maybe both.

'You can't trust Tricky.'

'Exactly.'

Thinking of Mum's boss – all that she'd said of him over the years – Ben suddenly had a horrible thought: 'Do you think he could be involved in Mum's disappearance?'

'No, Ben, no, he's a twisted malevolent schemer, but not that bad.'

'Are you sure?'

'It's dirty work, abduction, Ben, if that's what you mean. Your mum won't have been abducted. Why would anyone do that?'

'No idea.'

'You're so tired and so frightened you're putting two and two together and making twenty. Don't worry about that Ben.'

'*But where is she then*?'

'I only wish I knew. One minute,' she said to someone else. 'Sorry, Ben, I've got to go. I'll talk to Tricky on Monday, promise.'

'Thanks, Debs.'

'You'll find her, Ben. If anyone can, you will.'

But it was over a day since she'd disappeared and he still didn't know why or where she was. He went to see Jess and Aunt Miriam, who were both in Aunt Miriam's study.

'The meeting was definitely in Oxford, Debs reckons.'

'Okay. We'll try there tomorrow first. But not tonight. It's too late.'

'Every night we don't look is another night she's missing,' said Jess. 'I'll phone round now.'

'But no one would help you, not at this time.'

'Jess is right. We need to search.'

'We can't, Ben. If it would do any good I'd walk the streets all night to find her, you know I would. But it won't.' Ben nodded, feeling wretched inside. No, the kidnapper would make sure she couldn't be easily found. 'Get to bed, darling. After last night you must be shattered. A good night's sleep will do you the world of good.'

'Okay.' He wished them goodnight, then went to clean his teeth, changed into his nightwear and returned to his phone. He read her text once more, wishing he'd not cleared his Inbox last week, else there would be lots more of her messages to see. In the faint hope that they would let her see her phone he typed:

Love u mum searching 4 u stay strong love Ben xfe

He switched off the light and climbed into bed. He'd slept in it many times before but it was the first time he'd had no idea where Mum was, or if she was safe.

Miserable, anxious, yet exhausted, he drifted off into a fretful sleep.

Chapter 7

Off to Church

On Sunday morning Ben woke, wondered where he was for a few muzzy seconds and then, as he remembered, the gnawing fear returned. He got up. Time to do something about it. First he checked his phone, just in case – but no, Mum hadn't replied. There were new messages from Jonno, Naz and Dan who were offering condolences and help. News had got around then.

Quickly he tapped in a reply.

Will let u know, thx

He pulled on some jeans and went downstairs. Jess was dressed (green and purple again) and setting the table for breakfast, whereas Aunt Miriam was still in her dressing gown. The delicious fragrance of sizzling bacon announced she was back to cooking – Sunday breakfasts were one of the best things about staying with them.

'Hi Ben,' Jess greeted him brightly.

'Morning, Ben. Sleep well?' asked Aunt Miriam. Ben could tell she hadn't. Very pale except for the dark circles around her eyes, she looked like an inverse panda.

'Better than last night. Is there any news?'

'I'm sorry darling, no. I've been searching all night online, but I can't find her. It's awful how many people are missing in the UK alone; so many children.'

'Maybe that's why the police focus on them,' said Jess. 'But I wish they had time for adults too.'

'Indeed. It's desperately sad.' Aunt Miriam sighed heavily.

'Would you like a coffee?' Ben offered.

'I've had three already, I'd better not. But thanks. You can call Freddie and Henry instead. Don't bother Robert. He likes cold sausage sandwiches when he emerges from his lair.'

'I could have one later too. I'd like to find that meeting in Oxford,' Ben said, just in case she'd forgotten.

'After breakfast. No one would appreciate being rung before nine on a Sunday,' said Aunt Miriam firmly, so he went to call the others. Freddie was coming downstairs, so Ben's task was simply to knock on his uncle's study door and shout, 'Breakfast's ready.'

'Keen to be off on your treasure hunt?' said Freddie, digging for information already.

'No, just hungry.'

He knew there was lots of time – St James's church wasn't far, it would take fifteen minutes to walk there, no more.

Hungry now, Ben tucked in to his breakfast. Freddie tried to probe again, but Ben deflected this by asking Uncle Henry if he had any forthcoming publications, to be rewarded with an incomprehensible but lengthy summary of an imminent paper, allowing him to plough through the tasty breakfast in peace.

After breakfast Uncle Henry beetled back to his study and Ben and Jess cleared the breakfast dishes whilst Freddie finished his coffee.

'Have you any school trips coming up?' Jess asked.

'No. What about you?'

'Pompeii maybe?' she looked at her mum.

'Don't ask me, ask your father.'

'You lucky thing. Our school trips are to places like Staircase House and Manchester Museum.'

'It's a good museum. Dinosaurs and mummies.'

'But not Italy.'

'Where's Staircase House?'

'Stockport.'

'Why's it called that?'

'It has a staircase.' Her wounded expression made him feel bad. She didn't deserve that. 'No, sorry Jess. It's been in the marketplace for centuries and has a *historic* staircase and loads of rooms.'

'Why is it a museum?'

'Each room's set up from a different time in the house's history. We had to be medieval peasants, wrapping apples and doing stuff to candles, can't remember. Oh yeah, they were tallow. Smelt rank. There's a posh dinner table too. Your dad would love it.' Ben cleared the final mat – another of Uncle Henry's insane demands, since they'd have to be replaced for lunch, then dinner. (No-one bothered when he was at work, not even Aunt Miriam).

'I'm going to get ready,' said Aunt Miriam.

'Can I borrow your study to start the ring round of Oxford?'

'Why don't you two take a few hours off? I know Oxford better than both of you, so I could do it.' She checked the clock. 'I'll be ready not much after nine.' Aunt Miriam, Mum and Uncle Henry had all studied at Oxford.

'Could you take a couple of hours later on?' asked Jess. 'Ben's got his homework quest to do.'

'On a *Sunday*?'

'I know,' said Ben. 'If I knew how to bring her back I'd do it right away but while I don't, it's something to do. It'll improve my grades at school. Mum would want me to do it,' he added, sure that at least his last sentence was true.

Aunt Miriam sighed heavily. 'That's true, she would. She'd be so proud of you right now.' Her eyes filled with tears, which she attempted to blink back, but one escaped. Jess rushed to cuddle her. Ben felt his eyes prick with unshed tears, and determined to keep it that way, muttered that he'd grab a shower. He hurriedly left the room.

He was emerging from the bathroom rubbing his hair dry as Aunt Miriam reached the top of the stairs.

'I'll log you in, Ben, but I've asked Jess to do her practice first. You're setting us a fine example. We can't let everything else slide whilst we're searching for your mum. A raging tiger wouldn't stop me bringing her back, if I only knew how to do it.'

'We will soon,' Ben assured her, the vision of Aunt Miriam fending off a raging tiger causing his lips to twitch with amusement. Mum would find it funny too. He must remember to tell her.

Alone in her study, to the distant strains of Jess's violin, Ben started calling the Oxford hotels. (Aunt Miriam had advised that the colleges took longer to get going on Sundays.) He worked down the names suggested on a travel website and had just finished those (no luck) when Jess came in. Jess was more methodical (too methodical in Ben's opinion) and was appalled he hadn't made a list.

'You could forget and ring a hotel twice, or even worse, miss one out, and that might be the one where the meeting was held.'

Ben admitted she had a point, and worked to her system from then on. By mid-morning they had found a few conferences, but nothing involving agrochemicals, or even the broader chemical industry. Unless Mum had a secret passion for scuba diving, she wouldn't have been at any of them.

'Well that was a complete waste of time,' Ben complained.

'Not according to Sherlock Holmes. He said that if you eliminate the impossible, what you are left with is the truth.'

'Yeah but he's fictional.' Seeing Jess's face fall, Ben quickly added, 'Though I suppose he had a point.'

'I don't suppose it's worth trying guest houses?'

'When have you ever seen a guest house with a meeting room?' Ben snapped and, seeing the hurt in Jess's eyes, immediately felt bad. 'Sorry Jess, I'm just so worried about Mum. I didn't mean to bite your head off, I'm just so scared for her.'

'I know. Me too. So let's find her. Shall we start on the colleges?'

'Yeah.' There was a helpful list on the University's website, with each college's phone number just one click away. The first few colleges denied any meeting, but eventually they got a positive response.

'Yes, we did have a meeting on Friday night, a pre-gaudy drinks party,' said a woman at Brasenose.

'Gaudy?'

'An old members' reunion. Was your mother at Brasenose?'

'No, St Saviour's. And I think it was a business meeting.'

'Then it wouldn't be here, not this weekend. We're completely booked up with the gaudy.'

After a few more fruitless calls, Aunt Miriam entered with two mugs in her hand. 'Hot chocolate for the two workers. Any luck?'

'Not so far, no. We've eliminated all the hotels, now we're onto colleges,' said Ben taking a sip of the overly sweet drink. His mouth was dry after so much talking so he'd have preferred water, but Jess was relishing it.

Familiar footsteps outside. Uncle Henry marched in.

'My mother says you've cancelled tonight!'

Aunt Miriam turned to him. 'No, Henry, I told her about Sue and she said she wouldn't come. She said I had enough on my plate.'

'It's no trouble to feed her!' It was. Ben knew Aunt Miriam went to enormous efforts for Uncle Henry's beloved (posh, wealthy and daunting) mum: special menus, four or more courses, everyone dressed up. Ben had had to endure a few of those delicious but terrifyingly formal meals and he was heartily grateful there wasn't to be one that night.

But Uncle Henry wasn't.

'Your nephew's welcome, but my mother isn't!'

'My nephew has nowhere else to live. Your mother has a mansion.'

'It's not a mansion!'

'Okay, it's a beautiful elegant spacious house in the most expensive village in Britain, and she is sufficiently wealthy to dine out whenever she pleases, or to see out her days in Claridge's should she so wish. Your mother can cope perfectly well tonight and has very kindly offered to do so.'

Still seething, Uncle Henry stalked out.

'Sorry,' Ben said.

'It's no problem at all, Ben. His mother didn't mind one little bit. She has more compassion in her little finger than that maddening man I married. Anyway back to more important things. Have you tried St Saviour's yet?' It was the family college. She and Mum and Uncle Henry had all studied there. It was where Aunt Miriam and Uncle Henry

93

had met. (So it had a lot to answer for, Aunt Miriam sometimes joked – or maybe not?)

'No. We've just finished Hertford,' Jess replied. 'We're working alphabetically.'

'Of course you are. Right, I'll take over now, and call … Jesus,' she said, consulting the list. 'Seems very appropriate on a Sunday.' Ben smiled.

'Thanks. Hope you have more luck than we did. So far this morning's been a complete waste of time.'

'No it isn't. We've narrowed down the possibilities,' said Jess.

'Maybe. But I'm starting to think maybe Debs was wrong about Oxford.'

Jess looked horrified. 'We can't ring every hotel in England!'

'We might have to, if we can't find Mum's meeting any other way.'

'After Oxford, I'll try Cambridge, then London. I'll have something for you when you get back,' Aunt Miriam said.

'I hope so. Thanks.'

It was much nicer walking towards St James's with Jess than it had been getting the bus to Manchester with Freddie. It was a sunny morning, so Didsbury village was bustling with coffee seekers, but because they had left early, short delays behind Sunday loiterers weren't a problem. Plus Ben knew the format now – there would be an envelope, he'd find it and it would tell him (tortuously, but with the help of Jess and the internet he'd get there) where to find the next clue.

The crowds thinned as they left the village, so they speeded up.

'I hope we can spot the kidnapper,' said Jess as they turned onto Stenner Lane where the church and Fletcher

Moss were both situated. 'Oh hang on, he or she wouldn't be here, would they? I mean, who's guarding your mum? And where?'

'I wish I knew. If it's Goatee Man I feel sorry for her. Of course I do anyway,' Ben quickly added, realising he'd said something stupid. 'But the person writing the Einstein Code is clever, and they weren't.'

'No. The author's local though.'

'How do you work that out?'

'You'd have to be fairly local to know of St James's church, wouldn't you?' she said as they arrived in front of it. Its square tower rose high above the pavement. Now Ben looked at it afresh. He could tell the arched windows were historic, but from the 13th century? He was surprised they were so ancient, yet had survived. Worryingly the wooden entrance doors were shut.

'I guess that means they're having a service,' Jess said.

Freddie rode up on his bike.

'You two took your time didn't you?'

'Where've you come from?' asked Ben, suspicious Freddie had been snooping in his bag.

'Fletcher Moss. Nice day for a ride.'

'How did you know when to be here?'

'Simple. I checked on the service times. You didn't leave between Holy Communion and Family Worship, so I guessed your next appointment would be after eleven-thirty, when Family Worship is due to finish.'

'And if we hadn't turned up?' said Ben suspiciously. Freddie shrugged nonchalantly.

'I'd have gone home again.'

'Have you nothing better to do than spy on me?'

'Why are you using Jess to help you and not me?'

'Because she's nicer.' Freddie looked wounded, but Ben was in no mood to pander to his feelings. 'So stuff off, yeah?'

'Fine,' he huffed. 'I'll take a look around. I love old graves.'

'Weirdo,' muttered Ben as he went off.

'You don't have to live with him.'

'I do until I get Mum back.'

'True.'

But the service didn't end at 11:30 as he'd predicted. It was getting uncomfortably close to the deadline when the doors were finally opened and people started emerging from the church: families, pensioners, but no Goatee Man.

'We wouldn't know what the others look like.'

'I think I'd have spotted Nixon. I saw him on the website, remember,' Jess explained in response to Ben's startled look.

'Let's get in there.'

There was still a steady stream of worshippers emerging so they progressed slowly, scattering excuse mes and thank yous as appropriate.

It was almost twelve by the time they entered the church. Ben half-expected Freddie to accompany them, but he was nowhere to be seen. Two elderly ladies, who were clearing a trestle table of used mugs by the entrance, gave them a welcoming smile. Two men further down the church were standing chatting, but both looked far too respectable to be involved with kidnapping.

'Is it all right if we look around?' Ben asked.

'Certainly,' said one of the ladies, smiling encouragingly.

They walked down the central aisle in search of the Mosley monument. Jess spotted it first, on the right of the church, an ornate monument with the grandly dressed figure of Nicholas Mosley kneeling over the much smaller figures of his two wives and four even smaller descendants.

'Typical!' said Jess. 'Subjugation of women yet again.'

But Ben was more bothered by the lack of an envelope. The church was very dark towards the altar, making him jittery (who might be lurking there?) so he was relieved to quickly spot an envelope nestling behind a nearby radiator (painted a rather startling red). The two men were still deep in conversation and the ladies were clearing away coffee cups, so while they were distracted he pocketed it.

'Aren't you going to read it?' Jess asked.

'Let's get out of here first. Anyone could be hiding in the shadows down there.'

'Don't say that! It gives me the creeps.'

They were both glad to get out into the sunshine – until they saw Freddie's bike.

'Let's ignore it,' Jess said – fine by Ben – so they turned down the path towards the lane, but before they had reached the graveyard exit, Freddie caught them up.

'So what does it say?' he asked. 'You'll need my help, judging from your performance last night.' Ben, anger bubbling up inside him, said nothing. 'Science isn't exactly your strong point, is it?'

'Get lost, Freddie. We can handle it,' said Jess.

'How do you know? What does it say?' Freddie persisted.

The bubble burst.

'IT'S NOT IMPORTANT! IT'S HOMEWORK, RIGHT? MUM'S WHAT MATTERS, NOT HOMEWORK!'

Looking alarmed, Freddie scurried off, but wasn't quite out of earshot when he taunted, 'So why are you bothering with it then?'

'Ignore him. He's just trying to goad you,' Jess said.

'It's working.' But also Ben was increasingly convinced that Freddie must know more than he'd let on. He watched him cycle off towards Didsbury wondering if he'd be so sneaky as to search his room. Was it him who'd switched off the socket? Would he be so nasty? Probably, yes. He was desperate to be begged for help. But Ben didn't need him. He had Jess now.

'I can see you're fuming, but perhaps you had better check the next clue, just in case we've got to get somewhere fast,' she said tentatively.

Ben looked at her and tried to relax his taught cheek muscles into a smile.

'Sorry, Jess. You're right. Sorry I let him wind me up so much.'

'He tries to wind everybody up. It just works better with you because you agree he's better than you.'

'I don't. He's a total snot bag.'

'Yes, but he's cleverer than you and that gets to you. He's cleverer than *everyone*, Ben, but that's not everything. You're kinder and nicer and could beat him hands down over any distance he chose.'

'Not on his bike I couldn't,' Ben responded, softening a little. 'He looks down on me like some dimwit country cousin.'

'He's scared of you.'

'*Really*?'

'Really. Freddie suspects he wouldn't survive in a state school.'

'He wouldn't, the way he goes on.'

'Exactly, so he admires you because you do.'

'It's not that tough, our school.'

'I know, but Freddie doesn't. He thinks you're all dealing drugs and fighting off flick knives every day.' Ben grinned at her. 'What does the clue say?'

He opened the envelope and held out the letter so that she could read it too.

Clue 3

One man switched a torch on,

Thought: 'Light beams are not free,

They come from mass the torch has lost.'

Hence Fat Man finished me.

To find Clue 4:

Sit down on some maths,

Lean back on a bear,

Search right by an eagle,

Clue 4 will be there.

Today 13:00

'Ben, that's practically now!' Jess panicked.

'Great! The sooner I get Mum back the better,' he responded cheerily, heading downhill towards the park.

'We've got to get back for lunch.'

'You do, Jess. It's your family. But I'm going to get my mum and nothing on earth will stop me.'

'Sure, Ben, sorry. You know what Dad's like. Where are we going?'

'Rory's bench. It's that carved bench in Fletcher Moss near the café – the one with bears and robots.'

'Oh I know. Why's it called Rory's bench?'

'After a boy from Parrs Wood who got knocked down.'

'That's sad.'

'Yeah, but it's an amazing way to be remembered. I can't understand the clue. Can you?'

'I think it's talking about Einstein. He imagined a torch being switched on, and losing one unit of light – that's a photon, yes? One unit of light.'

'With you so far.'

'Good. What energy does the photon have?'

'I dunno.'

'It's moving, so it's kinetic energy.'

'What?'

'You must have done it, Ben. Kinetic energy is mass times velocity squared. So what energy does the photon have?'

'Its mass times its speed squared,' Ben hazarded.

'Exactly! Which is c, the speed of light in a vacuum. So by the principle of conservation of energy, the energy lost by the torch, E, equals mc^2.'

'It's that simple?' Ben looked at her, surprised. The most world-shattering equation was down to simply switching a torch on and thinking? But most people didn't think, that was the point. 'Einstein must have asked questions about everything,' he said, smiling at her. 'Like you.'

But then he stopped, tense as an antelope sensing a lion. The white Mercedes was parked, right by the Fletcher

Moss entrance. The windows were a fathomless black; it was impossible to tell whether they were in the car, or not.

'It's them, Jess.'

'You can't be sure.'

'I am sure.'

'Shall we go back to the Wilmslow Road entrance?'

'It's too late. Let's run.'

Jess was fast. She matched his speed into the park, keeping a wide berth of the car. But nothing happened as they passed it.

'Even if it is them, they won't do anything here. It's far too busy,' Jess said.

The park was indeed packed. There were families, cyclists and dog walkers to contend with, so they slowed to a jog, evading slow-moving people by veering onto the grass.

'If you need to answer the clue, Ben, Fat Man's the nuclear bomb the Americans dropped on Nagasaki, so Nagasaki's the answer.'

'Why all that stuff about Einstein then?' Ben asked as they passed the tennis courts.

'That's how nuclear bombs work, mass being turned into energy. His equation tells you how much energy you'll get. Since the speed of light's huge, a little bit of mass gives you an enormous burst of energy.'

'Oh right, yeah.'

They headed left past the Petunia Triangle, as Mum had called the flowerbed ever since it was packed with petunias one spring. It was still full of colourful flowers, but petunias? Ben had no idea.

The café was open – good, perhaps he'd treat Jess to an ice cream for her help. But first he wanted to find the clue.

They were slightly early, so he wasn't sure it would be there yet, but he soon found it, planted under a large stone.

As Ben straightened up clutching the envelope he noticed a tall man turning the corner by the café, a tough guy with a paunch. And also a goatee beard, a shaven head and, as he spotted Ben, a look that would terrify anyone.

He bared his teeth like a hostile dog.

'It's Goatee Man!'

He started accelerating towards them.

'*Come on*!'

The path was too crowded, so Ben ran onto the grass verge with Jess in hot pursuit. Being small, she had a much shorter stride, but for a twelve-year-old titch her speed was amazing. But he'd drawn her into danger. He should have realised Goatee Man would attack. The kidnappers knew exactly where he would be and when he'd be picking up the clues. He shouldn't have brought Jess with him. He could have found Rory's bench without her.

He looked back. Goatee Man was closing on them.

A small boy darted in front of them, giggling. Ben swerved round him but Jess had to wait. A dog leapt at Ben, yapping excitedly. Again he swerved, knocking into Jess, but she kept going. She was so tough, but so small. Ben looked back again. They were still ahead of Goatee Man and near the exit now. But as they moved onto the path a family (mum, dad, two young boys) entered the park, blocking their way.

'Help us, please!' Jess begged. Ben looked at her aghast.

'What's up?' the mum asked, looking concerned.

'He's after us.' Jess pointed to Goatee Man. He slowed to a jog.

As the dad put a protective hand on Ben's shoulder he realised Jess might have been right to ask for help. Goatee Man wouldn't dare try anything now. Would he?

'Why are you chasing them?' the woman demanded militantly.

'I'm not chasin' them. I'm late,' he replied in the Mancunian tones Ben remembered. He roughly shouldered the dad aside and exited the park, pulling his phone out of his jeans. His accomplice could drive here in two minutes from where they were parked.

'Do you want us to call the police?'

Ben spotted an approaching 42A.

'No thanks. We'll get that bus.' He stepped forward and stuck out a hand, mentally thanking whichever genius had thought of sticking a stop so close to the entrance. The indicator light flashed and the bus started pulling in.

'He was lying, wasn't he? It's terrible, menacing you like that. Are you sure you don't want the police?' the kind mum asked Jess.

'We're fine, thanks to you,' Ben told her. 'Come on, Jess. This must go through Didsbury. Doesn't it?'

'Every bus here goes through Didsbury.'

'Come on then.' Ben took her hand again, like he used to many years ago, to lead her onto the bus. He hadn't found the encounter with Goatee Man half as scary as Friday night. Was he toughening up? Or was it because he'd been more concerned about protecting his cousin than himself? He didn't know, but he was glad he hadn't been as scared in front of Jess. He paid for their fares from the emergency fund.

'Let's sit down and look at the next clue.'

'Oh no! What if he was running after us to *give* us the next clue?'

'No way, Jess. You didn't see how he looked at me. He hates me.'

'He should be in jail.'

'Tell the police that,' said Ben, opening the letter.

Clue 4

Though we call it a Dog
To us it's brightest of the bright,
You'll see it nearly nine years ago
If you look up tonight.

To find Clue 5:
You can see my bones here
But to see me roam,
Visit the Hydra Supercluster,
And look back at my home
Tuesday 4th April 11:00

'Tuesday!'

'Oh Ben, I'm sorry. But at least we won't be late for lunch.'

'I don't give a stuff about lunch!' Two more days of silence. Two more days without her. Two more days of misery. It took all of his resolve not to weep.

Chapter 8

Message From Mum?

'Phew!' Jess exhaled as she slammed the door behind them. They had run most of the way back, in case the Mercedes had followed them, but on Jess's road had slowed to a walk.

'They're not after us, see?' Ben had said to try and reassure her.

'They were, Ben, and you know it. I'm not going to let them get you, you know.'

'Nor me you.'

She looked so relieved to be home. For a fleeting second Ben imagined going home too, but was distracted by Robert, who was ranting in the kitchen.

'That's so not fair! Ben's a guest. *He's* allowed to stay.'

'He's family. She's not,' Aunt Miriam replied firmly.

'Of course she's not family! That'd be weird.'

'We've discussed this very many times, and you know your father's rules.'

'But they're so last century!'

'We *are* last century.'

'He can't rule my life!'

'In this house he can. You have to abide by our rules while you live here.'

'But *he* doesn't, does he? Your darling nephew. He can do anything he likes.'

'Robert! Ben's going through enough without you getting at him.'

'Ben, Ben, Ben,' Robert chanted sarcastically as he emerged into the hall, where Ben and Jess were listening. He pounded up the stairs, ignoring them. Ben wondered if it was true that he got away with far more than them. He didn't have to do music practice, but the rest of his behaviour was constrained by Uncle Henry's rules and he often tried to help Aunt Miriam, unlike Robert.

Still he went into the kitchen a little shamefacedly.

'Hello you two,' said Aunt Miriam, who was chopping carrots. 'I'm doing a late lunch because we had a cooked breakfast.' On Sunday they called their second meal lunch even at 4pm, which was early dinner in Ben's view. The oven was on, but there was only a faint smell, implying food was hours off. He was hungry after the chase and the worry. 'Do you want a drink?' she asked.

'Just water, thanks. I'll get it,' Ben added hurriedly. 'Do you want one, Jess?' he asked as he opened the glass cupboard. Aunt Miriam had a half-filled glass beside her.

'Please.'

'You two look hot. Have you been running?'

'Yes. We raced home,' said Jess.

'In coats? Today?' The cool early morning had developed into a very warm afternoon.

'That's why we're hot,' said Ben, giving Jess a warning look. *Don't tell her.* She shook her head, showing she understood. Good. He handed over her water.

'What was Robert after? Bianca staying over?' she asked.

'Yes. He never lets up, but your father will never give in, and I'm caught between them, like Scylla and Charybdis.'

'What?' asked Ben.

'Two deadly sea monsters between which Odysseus had to navigate. Or sometimes a wall of moving rock and a whirlpool.'

'Ah,' said Ben nodding. 'Caught between a rock and a hard place?'

'Exactly.'

'So which is Robert?'

'The hard place. And Henry's my rock.' Ben rolled his eyes. His uncle was hardly that; Aunt Miriam was *his* rock. But he understood Aunt Miriam's good mood when she added, surprisingly casually, 'I found out where the meeting was.'

'*What? Where*?' Ben asked, stunned.

'St Saviour's, would you believe?'

'Mum's old college! And yours,' Ben added quickly.

'That's right.'

'How did you find out?' Jess asked.

'The porter told me. He wasn't meant to – it was incredibly hush-hush he said, but he'd heard it was SPC.'

'How?'

'Someone had recognised someone I think.'

'Mum?' Ben asked hopefully.

'Doubt it. He would have said.'

'Who was there?'

'He couldn't say. It could lose him his job.'

'But it might bring Mum back.'

'It might tell us who took her,' said Jess.

'Took her?' Aunt Miriam said. Ben glared at Jess.

'It's possible she's been kidnapped,' Jess said.

What on earth was she doing? Ben was so alarmed he had to turn away so that Aunt Miriam wouldn't notice.

But she calmly replied, 'Hardly, darling. Why would anyone kidnap her?'

'I know.'

'It's your detective books that do it. You imagine mysteries everywhere. I've left a message for Marcus about St Saviour's,' Aunt Miriam said.

'I'll tell Debs,' Ben replied. He used his mobile, left a message, then opened up Mum's last text, the only word he'd had from her since Friday morning when she'd left for work, calling, 'Have a great day.'

If only he had. If only she had. Wistfully, he viewed her text.

V late night cld even be midnight sorry. Go to M's. Mum xxf

What had she been thinking as she sent it? How had she been feeling? She would probably have been as disappointed as him that their Friday night celebration was going to be ruined. He reconsidered her new sign off. Maybe it was intentional, rather than a mistake. Maybe it meant lots of love forever. He traced it out on his keypad, and as he did so a part of his mind registered the numbers he was touching, because they were of such significance to him.

'993!'

'What?' Jess, busy setting the table, turned to him.

'993. Don't you remember?' he urged Aunt Miriam. 'Mum's rising star, the best product she never had?' SPC993 was a fungicide that had looked set to break all records. It cured a wider spectrum of fungal diseases than any existing fungicide on every crop tested. It was both protective and curative. With new chemistry, there was no resistance to it (yet), so the world's farmers would have been desperate for it. Mum had talked excitedly about the stunning results they were getting from field trials every night. Until the disaster.

'It was scrapped, wasn't it?' Aunt Miriam said.

'Yeah, it failed tox tests.' Since they were used on food crops, all products were tested for toxicology as well as efficacy.

'Tox tests?' asked Jess.

'Whether it harmed baby mice and rabbits.'

'Eugh, that's horrible! They test them on babies?'

'They have to, Jess. It wouldn't be safe for human babies otherwise.'

'We should farm without agrochemicals then.'

'Tell that to a starving country. Agrochemicals give more food per acre of land,' said Aunt Miriam. 'To feed seven billion humans and rising we need them.'

'Mum thinks so,' agreed Ben. 'But is she sending me a code? That the meeting was about 993?'

'*Code*? What do you mean?' Jess was intrigued, so he showed her the text and explained.

'It could be. She's read all the mysteries, Ben. She'd know about codes. Peter Wimsey is always cracking them.'

'Who?'

'Another fictional detective,' Aunt Miriam said. 'I can't see why there would have been a meeting about 993.'

'Maybe they found a mistake in the tox tests! Maybe that's why she stayed late. She would have done for 993.'

'You're only surmising, Ben. Much more likely she was just telling you she'd always love you, like she does.'

'Debs would know! I'll call her.'

There was still no answer so he left another message.

'Mum, can we go on your computer?' Jess asked when she'd finished setting the table. It was a pain to have to beg for computers. Most of Ben's friends had laptops or tablets, but Aunt Miriam believed too much computer time was harmful for developing minds, so the only other computer in the house, apart from hers and Uncle Henry's, was Robert's. (They'd given up on his mind years ago, Ben reckoned.)

'On your own time, yes. I can't see there's much else to do.'

'Missing persons' sites?'

'I've just checked them. Nothing. Until Marcus or Debs comes back to us there's nothing we can do, unless we try ringing round hospitals again, but on Sundays they're so badly stretched, I don't think we'd get anywhere.'

'Okay. Come on, Ben. Is that okay, Mum? You don't need help with lunch?'

'I should be able to cope with roasting a leg of lamb. That's fine. Go and enjoy yourselves.'

On the way upstairs, Jess whispered, 'I really want to crack that clue.' Since they had until Tuesday, Ben was more interested in the 993 idea, but, forced to wait until Debs responded, he agreed. Whilst the computer warmed up they chatted about Goatee Man.

'He was definitely after us,' Jess said.

'Me I think. Not you,' Ben replied, again attempting to reassure her.

'Why?'

'No idea. Why Mum?'

'I wish I knew,' Jess replied. 'But at least we know it's him dropping off the clues.'

'And you know he exists.'

'I never doubted you, Ben.'

'No, you didn't. Thanks Jess. Right, let's crack that clue.' He unfolded the letter (Freddie was playing the piano downstairs) and spread it out on the computer desk where they studied it together.

<u>Clue 4</u>

Though we call it a Dog

To us it's brightest of the bright,

You'll see it nearly nine years ago

If you look up tonight.

To find Clue 5:

You can see my bones here

But to see me roam,

Visit the Hydra Supercluster,

And look back at my home

Tuesday 4th April 11:00

'Isn't it about seeing into the past when you look at stars, like Freddie was going on about last night?'

'Exactly,' confirmed Jess, opening up the internet. She searched for Hydra Supercluster and clicked on the top-ranked site. 'Yes! 150 million light years away,' she exclaimed, as if that explained everything.

'What?'

'If we went to a star 150 million light years away and looked back at earth, what would we see?'

'Nothing. It's way too far.'

'Yes, but if you imagine you had a really powerful telescope, so powerful that you could see life forms ...'

'What? Trees? Birds? Dinosaurs?'

'Exactly! Dinosaurs. They were alive then, but now they're fossils. Some of them at least.'

'So we want dinosaur bones?'

'Exactly. We want Stanley.'

'*Stanley*?'

'The T Rex in Manchester Museum,' said Jess. 'He's Stanley. And T Rex was alive then, so it fits. It could be one of the other skeletons there too. I can't remember all of them. But I bet it's Stanley.'

'Okay,' said Ben, inwardly amused that Jess was naming a skeleton, as if it were a pet. 'So what about the clue? It's going to be a star nine light years away isn't it? With the same name as a dog.'

'Yes,' said Jess, searching online. It led them straight to Sirius, also known as the Dog Star, the brightest star in the sky because of its proximity – 8.6 light years away from earth.

'Close to the sun,' said Ben.

'No, that's under eight light *minutes* away, not years.'

'Oh yeah.'

'Look at these faces,' said Jess, opening up the SPC site and going to Meet the Board. 'Do you recognise any of them?'

Five men, one woman, all in suits, all white, the Executive Directors of SPC: Lord Charles Hanbury, white-haired Chairman; Sir John Knox, small, unsmiling Chief Executive; Ian Curtis, fiery-faced Finance Director; Peter Nixon, droopy-faced Operations Director; Hazel Finch, glamorous Human Resources Director; and their ally Marcus Wright, the Commercial Director.

'I only recognise Marcus. Maybe they're Pete and the Chief,' Ben mused, pointing to Nixon and Knox.

'They look mean enough. But how can we tell?'

'I dunno.'

The doorbell rang. Unable to quench the hope that it would be Mum, Ben shot downstairs followed by Jess. They joined Aunt Miriam as she opened the door.

'Hello. You must be Bianca,' she said.

'Yeah. Is Robbie in?' said Bianca, plastered in makeup (off-putting to Ben but he could see she would be attractive to many). She had large eyes, pouty lips and was wearing a very tight top, a very short skirt – and very high heels, Ben noticed, as she sashayed down the hall. 'These make me wanna puke. Dunno why you don't rip them out,' she commented of the gaudily tiled floor.

'They're far too valuable to remove,' Aunt Miriam explained, seemingly unfazed. But Jess was.

'She's horrid,' she whispered.

'But you like everyone.'

'Not her.'

'How come you know her when your mum doesn't?'

'She was here last week whilst they were at work.'

'Were you off again?' It was so not fair. His cousins enjoyed lots more holidays than he did.

'Yes.'

'Lucky you.'

'You wouldn't say that if you'd been here with Robert drooling over her and them lording it over us.'

'Nightmare.'

'Yes. I stayed in my room, doing homework. Good job. I won't get much done this week.'

He'd complained to Mum about their three week Christmas break.

'But they get much more homework,' she'd said.

'Yeah, and loads of time off to do it.'

'It's how they get good grades, Ben. They're force-fed knowledge. If you're interested in sitting for Freddie and Robert's school, I could perhaps afford it, if we give up foreign holidays and football perhaps.' She was unable to keep the amusement from her lips.

'Tempting offer. I'll think about it.'

'Just imagine getting the bus with Freddie and Robert every day.'

'Okay, that clinches it. No way.' She'd laughed at that – she laughed so much, which made him laugh too. Life was so much happier at home than in the high pressure Winterburn household. How he missed her as he sat down amongst them for the now very late lunch.

Uncle Henry entered, saw Bianca and looked outraged.

'So *she's* invited, when my mother isn't?'

'Henry, she's not called she, she's called Bianca.'

'I don't care what she's called, why isn't my mother here?'

'Because I haven't the time nor the energy to produce a meal fit for her. She's an elegant lady with wonderful taste and I like to make a special effort when she joins us,' she added, buttering him up. 'Would you kindly pour the wine before the meal goes cold?'

He started opening a bottle, the only domestic duty Ben ever saw him perform.

'Do you want wine?' he asked Bianca. 'Are you over eighteen?'

'Just,' she said. Freddie and Jess snorted.

'Twenty-five more like,' Jess murmured to Ben.

'Are you driving?'

'If there's wine, I could stay over.'

'You couldn't!' Aunt Miriam snapped back. 'Sorry, Bianca, we don't allow Robert female guests.'

'Yes you do. I'm female,' she said, pushing forward her chest. Robert practically drooled.

'Overnight, I meant.'

'God, you're old fashioned aren't you?'

Ben looked at Jess, eyebrows raised.

'*That's nothing*,' she whispered.

Bianca was pulling Uncle Henry back. 'I will have wine. I'll leave my car here and get the bus.'

'I'll drive you,' Robert offered. Ben had never seen him volunteer to do *anything* for *anyone* before. He was clearly hooked.

When they started eating, the interrogation of Bianca began. It made a welcome change from science. Uncle Henry started on educational achievements. When she said she hadn't a degree, Ben half expected him to ask her to leave.

'Instead I work.'

'Doing what?'

'As a beauty consultant.'

'*Beauty consultant*?' he repeated with withering scorn. 'What on earth's that?'

'Facials, make up, treatments,' she replied, seemingly undaunted.

'Treatments?' inquired Aunt Miriam.

'Fillers mainly, you know, Botox and things.'

'Who uses Botox?'

'Everyone. From seventeen to seventy, they all love it.'

'*Seventeen*? Teenagers volunteer to have a lethal toxin injected into their faces?' Aunt Miriam looked horrified.

'Not volunteer, they have to pay. It costs a bomb, but they love it, so they keep coming back for more. Like me with this wine. Is there any more?' Now Uncle Henry looked horrified. No one *asked*, he *bestowed*. Robert reached for the bottle and refilled her glass, earning a glare from his father, but he was oblivious, ogling her.

'It's all right, Henry, there's another bottle just behind you,' said Aunt Miriam, indicating the one atop their gargantuan dresser. 'I want to sleep tonight.'

'So you inject a toxin into their faces?' Uncle Henry said, opening it.

'Not me, no, the doc. But I get a staff discount.'

'You mean you've had Botox?'

'You have to, living in Manchester. It ages you fast. Pollution ruins your skin.'

'Well I've lived in Manchester almost all my life and I've managed,' Aunt Miriam said.

'That's because you're fat. I know you're old but your face won't show wrinkles like a thin person's.'

Poor Aunt Miriam! She flinched.

'Mum's not fat!' Jess protested. 'Or old!'

'The owner's fat too,' Bianca continued, ignoring her. 'He can afford to be. He makes a packet and I get peanuts. One of these days I'm gonna get my own salon.'

'What's stopping you?' asked Uncle Henry.

'Bread. Dough. Wonga,' said Bianca, draining her glass and holding it out for a refill. Robert rapidly obliged.

'Does she mean money?' Uncle Henry asked his wife.

'Yes. It's not Swahili, darling, it's slang. Now has everyone finished?' (Nods and murmurs of agreement

116

round the table). 'If you could clear the table, I'll get the puddings out.'

Bianca, Uncle Henry, Robert and Freddie seemed to have gone suddenly deaf, so Jess and Ben cleared up as usual. She filled the dishwasher whilst he stacked the serving bowls, roasting tins and pans by the sink for washing later. So much faff! All to please his grumpy uncle, who never served, cleared or washed the mounds of pots he insisted upon.

Over pudding (delicious, home-made chocolate cake or warm apple pie and ice cream) Bianca said, 'Ben, you're here because your mum's missing, yeah?'

'Mm,' he confirmed briefly through a mouthful of apple pie.

'But aren't you worried about her?' A surge of indignation made him choke. Whilst he recovered Jess answered for him.

'Of course he's worried. He's desperate to find her. Ben's really close to his mum.'

'Well why aren't you looking for her then? If it was my mum, I'd be out looking for her, not eating.' (Bianca hadn't touched her pudding, she was knocking back wine instead.)

'If we knew where to look, we would,' said Aunt Miriam, even more tight-lipped. 'But unfortunately we don't. We're hoping that any second now she'll call us, or walk through that door.'

'You can't wait for her to come to you, you've gotta get out there and bring her back.'

'*Where*?' Ben demanded, stung by the injustice of Bianca's words.

'I dunno, do I? Have you tried the police?'

'If only you'd thought of that,' Freddie teased, grinning.

'Of course we have,' snapped Aunt Miriam. 'But they're too busy to look for missing adults.'

'We've tried hospitals and hotels and colleges,' Jess added.

'Well that's a waste of time. Why would she be at a college?'

'We're looking everywhere we can think of. But we also need to eat,' said Aunt Miriam.

'You've never stopped, from the size of you.'

'That's so horrid!' Ben protested.

'And inaccurate,' added Freddie. 'She needs to work and sleep too.'

'And cook and clean and wash and iron, but right now I've one priority and that is to find my sister!' Aunt Miriam said angrily. Her face was pink – from embarrassment or anger?

'More wine?' asked Freddie happily. How could he enjoy seeing his mum being attacked so? He poured the relics of the second bottle into Bianca's glass without waiting for a reply. She glugged it down immediately.

'Careful, Freddie. *In vino veritas*,' warned Aunt Miriam, meaning, 'In wine there is truth', Ben recalled.

'In vino hogwash, more like,' said Jess.

'Right, coffee time. There's quite a few pots to wash,' Aunt Miriam declared, getting up. 'The dishwasher's full. Ben and Jess have done enough today. Freddie and Robert, it's your turn.'

'But I've got company,' Robert complained.

'And your guest has eaten. Well, drunk,' amended Aunt Miriam, noticing Bianca's untouched pudding. 'I'll get back to the online search for my sister,' she added bitingly, but it sailed over Bianca's head. She was a tough cookie, Ben thought. Robert had better be careful.

Freddie started running the water as they walked towards the door.

'I'll try Debs again,' Ben said.

'I'll help you, Mum,' offered Jess.

'In a few minutes, Jess. There's something I need to sort out first. I'd like a coffee in my study, please, Freddie.'

'*What*?'

'I'll have one, too,' said Uncle Henry.

'In my study with me, please, Henry, I want to talk to you,' said Aunt Miriam.

'*Now?*' Her husband looked as astounded as if she'd suggested a quick jaunt to the moon.

'I know you've got work to do, you always have work to do, but I need five minutes of your time. Is that too much?'

'All right,' he huffed. He followed his wife out.

'We'll have coffee too, FartFace,' said Robert.

'Four coffees then, two in Mum's study, two in the kitchen. What about you, Jess? Mint tea in the bath?'

'Normal tea, thanks,' she said. 'I'll wait and carry one up for you.'

'Thanks a bunch. And for you, Ben? Double espresso with a side of ass's milk?'

'Nothing, thanks.' Ben was keen to escape for some peace.

But upstairs Uncle Henry and Aunt Miriam were arguing in her study.

'Over my dead body!' he was protesting over something or other. It could have been one of a million things. Shaking his head – he felt so sorry for Aunt Miriam sometimes – Ben entered the guest room, thankful he had a door to shut on the Winterburns. He looked at the photo of

Mum smiling, wishing he could cuddle her right now. He couldn't hang around until Tuesday.

He tried phoning Debs again. This time she answered.

'Hi Ben, what's all this about 993? I was just about to call you.'

'Thanks Debs. I think Mum might have been telling me it was a 993 meeting in code.'

'In code? Does she often talk to you in code?'

'No.'

'Me neither. Why 993?'

'Just a sign off. Debs, could there have been a mistake in the tox tests? Could it be alive again?'

'Alive again? Nothing would be alive if we sprayed 993 onto crops, Ben. We'd all be dead as dodos.'

'So there's no chance of restarting development?'

'No way, José. Anyway as the Development Manager I'd know about it before Sue. There couldn't be a 993 meeting without me. And SPC wouldn't touch it with a bargepole. It's dead in the water, Ben. Over. Kaput. Sorry, but she can't have meant 993.'

'Right, thanks. It was just an idea.'

'Keep having 'em. One of them will bring her back.'

'Yeah. I've had another. Could I come into SPC tomorrow? To try and find Pete?'

'I don't think so, Ben. I don't think it would be appropriate.'

'I've got to get Mum back!'

'All right, Ben, I know, don't shout. So do I. I'm so worried about her.'

'Pete knows where she is and he must work for SPC. I've got to find him.'

'It's the headquarters of a major multinational, not a den of thieves, Ben. Though sometimes it's more like a madhouse.'

'I know. But it's the only way I'll get Mum back.'

'Have you had no luck with hospitals?'

'No. I've got to find out about that meeting, the Pete and the Chief. They must be from SPC. *Please*?'

'Tricky will go mad.'

'Tricky doesn't need to know.'

'He'll find out. You know him.'

'*Please* Debs. For *Mum*.'

'Okay, it's worth a try. I could say you're on a school visit or something I suppose. But not on your own. Bring your cousins or something.'

'Okay,' Ben agreed eagerly. He'd have agreed to take Uncle Henry if necessary.

'I'm busy first thing. Would 11 o'clock do you, Ben?'

'Great, Debs, thanks. See you tomorrow.'

'See you tomorrow, Benbo.' Ben smiled. It had been her nickname for him ever since they'd watched *The Hobbit* together. He rang off. If there was any way to get to Mum without waiting for the Einstein Code, it had to be via SPC.

And somehow Ben had to find it.

Chapter 9

Tricky Dicky

On Monday morning he woke from such a deep sleep that for a few seconds he felt wonderfully relaxed, until with a jolt he remembered and the terrible anxiety returned. He checked texts – nothing from Mum, and neither Jonno nor Naz could join him in SPC today – got ready and went downstairs, where Jess, Freddie and Aunt Miriam were in the kitchen, having breakfast. It was 09:10, the kitchen clock said. He'd slept late. He joined them at the table and helped himself to orange juice and cereal.

'You slept well,' Aunt Miriam said, greeting him with a smile. 'Good. You needed it. So did I.'

'Aren't you working?'

'I've got a couple of days off. Compassionate leave.'

'Oh. Because of Mum?'

'Yes. Marcus will be mailing London hospitals today for us.'

'Oh yeah.' He tried to sound hopeful too, but knowing Mum was kidnapped was a crushing weight to bear. 'I'm going in to SPC to meet Debs this morning.'

'What for?'

'I must be able to find someone who was at that meeting with Mum and knows where she went.'

'You'd think so, wouldn't you? But Marcus doesn't think Pete and the Chief are from SPC does he?'

'No, but I do. Do you?'

'It's possible. If so they are very bad men, so please be careful. No accusations or confrontations, promise?'

'Promise.'

'You investigate there, I'll investigate here and by tonight we might have her home.'

'I hope so,' Ben responded. He'd give anything to make it happen, but what? Only the Chief or Pete could tell him. He had to find them fast.

'So do I. But back to that meeting. Did Debs think it was about 993?'

'What's that?' asked Freddie.

'The rising star that crashed and burned.'

'Rising star?' Jess asked.

'It's the Boston Matrix, one of Mum's marketing tools.' Jess was looking for more, so between sips of orange juice he expanded. 'You have stars, dogs, cash cows and problem children, right? You want to drop the dogs, milk the cows and turn the problem children into stars, if you can.'

'So it's used to differentiate between products?' said Freddie.

'Yeah, exactly.'

'Using what parameters? Profit and growth?'

'Something like that. I think it's market share and market growth. If it's got a rising share of a growing market, it's a star. And 993 was expected to be the biggest star ever, which is why it was so gutting when it crashed and burned.'

'Why?'

'It was too toxic,' Jess explained, allowing Ben to eat. 'Ben wondered if Aunt Sue's new sign off – xxf was it?' Ben nodded. 'He wondered if it was code for 993.'

'But Debs said no way,' Ben explained. The phone rang. Jess sprang up to answer.

'Oh hello … yes ... right,' she said. 'Ben, it's Debs for you.' Worried, Ben went over and greeted her.

'Hi Ben. Sorry, you can't come today.'

'*What*? I need to find Mum!'

'I know. But Ballantyne's the department head, and he says no.'

'Blast Ballantyne!' Jess came to stand by him, looking concerned.

'I don't really see why coming here would help.'

'To find Mum!'

'Sorry Ben.'

If Debs knew she was kidnapped, she wouldn't be acting like this. But he couldn't tell her.

'Tell her about Oxford,' Jess suggested. Ben nodded.

'There was a meeting in Oxford, like you said, Debs, in St Saviour's. We need to find out what happened there and if anyone there knows where Mum went after.'

'I'll find that out for you.'

'But Debs, I've got to come in! There's that meeting. And Pete *must* be from SPC.'

'Why aren't the police trying to find him?'

'Dunno but they're not. But we are.'

'Who's we?' Every face was turned towards him.

'Jess, Aunt Miriam – and Freddie,' he added reluctantly. What had he done really? Diddly-squat so far, apart from convincing the police Ben was a lying scumbag, treating him like an idiot and snooping (probably).

'Well why don't you bring your clever cousins and turn up in reception? Though Tricky's not got a shred of humanity, everyone else will feel desperately sorry for you and will do everything they can to help. Well most people,' she added. 'It's not on my invitation, mind. I'm just saying I can't stop you if that's what you want to do.'

'Okay Debs. Thanks.' Taking a deep breath, Ben put the phone down and explained to the others.

'I can't possibly sanction such a madcap plan,' said Aunt Miriam.

'*Please*?'

'But I'm going upstairs to try and find my sister and provided you three stick together you should have the wherewithal to get yourself to Wilmslow, or wherever you want to go – within a short radius, mind. No jaunts to London or anywhere, Freddie.'

'Sure Mum. Am I in charge?' Freddie was looking triumphantly at Ben, so Ben looked away, as if he didn't care. If Freddie was his passport to SPC he'd take him.

'No. You're accompanying them. No one's in charge,' Aunt Miriam said, removing Freddie's opportunity to lord it over them, which might have tested Ben beyond his limits before they'd even reached SPC.

'Okay. I'll protect you,' Freddie said.

'*You*? You're about as protective as a paper bag,' Ben riposted.

'Now boys, be nice.'

'I'll try,' agreed Ben.

'Who's paying for the train?' Freddie said.

'I am,' said Aunt Miriam. 'Straight there and straight back, okay?'

'Okay.'

'With mobiles switched on, please. If you're not back by two I'm calling the police. I'd take you myself if I didn't have work to do,' said Aunt Miriam, going to the cupboard where they kept the everyday plates.

'But you're on compassionate leave,' said Jess.

'Theoretically. But the History Department can't grind to a halt. I've a few work things to deal with this morning, unfortunately. But the rest of the time I'll be trying to find Sue and bring her safely home,' she said, handing two £20 notes to Freddie. 'Will that be enough?'

'Plenty. Okay, children, are you ready to hit the trains?'

'Freddie, stop it,' Aunt Miriam warned.

Jess stood up, walked round the table and squared up to her brother. 'You can either waste your time winding him up, or you can turn your enormous brain to unlocking the mystery of what happened to your aunt. One's easy and one's very difficult indeed. You can be the star that solves the mystery of the missing mum!' Freddie nodded, preening. Ben wasn't surprised. He'd have preened if Jess had spoken to him like that. If it stopped Freddie taunting and started him thinking, it was a genius move.

They gathered mobiles, coats and shoes, left the house and just made the Wilmslow train, which was lucky, because the next one wasn't for ages. On the train Freddie wanted Ben to repeat the events of the night, every detail now important and relevant to him.

'So Pete and the Chief work for SPC?'

'Yes,' Jess said. 'There are three suspects for Pete: Nixon, the Manufacturing Director; Swarbreck, the Regional – Manager, is it?'

'Not sure. Whatever they call the department heads this week,' Ben replied. 'They change titles as often as I change my socks, but basically he's Ballantyne's oppo. The other's Pete Parker, a new grad, but he wouldn't be in a meeting with Mum.'

'So two suspects really? Good. What about the Chief?' Freddie asked.

'Dunno. Could be anyone.'

'Not anyone. Pete's a senior manager, yes?'

'Well yeah, if it's Nixon, very senior indeed,' Ben replied.

'So if he calls the other man Chief, the other man must be senior to him.'

'Or woman,' Jess said.

'Yeah but there aren't any senior women. Except for Personnel, but that doesn't count,' Ben said.

'Why?'

'They're non-league.'

'Meaning?' Freddie asked, football being a foreign language to him.

'Everyone looks down on them, like you look down on state schools.'

'I don't,' he lied.

'Why?' Jess asked, again.

'Because they don't make any money or grow profits like Mum does. A senior commercial man would never take orders from even the Personnel Director, especially if she's a woman. The bias against women drives Mum nuts.'

'Not surprised. She's a raving feminist isn't she?' said Freddie.

'Not raving, no. She just believes women are as good as men. So do I.'

'Better in some ways,' said Jess.

'Yeah, I know,' Ben said impatiently. There were far much important things to think about than gender politics. 'Look, you might be right, Freddie. That's good thinking. If Pete's Nixon, there are two guys above him, that's all: Knox and Hanbury.'

'Really? Oh well, that's very easy then.'

'What if it's Swarbreck?' Jess asked.

'The whole Board are above him.'

'Then there are lots of suspects to rule out.'

Ben was worried about their reception at SPC, so was largely silent as they walked from Wilmslow to the site. The suburbs thinned surprisingly quickly and he was even more surprised to enter the site, which could have been set deep in Cheshire countryside. They descended amongst beautifully sculpted parkland towards a central lake sparkling in the sunshine and a glass-fronted building positively gleaming grandeur.

'They're clearly rolling in it,' said Freddie.

'Mum says they're poor compared to Pharms.'

'Is that SPC Pharmaceuticals?'

'Yeah.'

'Not that poor, clearly.'

They entered reception, a vast space with a long curved wooden desk behind which two receptionists sat. Ben approached the woman nearest him.

'Hello, I'm Ben Baxter and these are my cousins Jess and Freddie and I'm trying to find out why my Mum's disappeared.' Their faces crumpled in sympathy, causing Ben to choke up, so he was thankful for Jess's intervention.

'Did you see her on Friday afternoon?' she asked.

'No I didn't,' the receptionist replied. But her colleague looked over.

'I last saw her at lunchtime. She marched out to the car park with a face like thunder. I remember, because she didn't speak, whereas normally she's very friendly indeed.'

'So she didn't say where she was going?'

'No. But I know who will know.' She rang an internal number. 'Hello, are you busy? I've got Ben Baxter, Sue's son, with his cousins in reception. Oh did he? Well, no, it wouldn't stop me either. Okay, thanks.' She rang off. 'Debs Moore is coming down.'

Ben smiled. 'Great. Thanks.' Good old Debs. He wondered if she'd uncovered anything about the meeting.

'Would she have been so agitated she might crash?' Freddie asked the receptionists.

'Oh no. She's a good driver.'

'We've been ringing round hospitals all weekend,' said Jess.

Debs soon arrived, her round face filled with concern. She had shoulder length brown hair and glasses and usually reminded Ben of a teacher but in her smart suit she looked more like a head teacher. She signed them in, got them visitors' passes and led them through the large double doors that divided the headquarters from reception. They walked past two massive conference rooms to four lifts. Debs pressed Floor 2.

'Tricky Dicky's been locked away in the Directorate – but you may have to keep your heads low.'

'Okay. Any news on the meeting?'

'No. No one knows a dicky bird, not Tricky nor Bob, nor Tony,' said Debs, referring to Mum's closest manufacturing colleague and another Product Manager as well as her odious boss. The lift arrived so they got it in.

'But even if Tricky said he didn't, he might,' Ben said.

'True. And he'll have you thrown off site if he sees you.'

'As if he's trying to block us investigating,' said Jess.

'He's just a pompous prat,' Debs said. 'He thinks teenagers are mental write-offs.' Unfortunately that left Freddie with a point to prove.

'It looks a very lucrative business,' he said, as they emerged from the lift. 'Your colleagues in Pharmaceuticals do even better, I believe.'

'That's the beauty of patents,' said Debs.

'What's a patent?' asked Jess.

'Copyright protection – for twenty years generally. But you have to patent separately in each country, and register them separately too, which costs a packet and takes forever,' Debs explained, leading them down white-walled corridors past office after office. Ben was looking at the nameplates, trying to spot Mum's.

'What's registration?' Jess asked, as they passed the office of Lai Peng, the Technical Manager who worked with Debs and Mum. Where was Mum's, Ben wondered? But there was no way to break into his cousins' interrogation and Debs's helpful answers.

'Products have to be registered before they can be sold. We have to prove they work and that they're safe to apply to crops. We have to do efficacy trials and feeding trials and answer every damn question the regulatory authorities can think of – and they bowl you some right googlies, believe me – and by the time we've done that, if we've ten years left on the patent, we're laughing. Then generics undercut us and we're back to the lab.'

'Because they enter the food chain they can't be toxic, can they?' Freddie said.

'You'd be surprised how many things are toxic,' said Debs, stopping at an unmarked door. 'Table salt, for instance. No one in their right mind would try and register that for application onto crops. It's far too toxic.'

'So agrochemicals are safer than table salt?' Jess asked, goggling.

'Nowadays, yes. This is Judy's office, Ben.' Mum's secretary, as Ben thought of her, but she and Anna were shared between all the department – almost: Ballantyne had Amanda, his PA. There were four enormous L-shaped desks in the room, of which two were currently occupied.

'Ben! Lovely to see you, but I wish it were in happier circumstances,' Judy, the curly-haired woman, greeted him. They had often spoken, so Ben recognised her voice.

Introductions were quickly made – the other woman (blond, tall, dressed to intimidate) was Amanda. Ben asked if Judy knew where Mum had gone on Friday afternoon.

'No, sorry, I've no idea where she went. There's nothing in her diary.'

'So there was nothing planned. It was off the cuff, whatever it was,' Debs said.

'She was taking you to the dentist's,' Amanda said, from the far end of the office. Ah, her cover story for Ballantyne – Amanda told him everything, Ben recalled Mum saying.

'Yeah, but she didn't turn up,' said Ben. He mustn't drop Mum in it with her boss.

'Who didn't?' asked a man.

'Oh, hello, Peter,' said Amanda, standing up. Ben stared at Jess. Which Pete was this? Seeming too young for his white hair, he had a tanned face, a barrel chest and a taut stomach. He looked as powerful as a gorilla. 'This is Ben Baxter and these are his cousins Freddie and Jess. They turned up in reception uninvited, but understandably. They want to find out what happened to Sue.'

'How did they get in here?' he demanded, looking angrily from Debs to Judy and back.

'Reception called me. I brought them up to talk to Judy,' Debs replied.

'And Marcus. We're hoping to see Marcus,' Jess said.

'*Marcus*? Marcus Wright?'

'Yes. He's helping us, Mr … sorry, I don't know your name?' Jess added, impressing Ben.

'Ballantyne. Peter Ballantyne.'

Ben stared, stunned.

'I thought your name was Richard,' Jess said.

'These days I use my middle name.' Ballantyne regarded her suspiciously, and Ben stared at him suspiciously, the boss Mum had never trusted, the boss she had never liked – could Richard Peter Ballantyne be Pete?

'We know she went to a meeting last Friday evening. Do you know where it was?' Freddie asked.

'No, I don't.' His tongue flicked across his lips. 'It seems she kept all of us in the dark.'

'Yes, but why? It's not like her at all,' Ben said.

'To pursue her own agenda? Are we talking about the same woman?' Ballantyne responded with heavy sarcasm.

'Sue is a fighter. She will get things done, come what may,' Debs said.

'If she thought something underhand was happening, would she try and stop it?' Freddie asked.

'For sure,' Ben replied.

'Definitely,' Debs agreed.

'You need to get back to work,' Ballantyne snapped. 'Have you an appointment with Marcus Wright?'

'No. We were just hoping to see him. He promised to help,' said Ben. *Unlike you. You've offered nothing. No sympathy, no concern, no help at all. You've just been trying to stop us.*

'You'd better give him a call,' Ballantyne told Amanda.

'Was there a meeting at St Saviour's?' Freddie asked.

'St Saviour's? No, why would there be?'

'Our mum talked to a friend there and he mentioned SPC had been there last Friday. It's her and Father's old college.'

'Mine too,' he replied.

'Did you know Mum there?' Ben asked.

'No. I left before she arrived, but I haven't time for idle chitchat,' he snapped.

'We're trying to find out what happened to Mum!'

'Ben, cool it,' Debs warned.

'Mr Wright is free in fifteen minutes,' announced Amanda, putting her phone down.

'Had I better show them up there?' asked Debs.

'Yes. Get out them out of Strategy now and stick to them like glue. This is a major international headquarters, not a playschool. But you'll make the time up later.'

'Oh Richard, none of us work to rule.'

'Peter, please, Deborah!'

'Oh yes, I've known you for so long as Richard it sometimes slips my mind.'

'As long as nothing else does. Where are you going now?'

'Could we see Bob in Operations? He might know about the meeting,' Ben said.

'Yes get them out of Strategy,' Ballantyne said again. 'Operations, the Directorate, then home. Understand?'

'Yes,' Ben said. He understood perfectly. Ballantyne wanted to stop them investigating. 'Can I ask, before we go, did you do a physics degree?'

'Why?'

'Just wondering what qualifications you need to work here?'

'A first from a Russell Group university or an Upper Second from Oxbridge.'

'A science degree?'

'Not necessarily. I read PPE: Philosophy, Politics, and Economics.'

'But do you know about Einstein? And Hubble? And the Doppler Effect?'

'Of course,' he said, but he gave nothing away. His face was blank, his eyes grey and hard as stone as they regarded Ben. Ben stared at him with equal hostility.

'Come on, Ben, let's go,' Debs said, so he broke away from the staring match and followed her, Jess and Freddie out of the office.

Ballantyne watched them down the corridor, so Debs ducked out to the staircase.

'Why's he changed his name?' asked Jess.

'He found out about his nickname. He reckons changing it will stop us calling him Tricky Dicky. It hasn't of course. Right you want to check out the Petes, don't you – oh no.' Her jaw dropped as she too realised. She stopped. 'Oh hell. You don't think – hang on.' Footsteps could be heard descending the stairs above.

'Yes I do think,' said Ben.

'I'm so sorry I didn't think of him,' Debs apologised as a trio of men passed, deep in discussion.

'It's okay. You and Mum think of him as Richard.'

'He'll know about you going to your mum's sister's, too,' Debs said rapidly and so quietly that they all had to lean in towards her. 'It'll be in her Personnel file. The only bit I can't swallow is, if Ballantyne wanted something doing, he'd do it himself, and certainly not delegate to inept hoodlums.'

'So you agree Mum's disappearance could be because of SPC?' said Ben.

'If there's been foul play, yes. She's worth her weight in gold to me as a friend, to you as a mum and to your aunt as a sister,' Debs said. 'But to the wider world her greatest value is her agrochemicals expertise.'

'Ballantyne's had her kidnapped. I'll bet he has.'

'Careful, Ben! Walls have ears,' Debs said. 'And he's a very dangerous enemy to make.'

'Before you jump to the conclusion it's him, we have to check out the other suspects,' Jess said.

'Okay. For you, I will. But I'll bet you anything you like it's him. The only problem is, how to prove it.'

'He's the most devious man alive. He doesn't even let his right hand know what his left hand's doing. If you're up against him, I pity you. But I can't believe he'd be quite so callous,' Debs said.

'I can,' said Ben.

Mum had always hated him. Did he hate her too? And if so, what had he done about it?

A shiver ran down Ben's spine.

Chapter 10

Golden Boy Gets Tough

'Don't mention it out here,' Debs warned, as they emerged into an open area containing photocopiers and printers. She approached a bespectacled young man in shirtsleeves. He was small, slight and had very pale skin, as if he never went outside.

'Ah, Pete. Can I introduce you to Ben Baxter, Sue Baxter's son and his cousins Freddie and Jess? This is Pete Parker, one of our graduate trainees.'

'I'm just on my way to a meeting.'

'So are we. It won't take long. I don't know if you've heard that Sue Baxter is missing?' said Debs.

'No.' Not a flicker of emotion crossed his face – surprise, distress, nothing. He too looked as if he couldn't care less.

'She might have been at a meeting in Oxford last Friday afternoon. Were you?'

'No. I had Friday off.'

'Did you go away?'

'Paris with my girlfriend,' he eventually replied, though he looked as if he'd rather tell her to get lost. It was a sign of her seniority, Ben realised – so presumably Mum would get treated with equal respect, he thought with a spark of pride.

'Is Bob in yet?'

'Out all day. He's in Grangemouth.' SPC had some manufacturing facilities up there, which Mum occasionally visited.

'I spoke to him earlier, hoped he'd be in later. Okay. Better get to that meeting,' said Debs, leading them further into the department. 'Regions is through here,' she announced loudly, adding in an undertone, 'Cold fish, isn't he?'

'I didn't like him,' said Jess. 'He never said sorry about Aunt Sue.'

'He didn't, did he? I've never liked him either,' Debs confided.

'Who's Bob?' asked Freddie.

'The Fungicides Production Manager. I spoke to him earlier. He knows nothing about that meeting.' They passed under a sign saying "Regions". 'Peter Swarbreck's office is the first one you come to.' She knocked and a deep voice told her to enter. She ushered them in. The office was big and bright, with three large windows looking out onto parkland. There was a desk on the left, and in front of it a circular table. The man sitting behind the desk had dark wavy hair and eyes shrouded by large spectacles.

'Hello Peter, these are the students I mentioned. One of them happens to be Sue Baxter's son, Ben. You've heard about Sue?'

'I have. Terrible news. Very distressing.' He rose from the desk and revealed his height – about six foot four, Ben estimated – and muscular build. 'Please sit down,' he said, gesturing to the central table. He remained barricaded behind his desk. 'When did Sue disappear exactly?'

'Friday lunchtime,' replied Debs. 'On her way to the car park.'

'She may have gone to a meeting in Oxford that afternoon,' Ben added.

'Oxford? Why?'

Jess jumped in before Ben could formulate an answer.

'We rang round colleges, we've rung everywhere, and one of them said SPC had a meeting there last Friday.'

'SPC could mean any division: Pharmaceuticals, Paints, Colours and Fine Chemicals, any of us. We're a big family.'

'You sounded surprised when Ben mentioned Oxford,' sad Debs.

'No, I was surprised she'd driven. Tackling the M6 on a Friday afternoon would be madness. She'd take the train.'

'So her car would have been on-site all weekend.'

'It would still be here now!' Ben realised, remembering she'd been seen marching to the car park, but not getting into her car. Perhaps she got a lift to the station? Or a taxi?

'Worth checking with security,' said Swarbreck.

'Thanks, Peter,' said Debs, standing up. 'We'd better be on our way.'

'I thought they wanted to know about careers here?'

'They did, it's just that with his mum disappearing, it's somehow driven everything else out of our minds.'

'Not you, Deborah, I hope. I need some news on 562 for the UAE. Urgently. I've had them on the phone twice this morning already.'

'I'll come back to you by lunch,' Debs promised, opening the door to leave.

But Ben had one more question. 'Do you know where I stay when Mum's away on work trips?'

'No! Why would I?' He looked so startled that Ben ruled him out immediately.

'Come on, Ben. Sorry, Peter. He's very upset, as you can imagine,' Debs said.

'Of course. I hope you find her soon, for us as well as you. Who will be covering her products?'

'Richard – I mean Peter – and I as usual. But I hope she won't be away that long.'

'Don't we all? In the meantime, 562 UAE, don't forget.'

'I won't.'

'That was a stupid question,' Freddie told Ben, as they left the office.

'It was a great question!' Jess protested. 'You can't fake surprise like that. He had no idea why Ben was asking.'

'I agree,' said Debs. 'Just general chat out here, right?'

'Why are agrochemicals tested on baby animals?' Jess asked immediately.

'To see if they develop as expected. To make sure they're safe for human babies. And also pregnant animals have to be fed our agrochemicals, unfortunately.'

'Why?'

'Because of thalidomide. Unexpected deformities were seen in babies of mums who'd had morning sickness and were therefore prescribed thalidomide. The link wasn't made for years so lots of babies were affected and tragically many of them died. It's a racemic chemical. Do you know what that is?'

Of course Freddie did. 'It exists in two mirror image forms, like hands.'

'Yes. And one was harmful and one wasn't, but it was sold as a mixture, because that's what occurs naturally. The mums that were fed it weren't affected, but the babies were. So all chemicals fed to humans directly like pharmaceuticals, or indirectly, like agrochemicals, have to be fed to pregnant females to check that their babies are okay.' She paused at the lifts. 'Marcus is in the gods.'

'Sorry?' said Jess.

'In the Directorate on the top floor, and I'm not flogging up there in these heels.'

In the lift Freddie resumed his attack on Ben. 'If he's Pete, he doesn't know that you know, does he? He wasn't there. He didn't hear what they said. They'll have covered their conversation up, it was a mistake.'

'But Pete must have told them where we lived. He told them about me going to yours.'

'I know.'

'You mean you believe me now?'

'Yes, now I can see how it might all fit together.'

'If you know anything, Freddie, tell me!' The lift stopped. They emerged into a small lobby, with a keypad-protected door in front of them.

'It's all right, no one can hear us here,' Debs said.

'If 993's toxic, could it be used a poison?' Freddie asked.

'Well yes, if you had any. But it's never been synthesized on a big scale, only in a lab.'

'But people here know how to make things on a big scale.'

'Some of us do. The Operations Department do.'

'Yes, but why use 993 when you've got cyanide and arsenic and strychnine?' asked Jess.

'Because it's odourless, colourless, very toxic indeed and there's no known antidote,' said Debs. 'Yes, from the point of view of a terrorist, I'd say it would be manna from heaven.'

'Does Swarbreck do a lot in the Middle East?' Freddie asked.

'Yes. A lot.'

'Lots of terrorists there.'

'Not just there!' Jess protested.

'No, but currently, most –'

'Careful Freddie, someone could emerge from the lift or through those doors at any time,' Debs warned.

Ben had been thinking, getting more and more frightened.

'She'd try and stop them, wouldn't she?' he said.

'Turning 993 into a poison? Faster than a rat up a drainpipe,' Debs said.

'So that's why they've kidnapped her.'

Alarm flashed across Debs's face.

'How do you know she's kidnapped? You've not received any ransom demands or anything have you?'

'No.'

'Oh good. If you do, let me know, won't you? But it's ludicrous to imagine Sue being kidnapped because of 993.'

'Why?'

'They'd want me. I'm the world expert, not her. It was still very firmly in development. Once they near commercial launch Sue takes over, but this didn't get within ten miles of the market. So if anyone was going to be kidnapped they'd take me. We'd better get into the gods.' Debs pressed the buzzer to speak to someone and said they'd come to see Peter Nixon.

'Why? We're seeing Marcus,' Ben said.

'Yes, but he's Peter and you want to find a Pete. Besides if they are making 993 or anything they'd need Bob or Frank or Pete. They're the old hands, the experts. Nowadays so much is done over in cheap overseas territories that they mainly specify and oversee rather than build, but those guys used to design the Grangemouth plants and check every pipe themselves.'

'Who's Frank?' Jess asked.

'Insectides guru. Currently in intensive care following major heart surgery. So out of the picture for a meeting last Friday.'

'Would you call John Knox the Chief?'

'No, he's either JRK or the Chief Exec. Never just the Chief.'

Nixon's PA, a tall, imperious woman called Cass, emerged from behind the door and led them into the Directorate. The lighting was low, the carpets were thick and there was no noise whatsoever: daunting in the extreme. Nervously Ben cleared his throat. Cass led them to Nixon's office, which was like Swarbreck's but double the size, and once inside, introduced them to Peter Nixon, an overweight man with greying black hair and a sallow, droopy face. He remained seated behind his desk whilst they stood in front of it.

'I'm sorry to hear about your mother, Ben. I take it she's still missing?' he asked in a faint but unmistakeable Yorkshire accent.

'Yes.'

'I'm afraid I haven't got long,' he said looking at his watch, 'so if you have any questions, fire away.'

'Do you know where I go whilst Mum's on work trips?' asked Ben.

'Why?'

'I think Ben's asking if you're close to Sue – as a colleague, I mean. He's very upset, as you can imagine,' said Debs.

'Course he is. I know Sue well, we go back years. We used to travel together before I moved up here. I know all about you, Ben, and how difficult it was for her when you were younger. She hated leaving you, you know. You stayed with her sister back then.'

'He still does. He's only thirteen,' Debs replied.

'*Thirteen*? Well you're a big lad for your age. Of course your mum's tall. But not as tall as you, I'd guess.'

'No, I'm taller than her now.'

'Is that all you wanted to know? I'm pretty pushed,' he said, again consulting his watch.

'Mum's old product 993. Are there any plans to relaunch it or anything?' Ben asked, watching carefully. But he looked amused rather than rattled.

'993? We couldn't spray that onto crops. It'd be genocide.'

'You designed the plant, didn't you?' asked Debs.

'No, that was Bob. Is that all? I really must crack on.'

'Yes. Thanks very much for seeing us, Peter.'

'Pleasure,' he said briefly. 'And good luck finding your mum.'

'Thanks,' Ben replied.

Outside in the oppressively silent passage, Debs said, 'We'd better talk to Becky. She's Marcus's PA. We can't just bang on doors up here like we do down there.' She led them to an office on the left and popped her head round the door. 'Hi, Becky. I'm told Marcus will see us?'

'Yes, that's right. I'll just check if he's free.' She phoned him and asked. 'That's fine. Just go in.'

M A J Wright, Commercial Director, the plaque on the door opposite proclaimed. Debs knocked before opening it.

'Hello Marcus, we were told to come straight in.'

'That's right.' Marcus rose from behind the desk and walked towards them. 'Ben,' he said, clapping a sympathetic hand on one shoulder whilst shaking hands with his other. 'I can't believe it. You must be tearing your hair out. Unless there's been any news?'

'No.'

143

'We've got nowhere with hospitals yet either. But I need to talk to you. I'll buzz Becky to get us some drinks. Please, sit down.' He gestured to the table (circular but twice the size of Swarbreck's) then phoned Becky from the desk, so that when he joined them they were already seated. He sat near Ben. 'Have you checked her passport?'

'No. Why?'

'Well, if she's not in a UK hospital, she could be in one abroad. She could have popped over to one of the European NCs, she could be there and back in a day.' NCs were the National Companies, SPC subsidiaries (or sometimes joint ventures, Ben didn't understand the difference) that Mum visited and talked to about forecasts and strategy, and if there was a production problem, allocation. (Ben heard about it whenever there was. Doubtless everyone did. Under allocation, Mum had to decide how much to supply to every territory. It was never enough and she hated letting the NCs down.)

'But she was here at lunch. She wouldn't have expected to get back before midnight, would she?' said Debs.

'I don't know. It's worth checking out.' The door opened and Becky (smiley, young, pretty) entered, holding a notepad. 'Oh, Becky, thanks. We'd like drinks, please. What will you have? We've got tea, coffee, juice and still or sparkling water.' Ben and Jess chose apple juice and the others ordered coffee. 'With a water on the side,' Marcus added.

'Marcus, do you mind if I ask Becky to call security?' asked Ben. Becky, heading for the door, turned back.

'That depends what you want them to do,' he responded jokily.

'Tell us if Mum's car was left in the car park this weekend.'

'Good idea. Because Sue's so important to us all, we've been forgetting that as well as a missing woman, we've got a missing car. Yes, please check Becky. Finding that car could lead us to Sue.' He waited until Becky left then turned back to them. 'I believe you've been asking about an Oxford meeting.' His expression was much more serious – grim, even. 'How much do you know about it?' he asked Debs.

'Nothing. These guys tracked down St Saviour's.' Debs wrinkled her forehead. 'Remind me how?' she said, turning to Ben.

'We rang round everywhere we could think of. Aunt Miriam tried Oxford, and found St Saviour's,' Ben said, remembering Debs had supplied the Oxford lead, and not wanting to get her into trouble.

'Whew! You're persistent, aren't you?'

'Of course. We want Mum back. Someone there had recognised someone from SPC, so they probably studied there. It could have been Mum.'

'Lots of people here went there.'

'Ballantyne went there,' Jess pointed out meaningfully.

'As did I. It's where I met your mum,' Marcus said, seeming relaxed again. But that meeting had made him tense, Ben noticed, worried now.

'Was everyone here at St Saviour's?' Jess asked.

'Not quite. We tend to focus on Oxbridge when recruiting – a few other top universities too, but it's remarkable how many people here went to Oxbridge. At management level upwards, of course – I'm not suggesting the cleaners here need an Oxford degree.'

'Nothing wrong with Manchester,' Debs said, 'Where I went.'

'Was Peter Nixon at Oxford?' Jess asked.

'Not that I know of. But he's older than me; we wouldn't have been there at the same time. You'd have to ask him, I'm afraid.' There was a knock. 'That'll be Becky.

I'll get the door. Then we can talk.' Marcus went to the door and took the tray off Becky. 'Thanks, Becky. I'll take care of this. Any news on the car?'

'It wasn't here. The car park was empty.'

'So she went *somewhere* in her car,' said Freddie. 'As the receptionist said.'

No she didn't, but Ben had no stomach to point that out. He was far too worried about the meeting.

'Could you make sure we're not interrupted for the next half hour?' Marcus asked Becky. Debs looked surprised and checked her watch. Ben wondered what Marcus would tell them. He had a dry mouth so gladly accepted the drink, but refused a biscuit from the proffered plate. He was far too anxious to eat.

'I need to talk to you about that meeting.' Marcus regarded them seriously. 'It's an extremely sensitive commercial venture, of massive importance, that will only go ahead if there is complete secrecy. I mean *complete*. If anyone talks, the deal will be off, and if you go around asking questions about it, you could destroy the whole thing. I've got to ask you to stop.'

Ben stared at him, dumbfounded.

'He can't stop looking for Sue. She's his mum!' exclaimed Debs.

'I know. No one wants to stop him looking for Sue; we all want her back safe and sound. But if you say anything at all about a St Saviour's meeting outside this room, Debs, I'll have no option but to dismiss you.'

'*What*?'

'It would bring down the biggest deal you have ever imagined. Thousands of people's livelihoods depend upon it. It's vital that no one talks. It's so unfortunate that you've got the erroneous idea that your mum was there, Ben. She wasn't a part of these negotiations, please believe me. If you go asking about it again, I'll know straight away and I'll have no option but to bar you from site and let Debs go, which would be terrible, because she's one of our best assets.'

'I can't believe you're threatening me,' Debs said, shaking her head.

Marcus spread his hands, palms upturned. 'I've got no choice. It's bigger than me, it's bigger than you, it's bigger than any of us. But it will only work if nobody else gets wind of it. You could destroy SPC.'

'*Really*?'

'Really. And Sue wouldn't want that any more than we would. I completely understand why you've asked about it, I have no problems with your behaviour so far, but it's such an important issue that, as soon as I heard you were asking about that meeting, I had to step in immediately. It's a monster.'

'So you're sure Aunt Sue wouldn't have been there?' said Jess.

'Sure,' said Marcus, nodding.

'You don't know she was there,' Freddie told Ben. 'It was just that you were looking for a distant SPC meeting last Friday and discovered there'd been one at St Saviours.'

'You mean you've been putting two and two together and making five?' said Marcus sympathetically. 'I can understand that. I'd be tearing my hair out if I were you, Ben, I really would. Who told you it had happened?'

'I'm not sure. It was Aunt Miriam who spoke to someone. An old friend, I think,' he said, to protect the porter.

'Since there's no sign of her here I strongly suspect she went overseas. Check her passport.'

'She wouldn't have gone overseas without telling me.'

'She went somewhere without telling you.' He turned to Debs, who was looking mightily miffed, as Ben could understand. He was shocked Marcus had threatened her with the sack and worried for her. 'Forget everything I've told you.'

'Apart from the threat?' Debs retorted angrily.

'The same applies to me and to everyone involved.'

'You make yourself very clear, Marcus. Thank you for your time,' Debs said with all the warmth of winter.

Before they left, further assurances were sought that they wouldn't mention the St Saviour's meeting to anyone and that they'd let Marcus know about the passport, because then he would organise a ring round of the NCs to find out which she had visited, if any.

Becky shepherded them out of the Directorate, saying, 'Cass asked for your phone number in case we think of anything to help. I'd like it too, please, Ben.' Ben was usually reluctant to share his mobile number, but he happily wrote it down for her. A red-haired woman – Hazel Finch? – brushed past them, power dressed to the toes.

'Morning, Debs,' she greeted Debs.

'Morning.' Apart from that one word, Debs led them back to her office in grim silence. Ben was confused and Debs was seething. She let them all in, then closed the door.

'Please don't ask any more about that meeting. He meant it, I know. And if I'm sacked I can hardly help you find out what happened to your mum. But it's connected with Friday, I'm convinced of it. And someone knows something they're not telling us, Golden Boy for one.'

'Golden Boy?' echoed Jess.

'Marcus,' explained Ben. 'And Ballantyne. He's hiding something.'

'As always. I'll see what I can dig up, promise,' said Debs. 'But unfortunately I've got to back to Swarbreck right now, because I've got a meeting in ten minutes.'

Ben had an idea. 'If Mum flew abroad on SPC business, would Ballantyne have to approve the flights?'

'He would. He'd know where she'd gone.'

'Can we ask him?'

'I will, later. Promise.'

'And 993?' asked Freddie.

'Not a word about that either. It's the worst swear-word imaginable in our building, after all the millions we'd invested in it.'

'So the St … I mean the meeting on Friday couldn't have been about that?' asked Jess.

'You've got to be joking, haven't you? A billion dollar deal? We couldn't offload it for a bag of chips. Now come on, else I'll be late.'

'Would all the Board have been at that meeting?' Ben asked.

'No, not Nutcase. She's the female window dressing at Main Board meetings. She has zero commercial input.'

'Is that Hazel Finch, the woman we saw?'

'Yes. Now come on.' Debs shepherded them out of her office and down to reception, where she asked them to sign out. She shook Freddie and Jess's hands and enfolded Ben in a hug (embarrassing) but being in a rush, released him quickly. 'Check her passport. We've got to get her back,' she said, looking so emotional that Ben could only nod in response, whilst a wave of grief crashed over him.

On the way back to Didsbury he felt increasingly helpless. He'd started the day with such high expectations, but all he knew now was that Mum hadn't been at the Oxford meeting, that no one knew where she'd gone and if

Ballantyne was Pete, that no one would know where she was until he chose to tell them. He was a master of secrecy, Mum said.

'I think Pete's Ballantyne,' he said, to see what the others thought.

'I'm not so sure. Did you notice the way Nixon thought you were older than you are?' said Jess.

'Everyone thinks that, because I'm tall.'

'I know, but the burglars found you at home, didn't they?'

'They weren't burglars, they didn't steal anything,' said Freddie testily.

'Yes, but they didn't expect to find Ben. They'd know a good mum wouldn't leave a thirteen-year-old alone all night. But she might a sixteen-year old.'

'Jess!' scoffed Freddie. 'You're assuming everyone's been brought up like you. They haven't, you know. Not all children are as well parented as us. Lots of them are from disadvantaged backgrounds, or broken homes,' he said, with a loaded glance at Ben. 'They're the type that end up as burglars, not us.'

'Broken home doesn't mean bad home!'

'Statistics show that children without a father are more likely to do drugs, go mental or end up in prison.' It was a claim Ben had heard countless times from Freddie and his father. The only way Ben would do drugs was if his dad was Uncle Henry – that would definitely drive him off the rails.

'Can we stop arguing about single parents and broken homes and get back to what's happened to Mum?'

'I think Nixon could be Pete,' Jess said. 'He'd know where you lived, wouldn't he?'

'If he's travelled with her he would probably pick her up on the way to the airport, yeah. But Ballantyne's much creepier. He knows from day to day what Mum's doing and where she's going.'

'It's one of them: Ballantyne or Nixon or Swarbreck,' Freddie said. 'Maybe Swarbreck because of terrorists, maybe Ballantyne. He's the most dangerous, you can see it in his eyes.'

'And the cleverest,' said Jess. 'He'd know exactly how old you are, to the day, Ben. It's Nixon, I think.'

'It's one of them. But why have they taken Mum?'

'993, I told you,' said Freddie.

'Then why haven't they kidnapped Debs?'

'You need to work that out for yourself,' said Freddie, meaning he didn't know, else he'd boast about it, Ben thought. 'You also need to find out whether Ballantyne was in Oxford on Friday afternoon.'

'If you know anything more, you should tell Ben.'

'I don't know for sure. But I think I'm right. I think I'll tell Dad. He can call the police.'

'*No*! No police,' Ben snapped.

'We don't know enough to go to the police. And if we mention the meeting it'll get Debs sacked. We can't risk that,' added Jess, more calmly. Ben looked at her gratefully.

'If not the police, who's going to find her?' said Freddie.

'I am,' said Ben. 'I'll find her.'

'Will you really?' said Freddie, sitting back, arms folded, smirking. 'You don't know who Pete is, you don't know where she went and you don't know why she left in such a hurry.'

But I still have the Einstein Code, Ben thought defiantly. And if any Pete was writing the Einstein Code, he would bet every penny he had on it being Ballantyne.

Ballantyne was Pete, because of the Einstein Code.

Chapter 11

Thief?

They had promised Aunt Miriam they'd be back by two and they were cutting it fine. They had hardly got through the front door before Uncle Henry had confronted them. He looked furious.

'Five thousand pounds has vanished from my study. Which of you took it?'

'Not me, Dad,' said Jess.

'I haven't,' said Freddie.

'Nor me,' said Ben.

'Then where is it?'

'What five thousand pounds?' asked Freddie.

'To pay the roofer. He wanted cash.'

'Has Robert taken it? He's always broke.'

'But not a thief,' said Uncle Henry. 'I must ask you to empty your pockets.'

'Henry, lay off them,' said Aunt Miriam, coming into the hall as they were complying with the order. 'I know you're very worried.'

'Of course I'm worried! It's a lot of money – and a criminal offence,' he added, glaring at Ben.

'It may have just got lost,' Jess suggested – lame even to Ben.

'Of course it hasn't got lost! It was in the top drawer in my study and now it's not. If it's not back by six pm I'm calling the police!' On that bombshell he turned and stalked back to his study. There was silence until the door had shut.

Then Aunt Miriam said, 'I don't see how I can stop him. It was a ridiculous amount of cash to have in the house in the first place, I told him, but he wouldn't listen.'

'Is that why Dad's home?' asked Jess.

'Partly. He's supposed to be writing that paper. But he's not got far. He's been turning the place upside down, as you can imagine. It's such a lot of money.'

'So it went missing this morning?' said Freddie.

'Probably. He knows it was there yesterday because that's when Mr Macardle rang.'

'Who's he?' asked Ben.

'Our roofer. He was arranging to be paid this lunchtime, but now we don't have the money. Well we do, but in the bank, not here.'

'Bianca was here last night, wasn't she?' Ben said.

'What's that, No-Nuts?' said a voice from the stairs.

'Oh, morning Rob, or rather good afternoon,' said Freddie, making a big show of checking his watch. 'Time for breakfast is it?'

'Get real,' said Robert scathingly. 'You think Dad didn't drag me out of bed as soon as he'd found out?'

'Well you've not taken it. And none of us has. So it could have been Bianca.'

'No it couldn't! How would she know about the money in Dad's study?'

'You told her?'

'No! I didn't even know,' Robert shot back angrily. But Ben wondered if he was lying. There was no need for Freddie and Jess to pinch money, they were both flush, but Robert was always skint, he was the only one with a motive to steal his dad's money – or help Bianca to do so. And she was desperate for funds.

'Your dad was out of his study just after dinner. Where did Bianca go then?' he asked.

'Nowhere. She was with me,' Robert claimed. 'It's not her, Baxter, it's you!'

'No it's not!'

'Well if it's not there by six o'clock tonight the police will be here again, and I could really do without that. So can whoever took it please put it back,' said Aunt Miriam. 'Now, have you had your lunch?'

As soon as she heard that they hadn't, she shepherded them into the kitchen and, accepting Ben's assurance that he would never, ever steal from them, they made lunch together. She explained that Robert and Uncle Henry had already eaten. Ben was relieved he wouldn't have to face his uncle's glowering face across the table. It wasn't until they were all sat down that she asked about their morning.

'Ballantyne calls himself Peter now!' began Ben.

'Your mum's boss?' Aunt Miriam sounded as astonished as Ben had been when he heard.

'Yes. She's never trusted him.'

'So I suppose he's jumped to the top of your list of suspects? Be very careful, Ben. As I said, there is more likely to be an innocent explanation than anything else. How did Marcus get on with the hospitals? Did you see him?'

'Yes, but he didn't say much about that, just that they'd not found her yet. He was more bothered by the St Saviour's meeting. Mum wasn't there but it was so top secret that he threatened Debs with the sack if she talks about it.'

'Or we do,' added Jess.

'Oh dear. But Sue wasn't there?'

'No. He thinks she might be overseas.'

'But she'd have told us.'

'That's what I said,' agreed Ben. 'But he thinks something urgent might have come up.'

'Well it did, we know that.'

'And she might have gone to one of the NCs. He's checking them and said we should check her passport.'

'We will after lunch,' Aunt Miriam promised.

'But if Uncle Henry goes to the police about money … I've not stolen it, honestly.'

'I know, Ben, you wouldn't.'

'But does Dad?' asked Freddie. 'I think her disappearance could be to do with 993.' He outlined his theory about 993 being used as a poison.

'But it can't be, because they'd have kidnapped Debs, not Mum,' Ben said. Seeing he'd puzzled Aunt Miriam, he added, 'She knew more about it because it was still in development.'

'Not necessarily. If Aunt Sue thought any of her colleagues were dealing with terrorists, she'd be bound to stick her nose in,' Freddie said. Ben glared at him.

'She'd go to the police,' said Aunt Miriam. 'As will your father unless I can convince him otherwise. If you three can kindly clear up, then I'll go and talk to him. Then we'll check on your mum's passport.'

Whilst they were clearing up they heard shouting from the study.

'IT MUST BE!' roared Uncle Henry.

Freddie arched his eyebrows, Jess's eyes widened and they all moved towards the study, to hear more.

'He's got enough to cope with,' Aunt Miriam was saying when they got close enough to hear her more measured tones.

'It can't be anyone else! It's been here for over a week! If it had been one of our children, they would already have taken it. Besides, none of them have ever stolen.'

'Neither has Ben.'

Ben looked at Jess in horror. '*He thinks it's me*,' he hissed.

'How would you know? Sue would never tell you anything like that about her darling boy, would she?' Aunt Miriam said something they couldn't catch. 'Rubbish!' he exclaimed. 'If that were true, why aren't you stealing? You're missing her too, aren't you?'

'YES!' It sounded like Aunt Miriam had finally cracked. 'And you'll get the police in over my dead body!'

She marched out and saw them. Her lips were compressed into a tight line of fury.

But Ben was angry, too. 'I'm not staying here if he thinks I'm a thief.'

'I don't, as you evidently heard,' Aunt Miriam replied.

'But *he* does,' Ben said, pointing at his study door.

'Ignore him. He's been scattering around accusations like confetti. One minute it's me, the next it's Robert.'

'He thinks it's me,' Ben maintained.

'I don't,' said Jess.

'Neither do I,' said Freddie, surprisingly. Usually he sided with his dad on everything.

'Why not?'

'Where would you hide it? You've been nowhere without us. No, it's Bianca, I'm sure of it.'

'The problem is, how can you prove it?' asked Aunt Miriam.

'I'll think of something. Leave it to me.'

'And I'll search the house, in case Dad and Robert have missed it,' said Jess.

'Then Ben and I will go passport checking, shall we?'

'Please.'

In the car Ben sat reflecting. Now he knew Mum hadn't been in the Oxford meeting, they had no idea where she'd disappeared. Debs hadn't known about the meeting, Marcus hadn't and seemingly, Ballantyne hadn't either. So who had? Unless he could find the right person to ask in SPC, they'd have to phone every hotel and conference centre in the UK – and maybe even abroad, if Marcus's suspicions were correct.

'Don't worry, Ben, money's nothing compared to your mum,' said Aunt Miriam, smiling kindly at him as they waited at the Parrs Wood lights.

Ben smiled at her ruefully. 'If only Uncle Henry thought that.'

'Hmm.'

Going up Didsbury Road he had the strangest sensation that Mum would appear. He looked out hopefully, but saw no one he knew except a group of girls from school heading down towards Parrs Wood, where the restaurants, cinema and gaming centre were a magnet for teenagers. They were giggling together, so happy and carefree. In another world, Ben thought.

'Have you got your keys?' Aunt Miriam asked, pulling up at the house.

'No, they're back at yours.'

'Here,' said Aunt Miriam, handing over her keys. 'You should unlock, it's your house, not mine.'

'Can I stay here if Uncle Henry throws me out?'

'He won't throw you out. I won't let him. But no, you can't. Your mum would be locked up for neglect if you stayed here alone. We can't have that, can we?'

'No,' Ben agreed, unlocking the door.

So he'd have to stay somewhere else. He was not staying where someone thought him a thief. On the doormat was a pile of junk mail. He deactivated the alarm, let Aunt Miriam pass him and go into the lounge, then gathered the flyers up and dumped them into the recycling bin outside, as Mum usually would.

'I'm checking the answer-phone,' Aunt Miriam called as he returned to the house, reminding Ben he hadn't had his phone switched on since morning. 'Remember to pack a few more clothes while you're up there.'

As Ben walked upstairs he checked his Inbox. There were a few new messages, but one stood out. It was from a number, not a contact. He opened it.

YV IVFMRGVW DRGS BLFI NFN LCULIW UIRWZB MLLM

Ben stared at the jumble of letters, perplexed. Though probably rubbish, it looked weirdly like code.

'Is her passport there?'

'I'll just check.' He went into Mum's bedroom, which still looked as if she'd just left it that morning. He went round the bed and opened up the top drawer, where she kept the passports. There was only one there. Alarmed, he pulled the drawer out further, but it was otherwise empty. He flicked through the passport to find the photo page and saw his (much younger) face staring back. Her passport had to be there! He checked the other drawers, but there was no passport amidst Ben's childhood cards and drawings, an embarrassing number of which she insisted on keeping. With a sinking feeling, he straightened up. Marcus was right. She could be anywhere in Europe.

'What's up?' Aunt Miriam said from the other side of the bed. He hadn't noticed her entering the room.

'It's missing. Marcus is right. She could be anywhere.'

'We must tell the police.'

'No! They won't look overseas if they won't look here.'

'True. We need to know where she was.'

'Marcus said he'd ring round the European NCs for us.'

'How kind of him!'

'I'll text Debs and get her to tell him.'

As he did so, he recalled the weird message. It was so like the codes Mum used to set for him to crack. *Could it be from her?*

'Ben, what's happened?'

'Nothing. Why?'

'You looked so excited.'

'I was just thinking about Mum. Oh Debs said she'll tell Marcus,' he added, opening her latest text.

'Good.'

He urgently needed half an hour to crack the code.

'Can I stay here for a bit?'

'Sorry Ben, I have to get back.'

'On my own? I'll get the bus. Or walk.'

'No, it's too dangerous. Whilst your mum's away I've got to take good care of you. She'd never forgive me if I didn't. Are you packed?'

'No. I'll be quick.' He hurried to his room. He shoved a few pairs of socks and pants into his case and added three tops, two pairs of jeans and a hoody, then ran downstairs with it. Aunt Miriam loaded it into the boot of the car whilst he locked up, burning with excitement. It would be just like Mum to sneak somebody's phone and send him a secret code, so that they couldn't read it, but he could.

'I wish we could *do* something. I suppose we could check with the airport. They must have a record of last

Friday's flight and passenger lists,' said Aunt Miriam, on the way home.

'Good idea. I'll do that when we're back.'

Aunt Miriam smiled at him kindly. 'You look shattered, Ben. You have a break. I'll do it.'

Ben turned to her to deny it, but realised it might give him code-cracking space. There might be no need to phone the airport. Mum might be telling him how to find her. He wondered whether to tell Aunt Miriam – she'd be so thrilled if it was a message from Mum – but decided to wait until he cracked it and knew for certain.

When they got back Jess hurried to the door for an update, and looked so worried about Mum's passport that he again considered telling them about the text. But it would be much better to show them when he knew what Mum was saying.

'You'll be better off out of Dad's way,' she whispered. 'He's going nuts.'

'Okay,' Ben agreed. 'I'll hide in my room.'

As he ran upstairs he recalled the paper and pens Aunt Miriam had left for him. Perfect for code cracking. He opened the door and was pleased to see no one had removed them.

He took a few sheets of paper from the top of the pile she'd so thoughtfully placed on his bedside table and sat on the bed, carefully transcribing the code onto paper so that he could view it without scrolling.

YV IVFMRGVW DRGS BLFI NFN LCULIW UIRWZB MLLM

Ben had enjoyed code cracking in primary school (as had Jonno and Naz – they had all enjoyed Mum's codes). He always liked to start with the vowels and short words. So he started with the first word. Either Y was a vowel or V was a vowel – or y, as in by. He decided to try Y as a consonant first. Then V would be a, e, i, o or y. (He couldn't think of any two-letter words ending u.) V occurred twice in the second word, he noticed – so it was most likely e, Ben thought. He copied out the code substituting e for V.

Ye IeFMRGeW DRGS BLFI NFN LCULIW UIRWZB MLLM

But it didn't get him very far. Except that unless the first word was ye (surely not Shakespeare?) it was be, Ben reasoned.

be IeFMRGeW DRGS BLFI NFN LCULIW UIRWZB MLLM

Disappointed there were no more bs and es, he moved on to the last word. With two double letters, one of them must be a vowel – much more likely the middle letters. He tried L as a, e or o, discounting u and i as never doubled vowels (or hardly ever at least).

a: be IeFMRGeW DRGS BaFI NFN aCUaIW UIRWZB MaaM

e: be IeFMRGeW DRGS BeFI NFN eCUeIW UIRWZB MeeM

o: be IeFMRGeW DRGS BoFI NFN oCUoIW UIRWZB MooM

Idiot! L couldn't be e if he was right about V being e. Cursing himself for carelessness (again) he crossed out the second option and studied the two remaining choices. There was a much higher chance of L being o than a (unless it was naan – unlikely Mum was texting a request for a takeaway) so he ruled through the top option too.

Unless NFN was eye or eve F was probably a vowel – not e or o, he was using them, so it had to be a, i or u. He tried each out.

a: be IeaMRGeW DRGS BoaI NaN oCUoIW UIRWZB MooM

i: be IeiMRGeW DRGS BoiI NiN oCUoIW UIRWZB MooM

u: be IeuMRGeW DRGS BouI NuN oCUoIW UIRWZB MooM

The second word was helpful. He couldn't think of any long word with e and u as the second and third letters so he crossed through the last line, but couldn't decide which of the top two options was the better bet. He knew the rule *i after e except after c* was wrong as often as it was right – he and Mum had watched Stephen Fry explain it on QI – but he couldn't remember any of the QI examples and couldn't guess at the word. F was probably a, he decided, ticking the top option.

He'd forgotten the short cut! He quickly scribbled out the alphabet and under it put the code letter used.

A B C D E F G H I J K L M

     a

N O P Q R S T U V W X Y Z

  l   e   b

He stared at it, looking for a pattern, but none emerged – yet. He probably needed more letters. He returned to the code, noticing he hadn't got any letters in the third or sixth words yet. Either their shared letter was a vowel – meaning R was u or i, or they each contained a different vowel.

Hopefully R was u or i, which would be easier. He tried it out.

- i: be IeaMiGeW DiGS BoaI NaN oCUoIW UIiWZB MooM
- u: be IeaMuGeW DuGS BoaI NaN oCUoIW UIuWZB MooM

Neither seemed more likely than the other, he thought after considering possibilities. The second word ended in eW. W would most likely be r or d or s, he reasoned.

'Ben, dinner's ready!' yelled Jess, knocking on the door.

Blast!

'Okay, I'll be there in a second,' he called, gathering up the papers. He stuffed them under his pillow, then raced downstairs, because Uncle Henry hated late arrivals for meals.

But he didn't have to eat! He'd say he was sick. Mum might be telling him where to find her. He might be able to get her safely back home that evening.

There was *no way* he was putting food before that delightful prospect.

Chapter 12

The Mysterious Case of the Missing Money

Freddie was in the hall, grinning excitedly.

'We've got a six hour extension.'

'What?'

'Dad's deadline.'

'What deadline?'

'The Mysterious Case of the Missing Money. You know, the thing he wants you arrested for? If it's not back by midnight, he's phoning the police.'

'Oh stuff!'

'It's okay, I've got a plan.'

'Oh *double* stuff.'

As they entered the kitchen and he saw the others assembled round the table, he realised he'd be in trouble for that too. Bianca was back, surprisingly, making the prospect of joining them even less appetising than it had been.

'You're late!' Uncle Henry snapped.

'Sorry. I feel a bit sick. I might pass on dinner.'

'Come on, Ben, sit down. You just need food, that's all,' said Aunt Miriam. 'Freddie, pour your father a glass of Bianca's wine, please, and one for her, of course. Thank you again for this wine, Bianca.'

'S'all right,' Bianca said, sounding a bit drunk already. She was again heavily made up, with Robert hardly able to draw his eyes away from her extremely tight top.

'No, really, I'm not hungry.'

'SIT DOWN!' Uncle Henry bellowed. 'Your aunt has gone to the trouble of making your favourite dinner for you – mollycoddling you again – and you are not – NOT! – going to turn your nose up at it like the ungrateful wretch you are.'

Ben had no choice. Avoiding Uncle Henry's furious glare, he sat down on the chair Aunt Miriam had patted next to her, sheltering him from her irate husband, who was seated at the head of the table, as usual. She had made Ben's favourite – chicken and mushroom pie (plus a chicken, ham and leek pie for Jess and other fungi-haters).

'Thanks Aunt Miriam, it's really kind of you,' he said, hurriedly spooning some vegetables onto his plate so that Uncle Henry would start eating. Until everyone else was ready, he would never begin, even though he hated lukewarm food. He was so hard to please.

'At *last* we can start,' he said and everyone picked up their knives and forks, except Bianca, who instead drained her glass.

'Pass us the bottle,' she told Freddie, who was between her and Uncle Henry.

'Sure.' Freddie filled her glass almost to the top, which emptied the bottle, due to their ostentatiously large glasses, which apparently improved the taste of the wine. ('But not enough for me to risk breaking one at that price,' Mum had said, when he'd asked why she didn't have balloon glasses too.)

'Robert, could you pop down to the cellar and get us another couple of whites, please?' asked Aunt Miriam. 'A viognier would be lovely.'

'Two?' Uncle Henry said, glaring at her now.

'I'm off tomorrow and it helps me sleep. I need help right now.'

'Is that why you drink so much, Bianca?' Jess asked. 'To help you sleep?'

'I've got no trouble sleeping, I could sleep on a clothes line.'

'With a bum like yours I'd like to see you try,' Freddie said. Ben looked at Aunt Miriam, awaiting the reprimand, but it didn't come. Payback time for yesterday, he supposed – though Bianca looked pleased, not insulted.

'Men love my bum. They like a bit of meat. Not like you, you're dead skinny,' she told Jess.

'Jess is slim, not skinny,' Ben retorted.

'And fit as a fiddle. She's won hundreds of trophies for running,' retorted Aunt Miriam, exaggerating wildly, but nobody was going to tell Bianca that.

As Robert returned with the new wine, Bianca glugged down her gargantuan glassful as if it were water. Whilst Uncle Henry distributed the wine, making a big deal of Bianca's now empty glass, Ben slipped his phone out of the pocket and had another look at the code.

'What are you doing?' Jess whispered.

'Just checking for messages.'

'If Dad sees that he'll hit the roof and you're in his bad books already.'

'Okay.' Ben's eyes flicked to Uncle Henry. He noticed and shook his head ominously. He'd love to get rid of me, Ben thought. He'd love to have a chance to throw me out. Could *he* have stolen the money? To frame Ben and get him out of his house forever? Surely his uncle didn't hate him that much – did he? But what if he did? He'd have to plant the money on Ben somehow – oh no!

'What's wrong, Ben?' Aunt Miriam asked.

'It's okay,' he reassured his aunt, heart fluttering like a panicky bird. Uncle Henry would put it in his bag. He'd hide it in the same compartment where Ben had hidden the

Einstein Code! Had he found it? Was he even madder at Ben for hiding it from them? But surely Aunt Miriam would have raised it with him by now?

Or had they just phoned the police?

'Are you feeling really sick, darling?' Her kind face turned towards him. There was no hint of anger or betrayal, just concern.

'It's delicious. It's just Mum, y'know. And the other. Uncle Henry,' he added, nodding towards his uncle, who had started to relax with the food and wine, and was now rattling on about relativity with Freddie, Robert and (it would be funny if he wasn't so scared) Bianca.

'Freddie's got a plan to help you. Go along with whatever he says.'

'Really?' asked Ben, now convinced that she was still ignorant of the Einstein Code. She wouldn't be so relaxed with him – she wouldn't have been able to cook, he realised. Why hadn't he realised that sooner? He needed to be sharper to crack the code, but his brain felt sluggish, his senses dull.

'Really. It's important. Back him up,' Aunt Miriam said, and it took him a second to realise she meant Freddie's plan.

'Okay,' he agreed warily. Freddie's plans usually meant trouble for Ben, not help.

'The satellites have to be very high up to get round mountains and skyscrapers,' he was telling Bianca, brandishing the wine bottle.

'Yeah?' she said, pushing forward her glass. It was like watching a dog begging for chocolate drops.

'Yes, about 20,000 kilometres,' he replied, topping her up. Uncle Henry, of course, knew the precise figure.

Whilst he shared it, Ben surreptitiously started tapping in an emergency text.

Help urgnt

'Relative to us on earth, their time is slower than ours, so we have to adjust for it,' Uncle Henry told Bianca.

Can I stay at yrs? Pls

HHOH nitemare, he finished, sending the message to Jonno, Naz and Dan.

'It's quite simple,' said Freddie, sloshing more wine into her glass. 'Time slows down at high speeds or near massive objects like the earth. So we also have to adjust for the clocks on the satellites seeming faster than ours,' said Freddie, as Ben hurriedly swallowed the last of his broccoli.

'Finished,' he told Aunt Miriam.

'Pudding. Wait,' she said, looking towards her husband.

Ben took out his phone and examined the code again.

'But that's contradictory,' said Jess. 'They're high up, making their time faster, but they're travelling faster than us, making their time slower.'

'Not contradictory, they're opposing forces, that's all,' said Freddie.

'They're slower by about 7 microseconds due to their relatively higher speed, but 45 microseconds faster due to height, making them seem around 38 microseconds per day faster than us,' said Uncle Henry, emptying his bottle into his glass.

'Big deal,' said Robert, smirking at Bianca.

'Finished,' she said, draining her glass again. He refilled it, emptying the other bottle.

'I've only had a glass and a dribble out of three bottles. Robert, would you get another, please?' Aunt Miriam asked.

'What's it worth?'

'A happy home,' she said, looking at Uncle Henry, who was still waving his arms about, rhapsodising about relativity.

'It's ten kilometres error per day, and cumulative. You'd be setting the sat-nav for Basingstoke and ending up in Bahrain,' he said, chuckling as if he'd told a cracking joke. The combination of wine, food and physics seemed to have melted the ice in his manner. Ben wondered if that was the real reason Aunt Miriam had asked for more wine. She'd stood up to Uncle Henry on his behalf and she'd made him one of his favourite dinners when she was worried out of her skull about her sister. She was so kind.

Whilst Uncle Henry and Freddie regaled Bianca with yet more fascinating physics facts, Ben's message alert pinged. He looked his phone.

'Not at the table,' Aunt Miriam whispered.

'It's urgent,' he whispered.

'Be quick.'

Naz couldn't help. He was off to Birmingham to see his grandparents. Disappointed, Ben slipped the phone back into his pocket.

'Whilst I serve pudding, perhaps you'd pour us another glass, please, Henry. Relaxed is good, paralytic is not,' Aunt Miriam said, looking at Bianca.

'Mind if I pass on pudding?' Ben asked as he cleared the dishes from the first course.

'Why, Ben? What's up?' Aunt Miriam said.

'I want to find Mum.'

'So do I, sweetheart, we all do, but we can't search the whole of Europe. We need Marcus to find out where she went for us.'

'I'm quite full.'

'Nonsense, a growing boy like you. Anyway you don't want to antagonize your uncle any further, do you? Until we can sort that money out, will you please stick with us?'

She had a point, and until he knew what the code said, he daren't mention it to Aunt Miriam. So Ben had to wait whilst the remnants of the chocolate cake and apple pie were served and consumed.

'Give me ten minutes in Mum's study,' Freddie said to him. 'Mum knows about it, don't you?'

'Yes. If you sort that out, Freddie, I'll be delighted. Go now, both of you. I'll get Bianca and Robert to help with the clearing up,' she said. 'Unless, Bianca, you'd like to go with Freddie and Ben to the study? Take the wine with you,' added Aunt Miriam, clinching it.

Whilst Aunt Miriam quelled Jess's protests about not being included, explaining she needed her help downstairs, Freddie grabbed the half-full bottle and led Bianca out of the kitchen. She followed the bait, clutching the table to help her retain her balance.

'What's going on?' Ben asked Freddie.

'You'll see,' he smirked.

'Ten minutes, tops?'

'Sure. Trust me.'

'I know you far too well for that.'

Progress towards Aunt Miriam's study was impeded by Bianca's stiletto heels, which made her as tall as Ben, but much less steady on her feet with all the wine sloshing about inside her on a largely empty stomach. But eventually they made it. Freddie sat Bianca down at the desk, poured her a large glass of wine, clicked the computer on and told her he was about to change her life.

'Mmm,' she grunted, guzzling.

Ben found a space by the bookcase, and leant against the wall staring at the code. A text arrived from Jonno who said there was no space now his baby sister had arrived.

Floor? PLS

'Air hostesses never age,' Freddie said as Ben pressed Send. *What?*

He returned to the code as Freddie started babbling about science making people younger. The three-letter word – NFN – was symmetrical, probably a repeated consonant with a vowel in the middle, he surmised. But which? He'd used a, e and o, so it could be i or u. Bib, did, gig, pip … all seemed unlikely. Dud, pup, tut, mum … MUM!

'Isn't he, Ben?' Freddie said, insistently.

'Huh? What?'

'Xander's dad. Rolling in it, isn't he?'

'Oh yeah. Sure.'

'Cheshire mansion, flat in Mayfair, and holiday homes all over the place,' Freddie was saying as Ben wondered why Mum had signed off in the middle of the text. Of course! She'd thought she'd heard someone coming, but it had been a false alarm, allowing her to type more.

Bianca's bag crashed to the floor. Startled, Ben looked up.

'Gimme 'is number,' she said, bending and fumbling in her bag.

'You need to give me something first.' Ben stared at Freddie in disbelief. *Surely* he wasn't propositioning her?

'Whachawan'?'

'You need to get the five thousand pounds back to Dad's study tonight.'

'I didn't take it,' she said, of course. Freddie was brilliant with science, but clueless about people. His plan was doomed to fail – this was just a waste of time.

But Ben's mood brightened as an incoming message from Jonno told him that Jonno's dad had offered him a tent in the back garden. He typed his acceptance, as Freddie told Bianca that Xander (his best – and only – friend, as far as Ben knew) would be off his dad's hands soon, away at university.

'He's got a private plane, hasn't he, Ben?' Freddie added.

'He has,' Ben assured her.

'So lots of flying and lots of money. He keeps his personal mobile secret, but I know his number. You want it?'

'Gimme!'

'Go and find Dad's money and bring it back first. Now!'

'Okay. It's at home.' Ben stared at her, open-mouthed in amazement. How had he persuaded her to do that? But he had no sympathy for her. She was the thief, she'd admitted it. She stood up, wobbled and then righted herself, clutching the desk.

'You mustn't drive,' Ben said. 'Get Robert to give you a lift.'

'Don't dump him yet then,' Freddie advised.

'No.'

Another text arrived from Jonno.

Sorry mate Mum says no tent

'Stuff it!'

'What?'

'Jonno says I can't stay at his.'

'You'll be okay here in an hour.'

Ben stifled the urge to reply that he was never okay here, knowing the code could change everything. Mum might be back tonight!

'Here's your printout,' said Freddie, handing Bianca a sheet of paper. 'That's worth billions that is. But it's top secret. Promise you won't tell anyone?'

'Shh!' she said, finger on lips. She missed at first, but eventually stuffed it in her bag. 'Less go an' ge' Robbie.'

'He'll be downstairs. You'll find him soon enough,' said Freddie.

Ben followed her out.

'Hang on! I saved your hide. You've got to see how,' Freddie called.

Ben sighed and returned to the study.

'It's on the screen,' gloated Freddie, delighted with himself. Ben carefully made his way round a pile of books to see.

TOP SECRET

Einstein published two works on relativity.

SPECIAL – 1905

a) The laws of science (e.g. the speed of light) are the same for all freely moving observers

b) Nothing travels faster than the speed of light

c) $E = mc^2$

GENERAL – 1915

a) Space-time is warped by mass and energy

b) Time runs slower near large masses (e.g. clocks up towers run faster than on earth)

c) Time runs slower at high energies (e.g. clocks on planes)

SO FAST TRAVEL KEEPS YOU YOUNG

The longer you travel and the faster you go, the less you'll age compared to your earth-bound friends. So you'll stay young whilst they get old! But don't tell anyone. People spend thousands searching for the secret of eternal youth. Scientists have known it for ages!

Ben looked at Freddie. 'Is that why you were going on about his private plane?'

'Yep.'

'It can't really be true, can it?'

'It is. The only bit I've left out is how *tiny* the effects are. A round-the-world trip only saves you a second or two, because planes are so slow compared to the speed of light. But she could do the calculations for herself if she wanted. You can find the time and mass dilation equations all over the internet.'

'Yeah right. She'd struggle to switch a computer on, the state she's in.' Then something struck him. 'Time and *mass*?'

'Oh yes, didn't I mention that? Crazy I know, but it's been proved with electrons. They get four times heavier near the speed of light. So she might too.'

Ben goggled at him. 'Really? She'd be as fat as a … a … I can't think of anything that fat!'

'Sumo wrestler?' suggested Freddie. 'She could have a new career. But don't worry. Unless someone makes a giant leap forward in aeroplane design, it's not going to happen. Besides, in theory she'd lose the weight again as she slowed down … I think.'

'You *think*? So maybe not?'

'Maybe not.'

It was the first laugh they'd enjoyed together for years.

Ben returned to the spare room to code crack in a much more positive mood. He settled down on the floor, leaning back against the bed.

YV IVFMRGVW DRGS BLFI NFN LCULIW
UIRWZB MLLM

If NFN was Mum, then N was m – so M would be n, usually.

Hang on – they were adjacent in the alphabet. Could it be that simple? Then MLLM would be noon – quite possibly so. It might simply be the alphabet backwards! So a would be coded Z, b as Y and c as X ...

So excited that he could hardly write, he scribbled the alphabet out forwards, and underneath, backwards. He made a couple of errors but within a couple of minutes he knew he'd cracked it.

BE REUNITED WITH YOUR MUM

'Can I come in?' Aunt Miriam asked, tapping on the door.

'Just a minute,' he called, hurriedly hiding the papers under the duvet. He hurried out onto the landing.

'She's confessed, I believe.'

'Yeah, thanks to Freddie.'

Your mum, Ben thought as Aunt Miriam talked. It wasn't from Mum. Someone else was talking about Mum. Who then?

'I am so glad you are exonerated. I never suspected you for an instant, but Henry did.'

'I know.'

'I'm determined to get you a full apology.'

'That doesn't matter.'

'It does.'

'No, the money's what matters.'

'They're back, that's what I came to tell you.'

'Great. I'll be down in a couple of minutes.'

He returned to the bedroom, desperate to finish the text.

OXFORD – so it *was* Oxford – FRIDAY NOON.

Oxford? He'd have gone to Australia to get Mum back. Friday was a disappointment, but at least it was later that week.

He was getting Mum back!

'*Yes!*'

But who had sent it? Pete or the Chief? It was so complicated, now there were two codes to worry about and both so different. It was almost as if one was writing one, and one the other. Maybe the Einstein Code led to Oxford too, but this message was far preferable – direct, clear and it promised to reunite them.

Yes!

The Einstein Code was devious, impossibly clever and cruelly slow – it had Ballantyne written all over it. If he was Pete, then this must be from the Chief. Or was he the Chief? And Swarbreck or Nixon was Pete? But Nixon wouldn't take orders from Ballantyne – he was senior to Ballantyne. Would Swarbreck?

It was all too perplexing. It didn't matter, because now he knew how to get Mum back. He simply had to get to Oxford on Friday morning.

Aunt Miriam would drive him there. But he shouldn't tell her, because if "no adults" applied to the Einstein Code, it would also apply to this. Plus she'd tell the police. Yes, he'd keep it secret for now.

But as he went downstairs it was hard to wipe the smile off his face.

Bianca, Robert and Jess were in the hall.

'He'd bess not be lying,' Bianca was saying grimly.

'He's not. I know the man he's talking about. I've met his son,' Ben assured her again, surprised she could remember anything, she was so wasted.

'Who? Whose son?' asked Robert.

'Oh just a mate of Freddie's from school.'

'Divorced?' Bianca asked.

'His wife died,' said Ben, suddenly appalled at how little he'd understood the impact of Xander's mum's death. He'd thought him unfriendly and snobbish when they'd met (shortly after she'd died). Now Ben realised his standoffishness had doubtless been due to the wretched time he was having, rather than the snobbery he'd then assumed.

And now, unlike Xander, he knew he'd be getting Mum back. Just a few more days to endure, whilst Xander had a lifetime of missing his mum to endure. Poor Xander. And lucky him, so very lucky. He was getting Mum back!

'What are you so happy about?' Robert asked.

'You'll see.' On Friday! Together again! He jiggled his legs, unable to contain his exuberance.

'It's in the music room,' Freddie said, emerging from the study with Uncle Henry and leading him to the room where all the instruments were housed.

'Put it back now and he'll give you the number,' Jess hissed. 'Quick! Before Dad sees. Else he'll call the police. He will.'

'Call the police over what?' asked Robert.

'The money!' Jess told him.

'Oh yeah. What? Does that mean ...' Robert's mouth was agape, showing he'd had no idea what his girlfriend had done.

But, as Aunt Miriam emerged from the kitchen, Bianca told the boyfriend she was about to dump to shut it, then, clutching her bag, wobbled to the study as fast as her tight skirt and stilettos would permit. Aunt Miriam watched her, mouth tightly compressed.

'Isn't it fantastic?' Jess said.

'Yeah,' Ben agreed, unable to stop grinning.

But Robert didn't think so.

'Do you mean you took it?' he said as Bianca emerged.

'Borrowed. I've purrit back.'

'Every last penny?' Aunt Miriam said sternly.

'It washn't in pennies.'

'You have no right to take that tone with me!'

'No. Sorry,' Bianca said, cowed, as Freddie emerged from the music room with Uncle Henry. They were both laughing, for some reason. Freddie raised an enquiring eyebrow at Jess, who nodded, so Freddie let Uncle Henry return to his study.

'Now get out of this house and never come back,' Aunt Miriam said. 'Robert, take your ex home.'

'Gimme that number,' she demanded of Freddie.

'What number?' asked Robert.

'Your free pass,' Freddie said, giving it to her.

'You'd bess not be lying.'

'I don't think you are entitled to demand anything of my family, do you?' Aunt Miriam said angrily. 'Now get out!'

'See what science can do?' Freddie gloated, as she left.

'It was you, not science. You were amazing,' Ben replied.

But rather than preening, as he'd anticipated, Freddie looked astounded.

'You've never said that before.'

'You've never done anything so nice for Ben before,' Jess said. 'It makes a change from you goading him all the time.'

'I don't!'

'Please don't argue,' Aunt Miriam said. 'A crisis has been averted. Now we have to get exoneration, then we can get back to finding Sue.'

Oxford Friday.

'I've not seen you this happy for ages,' Jess said.

'It's great I'm off the hook,' Ben said 'Thanks, Freddie.'

'You're welcome. It was fun.'

Aunt Miriam knocked on her husband's study door and, after a brief conversation, they were all invited in. The walls were lined with books, except on the wall behind the computer desk, which was walnut and huge.

'I suppose you've come to apologise,' said Uncle Henry sternly, looking at Ben.

'Oh, no, Henry, I think it's for you to apologise to Ben,' replied Aunt Miriam. 'He didn't take the money, Bianca did.'

'If you look, Dad, it's back in your top drawer,' Freddie said. Uncle Henry opened it. His eyes widened and jaw gaped. It was the first time Ben had ever seen him so utterly discombobulated. How Mum would smile at the sight. Friday! He could hardly stand still, he was so excited. Freddie was beaming, he was beaming, Jess was beaming. But Aunt Miriam still looked very, very angry.

Uncle Henry counted the money and it was all there.

'Where is that girl?'

'Robert's taking her home,' said Freddie.

'There's no offence, Henry, no theft, no breaking and entering, nothing. She'll claim she didn't even know what it was.'

'Of course she knew what it was!'

'She was so drunk she wouldn't have known anything,' said Freddie.

'She knew how to steal.'

'Never mind whether she knew or not, there's no offence, Henry. Apart from you accusing Ben. Apologise, please.'

'I will not!'

'Dad, we heard you saying it was him,' Jess said.

'It's okay, really,' Ben said quickly. 'The main thing is, the money's back and it's all down to your super smart son.'

'Me and Einstein,' said Freddie.

'What?'

'Relativity. I told her fast travel keeps you young and gave her the number – well, she thinks it's the number of a man with a private jet.'

'What is it really?'

'A wine shop. She'll give them lots of trade.' Everyone laughed together, which hardly ever happened. How happy they would be on Friday, how delighted.

But no one would be happier than him. Except, maybe, Mum.

Chapter 13

Old Bones

Ben was so excited that he struggled to sleep. The prospect of being reunited with Mum was so amazing that he could hardly contain his exuberance at first, but as the house quietened and darkened he realised it was three more nights apart. It would be hard for him – but what about her?

For the first time he considered how she'd be feeling. She'd hate being confined, she'd hate being controlled and she'd hate more than anything being kept apart from him and home. She'd be so worried about him. Oh please don't let her know about Goatee Man and his mate breaking in and chasing him, he suddenly thought. She'd be desperate to protect him and unable to. It would torture her.

Torture.

Suddenly he felt sick. They wouldn't, would they?

No matter how many times he told himself that kidnappers looked after their captives, that it was in their interest to keep them alive and well, he couldn't get the disgusting idea out of his mind. In the dark recesses of the night his mind wandered to some horrific places, but as dawn broke and he finally dropped off he'd realised waiting wasn't an option. He had to find her fast.

He rose at ten past eight feeling groggy, had a very quick shower (it revived him a little), threw some clothes on and ran downstairs.

'Can I ring St Saviour's, please?'

'Why?' asked Aunt Miriam, who was sitting at the table drinking coffee. Jess was with her, on orange juice and cereal.

'If Mum was at that meeting, maybe she's still there.'

'Marcus swears she wasn't.'

'Maybe he didn't know,' said Aunt Miriam.

'Huh?'

'If she thought she should have been there but wasn't invited, it's just possible my dear sister may have decided to take matters into her own hands. There are plenty of hidey holes in St Saviour's.'

Oh yes, Mum had mentioned them, a whole complex of tunnels under the college from years back when being Roman Catholic meant risking death, but only a few students knew about them nowadays.

Ben waited until Jess had finished cross-examining her mum then said, 'I can't imagine Mum spying on a Board meeting, she'd be risking the sack, but it's worth asking St Saviour's, isn't it?'

'Definitely. It's 01865 ...' Aunt Miriam reeled off the number so fast he had to get her to repeat it before he could get it right.

He let it ring for ages, but there was no answer.

'There's probably no one there until after nine,' Aunt Miriam said. 'The porters don't live in the lodge, they have homes to go to.'

'So what if there's an emergency?' Jess asked.

'Students have mobiles and emails and all sorts of ways of being contacted, as do even the more up to date dons. I know a lot of Oxford lives in the past, but not all its residents do.'

'I have to be at Manchester Museum at eleven for that school science project,' said Ben.

He couldn't help hoping that the Einstein Code might get him to Mum before Friday – maybe two or even more clues today to make up for none yesterday? It was only fair. But Ballantyne wouldn't play fair, he was evil, he might do anything, Ben thought, his insides knotting again.

'We've got loads of time. Come and have some breakfast,' said Jess. 'I know which bus we can catch.'

Aunt Miriam turned to look at Jess. '*We*? I thought it was Ben's homework,' she teased.

'I'd be better alone,' said Ben, remembering their narrow escape from Goatee Man.

'But that's not fair! I helped you solve it!'

'I don't want any of you going out on your own. Suddenly I'm aware of how very dangerous this world can be. I'm not really happy with the two of you going.'

'Freddie could come with us,' suggested Jess. 'Three of us would be safe.'

Aunt Miriam took a moment to consider, then relented.

'All right, as long as you promise to stick together.'

'We do,' they assured her.

'Right come and get some breakfast then, Ben. You can't go out on an empty stomach.'

Not wanting to risk upsetting Aunt Miriam, Ben complied, but wolfed down his cereal, because all he could think about was Mum being in Oxford.

He redialled straight after breakfast.

'Morning, St Saviour's,' a man replied – at last!

'Hello, my mum's missing and she used to be at your college. Sue Baxter.'

'Ben, slower,' Aunt Miriam advised. But luckily (because it would drive him mad to have to go through everything slowly when he was primed for action) the man understood.

'Missing? Really? Sorry to hear that. Have you told the police?'

'Yes, but they're not looking for her, I am.'

'Good for you. How can I help?'

'She might be hidden in St Saviour's. She was at an SPC meeting there last Friday. It was when she went missing. She knows about your secret passages.'

'Secret passages?'

'What are they called?' Ben asked Aunt Miriam.

'Priest holes,' she said. He told the porter.

'I can tell your mum's an old Saviourite if she knows about them. Seeing as she is, I'll get someone to check. What's your number?' Ben started to give his mobile, but the man asked for a landline, so he gave Aunt Miriam's. 'Does your mum work for SPC?'

'Yeah.'

'I shouldn't really tell you,' the man murmured, 'but they've got two rooms booked for this Friday, the Norrington Room and the Old Library.' Proving the SPC connection.

'Thanks. Will you get back to me today, please?'

'Definitely.'

'Thank you.'

There was just time to text Debs before he left.

SPC meet Fri 7 Apr St Svrs. Who's going? Can u find out w/o getting in trble?

Her answer pinged straight back.

I'll try my best x

He was so preoccupied as they left the house that Freddie's barbs bounced off him, as inconsequential as the pink blossom falling from the cherry trees above, until …

'Just because SPC are meeting there, it doesn't mean your mum will be,' he said. By now they were sitting on the bus.

'She will.'

'Even if you're right and Pete works there, you haven't got a clue who the Chief is.'

'We know it's one of the Board or Ballantyne, but how do we prove it?' Ben asked.

'If it's Ballantyne, then Pete must be Nixon,' Jess said.

'Or Parker. Junior to Ballantyne, so more likely to call him Chief.'

They hadn't any clearer ideas than him. Ben lapsed into frustrated silence, thinking about the codes: the texted code and the Einstein Code. He suspected he was missing something obvious, but he couldn't think what.

'This is our stop,' said Jess, getting up. 'Ben, didn't Debs say Hazel Finch hadn't been at the Oxford meeting?'

'Yeah.'

'So that's five down to four,' she told Freddie.

'What?' Ben asked.

'Jess reckons there are four suspects for the Chief.'

'At most. If it's Nixon, there are two,' Jess said as they walked down the wide pavement towards the museum.

'I think you've got to take that to the police,' Freddie said.

'But they don't believe me about the break-in. Your dad saw to that.'

'But we know now they did. They left no evidence at all, did they? They're slick. They're clever.'

And they had Mum. It wasn't a comforting thought.

Their deliberations had got them as far as the museum entrance hall. Ben hadn't visited Manchester Museum for years, but for Freddie and Jess it was a second home, right by where their parents worked. Jess led the way up the stairs so he followed her. Arriving on the first floor, they were faced by a mass of people on the left and a mammoth straight ahead, which Ben headed for, but Jess pulled him behind the crowd, which was shuffling towards Egyptology.

'Wasn't that a dinosaur?'

'No. The dinosaurs are downstairs.'

'So why have we come up?'

'It's across the bridge. It's the only way.'

'It's gone half ten.'

'We'll make it.'

But the crowd was so slow-moving that Ben was worried they wouldn't.

'Why are there so many people here?'

'School holidays. Easter,' Jess said.

'Oh yeah.' It didn't feel like a holiday; it was the worst week of his life so far – and how much worse for Mum? She might not know about Friday yet, she might think she'd be their captive for months, or even years.

He had to think of a way to get to her today.

The first display room was crammed with Egyptian relics and lots of people gawping at them. It was hard to navigate a way through. They had to join a queue moving as slowly as a tortoise with a heavy limp. Ben checked his watch every few seconds, becoming increasingly worried.

It was as they slowly shuffled into the second chamber, under lighting so dim that anyone could be lurking in the gloomy recesses, that he realised something was wrong.

'Where's Freddie?' he asked.

Jess looked round too. She shrugged. 'Staring at a mummy probably. He loves all the grisly stuff.'

187

The room contained several mummies and painted sarcophagi, doubtless explaining the dimness of the lighting, but it unsettled Ben. He couldn't shake off the sensation of being watched, and his scalp prickled uncomfortably, as if infested with biting ants, as he progressed deeper into the darkness.

'Do you think he's okay?'

'Yes, he'll be fine.'

'Anybody could be hiding here.'

'GM doesn't even know who Freddie is, does he?'

But Ballantyne did.

Ben's mobile rang, making him jump.

'Hello?'

'It's only me, Ben,' said Aunt Miriam. 'The porter from St Saviour's said they haven't found her anywhere, I'm afraid.'

'Okay thanks.' Ben sighed. It had been a long shot, but he'd hoped his hunch would be right.

'You're all together, aren't you?'

'Yes,' Ben lied, looking round, but he still couldn't spot Freddie in the gloom. As he rang off he was dismayed to see a third room ahead. 'I thought there were only two.'

'It's Mediterranean – Roman as well as Egyptian.'

'Great,' Ben said, meaning the exact opposite.

The third room was brighter and less packed, allowing quicker progress, but time was so tight that Ben was starting to wonder what would happen if they missed the deadline. Would the clue be removed? Would he fail the Einstein Code? Would Friday's reunion be cancelled?

'Come on Jess. Run!' he urged as they emerged onto a brightly illuminated and almost empty walkway.

'It's down there,' Jess said, indicating the narrow staircase on the left, above which there was a T Rex sign.

Ben raced downstairs after her into the vast room in which the fossils were housed. The T Rex was at far end of the central aisle, with alcoves containing fossilised tree roots, dinosaur skeletons and information boards on each side. High partitions divided the sections. As they hurried down the aisle, Ben kept expecting to see Freddie, or even Goatee Man, but saw only family groups.

'Where would it be?' Ben asked, surveying the giant skeleton with incongruously tiny hands.

'It's not on him,' said Jess, walking round to check.

'Or under him.'

'What are you looking for?' asked a girl.

'A letter. Someone's hidden it here for me.'

'It could be here,' she suggested, looking through a stack of leaflets. Jess took the other leaflet stand, whilst Ben kept an eye on the girl, but she searched well, assisted by her little brother. But they didn't find it.

'It must be here somewhere,' Ben said with more confidence than he felt. It was a minute past the deadline now, but even if they were going to remove the clue, someone would have to come to get it and he hadn't spotted Goatee Man or any man who might be his partner in crime.

'Let's search the sections.'

'Yes, let's!' the girl enthused. Her mum smiled. She wouldn't be smiling if Goatee Man turned up. They headed for the first alcove on the left, accompanied by Jess and the young boy, so Ben took the next one, the plesiosaurs and ichthyosaurs alcove.

There were dinosaur models overhead and two impressive skeletons in display cases, one found at Robin Hood's Bay in North Yorkshire and the other in Somerset, Ben read as he searched the stand. He hadn't imagined any dinosaurs had lived in England, let alone such big impressive ones.

Would Goatee Man have managed to balance the envelope on top of one of the models? He'd have needed help to climb up – but it would be typical of Ballantyne to suggest something so tricky, thought Ben. He ran his fingers behind the Ichthyosaurs sign on the window ledge, looking back at the models, wondering how to get up there.

There was no need.

'It's here!' he cried, pulling out a familiar cream envelope.

Jess and the children darted round the divider screening off the next section.

'That's great, Ben, well done!'

'Thanks for your help,' he said to the children, hoping they'd go.

'Aren't you going to open it?' the girl asked.

'Not yet. Not until we're outside. It's only boring.'

'The fun was in finding it. We've got to go now. Thanks so much,' Jess said, waving goodbye.

She accompanied him towards the stairs.

'I didn't know they had dinosaurs in England,' he commented.

'Or would it have been Laurasia then?' Jess asked.

'Where? Oh never mind.'

'The northern supercontinent. Above Gondwanaland,' Jess couldn't help replying. She was a Winterburn after all, and they were on a mission to educate him.

Hands clamped his shoulders from behind. Startled, Ben jumped.

'Boo!' Freddie said.

Ben rounded on him furiously. 'That wasn't funny!'

'You look like you've seen a ghost!' Freddie gloated.

'Why were you hiding?' Jess demanded.

'To frighten Ben. He nearly jumped out of his skin!'

'Hilarious. Come on, let's get out of here,' Ben urged.

'You shouldn't keep wandering off. We've been worried about you,' Jess chided her brother.

'There's a live animal section now, have you seen? It's brilliant. A mini-zoo in a museum,' Freddie said.

He pestered Ben to open the envelope as they crossed the walkway – which was the bridge between the two halves of the museum, Ben could now recognise.

'Let's get out of here first.'

'Why? There might be two clues hidden in the museum, have you thought of that?'

'Yes, I had. Right I'll open it here. But no peeking,' he warned Freddie. Shielding it from him, he opened it.

Clue 5

The higher you go,

The faster it goes,

The faster you go,

The slower it goes.

To find Clue 6:

By St Mary's market

Travel back in time,

Be medieval peasants,

See how Georgians dine

Tuesday 4th April 15:00

'It's this afternoon, but not in here,' Ben said.

'Why are you so sure?' Jess asked. He showed her the clue.

'St Mary's is in Stockport market so I think it's there. In fact I know exactly where it is,' added Ben, scanning the clue again.

'Where?'

'Staircase House. It's in the marketplace. So is St Mary's, the church. It's got to be there.'

'Oh yes, you were peasants there, weren't you?' Jess recalled.

'They're all peasants in Stockport,' said Freddie. 'Have we time to get home for lunch? If not, it's on you.'

'I haven't got that much money. Let's get the bus.'

He tucked the letter inside his coat, and as they struggled to get through Ancient Worlds, Ben was thinking. Clue 6 this afternoon made it unlikely that Clues 7 and 8 would also be planted today. He couldn't bear another night apart from her– and what would she have to endure in that time? Anxiety gnawed at his guts every time he thought about her and what she might be going through.

He had to stop it somehow, but how?

As they emerged from the museum onto Oxford Road he suddenly had the answer. Goatee Man was standing just a few yards away, checking his phone. He was wearing a black vest under his leather jacket and a thick gold chain. He had entwined snakes tattooed on his neck. Ben strode towards him.

'WHERE IS SHE? WHERE'S MY MUM?'

He looked up, startled at first, but then smiled, a jagged wolf-like smile, which was even creepier than his snarl. But it didn't frighten Ben. He was stoked up with anger, ready to explode.

'Where is she? You know. Tell me.'

'I'll take you to her, 'ow's that?'

'Great.'

'No, Ben, don't!' Jess urged, pulling at him. He shook her off, following Goatee Man down the pavement, seeing the white Mercedes approaching, indicating. His lift to get Mum! 'KIDNAP! HELP! POLICE!' Jess yelled. Strangers turned and gawped.

'Shut up!' Ben snapped, moving towards the car. Jess threw herself in front of him, blocking his path.

It pulled in alongside them, dark tinted windows effectively concealing the occupants. Goatee Man yanked open the passenger door and jumped into the passenger seat but Jess held her ground, arms outstretched, blocking his path to the car.

'*GET OUT OF MY WAY*!' Ben screamed, lunging round her for the door handle. But before he could reach it, before Goatee Man had managed to close his door, the car pulled out, accelerating away from him. He fell against Jess, who clung to him. Even if he threw her off, the car was moving too fast for him to have a chance of catching it. Instead he turned on Jess.

'You *idiot*! They were taking me to *Mum*!'

'I *saved* you! They were kidnapping you too!'

'*I could be with her now*!' He spat out the words like bullets aimed directly at Jess's face.

'Not *now*. She's hardly just up Oxford Road,' said Freddie, turning up now the danger had passed.

Ben couldn't bear the company of his cousins. Fizzing with fury he stomped off, cursing Jess, cursing Freddie and most of all cursing himself. He'd been so close, seconds away from a lift to Mum. Why hadn't he pushed Jess away? He might have hurt her slightly, but what if he'd blown the chance of getting Mum back?

He stopped and groaned. He was a totally useless son. He was a complete and utter waste of space.

His mobile rang. Slowly he took it out of his pocket and answered it.

'Hello.'

'Sorry, Ben. I'm really sorry, but I couldn't lose you too. I couldn't bear it,' Jess babbled.

Ben sighed. He knew that feeling only too well.

'I know. I'm sorry too. I shouldn't have yelled at you.'

'If you come back, we can get the bus up here.' He hesitated. 'Ben, we need to get the next clue.'

'There might not be a next clue. I might have blown it.'

'You won't have.'

'I might have,' he told her, seeing her approaching now.

'The only way to find out is to go and get it this afternoon. Before which, we need to go home, else Mum will worry about us.'

He didn't have any energy to fight.

'Okay,' he agreed, ringing off.

'Sorry, Ben,' she said, hugging him.

'It's okay. You were protecting me.'

'Of course I was.'

'I wish you hadn't. I might be with Mum now.'

'Kidnapped, yes.'

'I got the car reg. so we can give it to the police,' Freddie said.

'No!'

'You'd only avoid the police if you knew she's been kidnapped. How do you know? Ransom demand?'

'No.'

'Good job. You couldn't pay it.'

'Freddie, that's horrible!' protested Jess.

'Maybe SPC will pay it,' Freddie said, ignoring her reprimand.

'Why would they do that?'

'If she's been kidnapped, it's because of work, isn't it? It's because of 993.'

'It's not 993! Debs said.'

'But Debs might not know. If your Mum found out about a terrorist plot using one of her precious fungicides, what would she do? Call the police, go to Debs or go to Ballantyne?'

'Ballantyne, I guess.'

'And if he's the Chief …' Freddie didn't need to say any more. Ben sat shaking his head, utterly sickened – and very, very frightened indeed.

Chapter 14

Aunt Miriam Puts Her Foot Down

When they got in, Aunt Miriam met them in the hall and asked them how the morning had gone.

'Apart from being chased halfway round Manchester by Ben's thugs, great,' said Freddie.

'*What*?' Aunt Miriam looked horrified. 'I'll call the police.' She had a phone in her hand.

'*No*!' Ben and Jess cho* rused.

'Why not?'

'They've gone,' said Jess.

'We didn't get their number plate, there's probably nothing we can tell them,' claimed Freddie. Ben looked at him, amazed. Why had he lied so blatantly about something he'd been gloating over earlier?

'Why not? There were three of you this time and it was broad daylight.'

'It all happened so fast!'

'What did?'

'I tried to get them to take me to Mum,' Ben admitted, before the others made it worse.

'Oh you poor darling. But *why*? Why do you think they'd know?'

'If she's been kidnapped, they must be in on it.'

'So you insist I mustn't tell the police, even though you've now got good descriptions of the men, and corroborating evidence.'

'Kidnappers and the police don't get on,' said Freddie.

'But why on earth would Sue be kidnapped?'

'Because of her job.'

Aunt Miriam considered this thoughtfully. Ben watched her nervously.

'We need to pool our thoughts. Come to lunch and tell me exactly what happened.'

Whilst they carried food to the table, Freddie gave her every detail of the morning – except the registration number – and because he didn't know Goatee Man was planting the Einstein Code clues he made it sound like a chance encounter.

'But what do they want with you?' asked Aunt Miriam, as they sat down.

'They want to kidnap him,' said Jess.

'They want him as bait, not as a hostage,' Freddie said, casually reaching for a slice of turkey.

'*What*?' Ben demanded.

'If your mum's been kidnapped, they can't have taken her for money, it must be because of her job. And they know she wouldn't be able to bear watching you being tortured, she'd do anything they wanted.'

'*Freddie*! That's too horrible for words!' protested Aunt Miriam. 'No one would be that cruel.'

Yes they would, Ben realised.

'You nearly walked right into their trap, didn't you?' Freddie said.

'It was to get to Mum.'

'Ben, you know they are very bad men, don't you?' said Aunt Miriam. 'And that you should never ever get into a car with them, or any other stranger?'

'Yeah, of course I do. With Mum missing, my head's all messed up.'

'It must be if you nearly walk right into the kidnapper's trap,' said Freddie. 'It's like a turkey volunteering for Christmas.'

'What's all this about a kidnapper? Ben, you haven't received a ransom demand, have you?' Aunt Miriam said.

'No, I haven't,' Ben said uncomfortably conscious of hiding so much he would normally tell her. He stared at the floor, dreading where the interrogation would lead.

'Ben? Have you?' persisted Aunt Miriam. 'Have you received a ransom demand and been hiding it from me?'

'No. No one's asked me for any money,' he said firmly.

'You're sure? You'd tell me if they did?'

'They haven't! I don't know who's got Mum, I don't know why and I DON'T KNOW WHERE!' Ben finished on a yell, frustration and grief boiling up inside him. He wanted to scream, to shout, to smash things. He stormed upstairs to the guest room, flung himself face down on the bed and bashed his fists into it again and again and again.

The piano started up (both Jess and Freddie played) and a beautiful melody started to calm him. A simple, yet haunting tune sang out above rippling triplets, with sonorous bass chords underpinning them.

'*Set me free,*' the melody sang. '*Let me go. Please send me home.*'

But the repeated '*No!*' in the bass became darker, angrier and stronger, whilst the melody, so expressive, so poignant, became even more plaintive. It almost hurt to hear it, so moving and emotional was the piece, perfectly encapsulating his grief.

As the magical music died away, he lay, his eyes wet with unshed tears. Now the piano was cheerful and brisk – and so very wrong. He yearned for the beautiful tune again.

He dried his eyes and went downstairs to the music room. Freddie was sitting at the piano. He looked up.

'Oh, it's you.'

'That last piece, the slow one, it was amazing. What's it called?'

'It's the same piece as this. I'm about to start the Allegro, the third movement. That was the first movement, the Adagio, from Beethoven's Moonlight Sonata.'

'It's not like moonlight, it's really sad.' Freddie nodded.

'He composed it by the bedside of a dying friend. You get it, but lots of people don't. You should play something.'

'No. But maybe I'll listen more. It's soothing, isn't it?'

'Not always. It gets angry in the allegro, then really sad again.'

'Angry he's dead?'

'Yes, I suppose so. It's a beast technically because it's got to be played really fast. I might slip up a bit.'

'I won't know if you do.'

'If you loved the Adagio you'll love the Adagio from Bach's Brandenburg Concerto too, and Schubert's Impromptus. But Beethoven's the best. You must know the Ode to Joy?' He sang a snatch of music.

'Oh yeah I have heard that somewhere.'

'You can sing that when you get her back,' Freddie said, smiling. Ben returned his smile, sadly.

As he returned upstairs, he was impressed by the torrent of notes Freddie was producing. It was weird, this being nice to each other, but Ben liked it much better than the constant sniping. Had Freddie matured? Have I, he wondered? Mum had always said they'd get on better when they grew up.

Mum. Missing her was a physical pain, a heaviness in his chest, as if his heart had quadrupled in size and weight. Ben had felt sad when his granddad had died, but nothing like this (and had been too young to much register his grandma's death). The only thing that would him feel better was getting Mum back home. But how?

The fact that the two codes were so different kept nagging at him. The Einstein Code was wordy, obscure and in an old-fashioned format. The text, however, was modern, direct and in proper code. Two different setters, surely?

The Einstein Code composer was clever, controlling and cruel, as if enjoying prolonging Ben's agony – and Mum's. Who else but Ballantyne? But was he the Chief, or Pete? Pete had told Goatee Man and his accomplice about their domestic habits, so Pete must be Ballantyne, Ben reasoned, since he was Mum's closest work colleague after Debs.

The only thing Ben knew for certain was that he daren't ignore any opportunity to rescue Mum. And Goatee Man would be in Staircase House soon, planting the clue, and the Mercedes would be parked nearby.

There was a knock on the door.

'Ben, it's me,' said Jess. 'Can I come in?'

'Sure.'

'We've got a problem. A really big problem. Mum's banned us from going out.'

'*What*? Why?'

'The men. And what you might do.'

'I won't do anything.'

'Promise?'

'Promise. We need the next clue. We can't miss it.'

'The only way is to get her to drive us.'

'She can't come. She mustn't see the clues. No adults, remember?'

'It's okay, I'll get her to go shopping. Food shopping,' she added in response to Ben's startled expression. (She usually hated shopping, except for bookshops.) 'There are supermarkets in Stockport town centre, aren't there?'

'Loads. She can take her pick,' Ben said, thinking fast. That would get rid of Aunt Miriam, but what about his cousins? If he had a chance of getting in the Mercedes, Jess would try and stop him again. 'Jess, it might be dangerous. Freddie might be right. I've got to take the risk, but you haven't. You mustn't.'

'No *way* am I letting you go alone! We're *together* in the Einstein Code. Together.'

'I know. I'll give you the clue as soon as I've got it,' Ben said, thinking maybe Jess could follow the Einstein Code whilst Goatee Man took him to Mum. He'd have to text her the clue.

'If you go alone to Staircase House, I'll tell Mum everything.'

'You can't!'

'I will.'

'But they might hurt Mum.'

'You need me, Ben.'

'I can find it alone.'

'No, you can't. I have to check you're not going wrong. Are you sure it's Staircase House?'

'I think so.'

'Let me see.'

He found the clue and gave it to her. She held it out for them both to read.

Clue 5

201

The higher you go,
The faster it goes,
The faster you go,
The slower it goes.

To find Clue 6:
By St Mary's market
Travel back in time,
Be medieval peasants,
See how Georgians dine
Tuesday 4th April 15:00

Ben looked at his watch in alarm. 'That's under two hours!'

'That's okay if you're right and it's in Stockport. The clue's time, obviously.' Ben remembered Freddie saying time slowed down at high speeds and near big masses like the earth, so he nodded. 'But the clue's a bit vague. Why do you think it's Staircase House again?'

'St Mary's is the old church in Stockport market, next to Staircase House.'

'Are you sure there isn't a St Mary's in a marketplace anywhere else nearby?'

'No. But they know I live in Stockport, so they know I'd know the market.'

'Okay, I'm convinced. Sort of. But I'm coming with you, Ben. If not I'll tell Mum.'

'Okay,' Ben said, vowing this time he'd shove her out of the way if she tried to block him. It was against his principles to hurt a girl – or anyone, he had never been violent – but to get Mum back, he'd do anything.

They found Aunt Miriam sitting in the kitchen with her hands round a mug. Freddie was there too, radiating smugness. *Why?*

'I'm sorry if I upset you, Ben,' Aunt Miriam said.

'You didn't upset me. It's missing Mum that upsets me. I'm sorry I shouted.'

Aunt Miriam smiled ruefully. 'Me too. We're all at sixes and sevens emotionally. The fact that we're mostly holding it together is amazing. Please sit down and have some lunch.' Which was still set out on the table.

'I've got a favour to ask. I've got to get to Staircase House in Stockport this afternoon for that science project.'

'No, Ben, it's not safe.'

'But I've nearly finished!'

She seemed surprised by the strength of his reaction.

'It's only homework.'

'But it's really important.'

'You can't argue against Ben doing homework,' Jess said.

'I wanted to have another go at the police.'

Unlike Ben, who was panicking internally, Jess kept her cool remarkably well.

'Don't bother with *them*, it's a waste of time.'

'But what are we doing to get your aunt back?'

'Everything we can.'

'I'll phone Debs,' Ben said.

'Then I'll phone Marcus,' Aunt Miriam resolved.

203

'Then take us to Staircase House? Please?' Ben tried again.

'What if you run into those men?'

'We won't. They drive everywhere. It's pedestrianized up there,' Ben said (partly true).

'They're hardly going to be visiting museums are they?' said Jess. 'But if they are, I'll be with him.'

'They're from Manchester, not Stockport. You could tell be the way he talked. Really chavvy,' said Freddie.

'Freddie!'

'Please, Aunt Miriam.'

'How long will it take?' Aunt Miriam asked, consulting her watch.

'Not long, ten minutes.'

'Maybe more, Ben. It doesn't say where in the house it's hidden,' Jess pointed out.

'Oh yeah. Maybe half an hour then,' Ben said, hoping it wouldn't take anything like that because they should have left already if so.

'So you could do a shop, Mum. There's no way those men would be visiting a museum.'

'Especially a *Stockport* museum,' said Freddie. Ben glared at him.

'Well we are running low on food, and I admire your determination to finish your homework, so if it helps, I'll run you there, provided you all go.'

'Okay. Thanks.'

'Staircase House charges for entry,' said Freddie.

'Why? Have you been?' asked Ben, startled. Freddie and Jess, being from Didsbury, were more familiar with the tourist attractions of London, Paris and Rome than neighbouring Stockport.

204

'Of course not. Firstly it's in scummy Stockport, secondly it charges.'

'Stockport's not scummy!'

'I think it's disgusting, having to pay for entry. Didn't your teacher consider that?' Aunt Miriam said.

'No,' Ben said, deeply uncomfortable now. He couldn't afford to pay for all three of them, or even just himself, probably.

'We don't all have to go, do we?' Freddie said.

'Yes. I'm not having Ben out on his own,' said Aunt Miriam firmly. 'I'll give you the money to get in.'

'Thank you. That's really kind of you. We have to be there by three,' said Ben feeling awful about her paying. She'd happily pay much more than that to get Mum back, he tried telling himself, but he still felt terrible about lying to her.

'Eat some more, Ben. It will only take fifteen minutes to drive there. If we leave at two-thirty, that should get you there in time.'

'I need time to find it. Can we leave at two?'

'I've never known you so keen on homework,' said Aunt Miriam. From her tone, Ben half-suspected she knew. But after a moment's consternation, he relaxed. She would never allow him out again if she knew about the Einstein Code. He gulped some more food down then cleared the table.

Afterwards Aunt Miriam went to call Marcus, so he called Debs.

'Any news?' he asked.

'Not really. They're schtum about that meeting, but there's definitely something up. There's a buzz about, but nobody knows why. Tricky's off Thursday and Friday. Off to Oxford he says.'

'*Is* he? Why?' asked Ben, deeply suspicious.

'It's an anniversary treat for his wife apparently. The best treat he could give her is to emigrate to Mars.'

'Sure is. Anything else?'

'Not about your mum, sadly. I so wish I knew where she was.'

'Me too. Sorry Debs, I've got to go. If I find her you'll be the first to know, okay?'

'I'd better be. Okay Benbo. Take care.'

'I will.'

He hurried downstairs to shepherd everyone into leaving, and after a frustrating few minutes they finally did. But it was after two now, there wasn't much time and traffic was heavy, particularly queuing to get into Stockport.

'Can we jump out here?' he asked, at the foot of Lancashire Hill.

'No! I'm taking you up there. I'm not letting you loose with those evil men around.'

'But we might be late!'

'Ben, it's a school quiz, not life or death,' said Aunt Miriam.

It is, thought Ben, lips clamped together to prevent him blurting out the truth. She'd be driving like a Formula One champion if she knew, but since she didn't he was forced to endure the agonizing inching forward the lights permitted.

Finally they pulled onto a supermarket car park, but there was another delay whilst Aunt Miriam went to get her ticket. Ben looked round but couldn't spot the Mercedes. Unsurprising, probably, given the number of local car parks, but disappointing.

Time was running out.

'It's up the market brew,' he warned, thinking of the steep cobbled slope and Aunt Miriam's slow walk.

'What's a brew?' said Jess. 'Besides a cup of tea.'

'It's the slope to the market. It's short, but steep.'

'Yes, it's always been called the market brew locally hasn't it? I think it's from Old English, bru for brow of a hill – or an eyebrow, if I remember correctly,' mused Aunt Miriam, accompanying them out of the car park.

'How do you know that?' Ben asked, awed.

'My roommate at Oxford. She was studying *Beowulf*, frequently out loud. It's a very different language written, but spoken it's similar to old Cheshire, Alan Garner says, so that must be how I understood so much.'

'Alan Garner of *The Weirdstone of Brisingamen*?' asked Freddie.

'That's right. I heard him on Radio 4.' What Mum and Aunt Miriam hadn't heard on Radio 4 wasn't worth knowing. They both enjoyed it chattering away in the background – but not this week, Ben realised. The only thing Aunt Miriam was interested in was news bulletins and missing persons' sites. Poor Aunt Miriam, she must be suffering so much more than she let on.

'Why do Stockportians ...' Freddie began.

'Stopfordians,' Ben corrected him.

'Whatever. Why do they use Old English, apart from being Neanderthals? Isn't Stockport in Lancashire?' Cheshire contained some of the richest villages in Britain, whereas Lancashire had a lot of former mill towns.

'No, it's in Cheshire,' Ben was pleased to tell him.

'Stockport's been here a long time. Have you seen the Roman road?' Aunt Miriam said.

'No,' said Freddie, looking miffed, so there mustn't be one in Didsbury. Hah!

'You don't need to come right up,' Ben told his aunt at the foot of the brew.

'I do, to pay. And if you think a brew's going to stop me keeping you safe, you're wrong,' Aunt Miriam replied haughtily. 'I'm not nesh you know.'

'What's nesh?' asked Jess.

'Soft,' Ben replied.

'Or weak. It's another Old English word still in use hereabouts,' Aunt Miriam explained, increasingly breathlessly as she tackled the brew. Freddie too was puffing by the time they got to the top.

'Hey! We could have used that!' he complained, pointing to the elevator. 'How modern, a glass lift. Stockport's finally reached the 1980's.'

'More than Didsbury has,' Ben retorted.

'You're so unfit,' Jess commented.

'Physically maybe, but mentally I'm sharp as a scimitar.'

'Modest too,' teased Aunt Miriam.

The market was quiet, so they had a clear path to Staircase House, but by the time they entered the reception it shared with Stockport Story Museum it was ten to three.

'Have you been here before?' the receptionist asked.

'I have, not them,' Ben responded. The tickets were taking ages to print out.

'Every room's from a different period in the house's history. So it's like travelling through time as you go through the house,' she told Jess and Freddie.

'Cool,' said Jess.

'You'd love it some other time,' Ben told her, accepting his ticket, 'but now let's get cracking. Thanks, Aunt Miriam. Bye.'

As they entered the first, dimly lit, medieval section, Freddie grimaced.

'Eugh. It's far too plebby here. I'm going on.' He hurried ahead.

'He's after the clue,' said Jess. 'He shouldn't run off with Goatee Man around.'

'He might have left already,' Ben replied, hoping he hadn't.

But as they progressed through the history-crammed house, Ben could neither find him nor the clue. His earlier fear that they'd frightened the men off for good was resurfacing by the time they entered the bedroom.

Whilst Jess searched the other furniture, Ben checked underneath the bed.

'Yes, there's a chamber pot there,' the attendant told him, misconstruing his intention. 'They used to live in bed to keep warm during winter months. They'd even entertain visitors from bed.'

'That's disgusting!' Jess exclaimed.

'They didn't have central heating then.'

Ben was so relieved to find the envelope hidden beneath the chamber pot that he banged his head.

'Ow!'

'Are you okay?'

'Sure.' He got up.

'What's that you've found?' asked the attendant, eyeing the envelope curiously.

'A clue a friend left for me,' said Ben, showing her the envelope. 'I'm Ben Baxter. We're doing a quiz.'

'Oh I see. How exciting!'

'Mm,' agreed Ben, itching to open it, but not while she was so interested.

'Is this your friend?' she asked as Freddie entered from the other door.

'No, he's my cousin.'

'Oh you've got it, have you?' he said.

'Yes. We should go now.'

'The exit's that way.' The attendant pointed to the doorway through which Freddie had emerged.

On the way downstairs, it occurred to Ben that there were plenty of places in Staircase House to hide all the remaining clues. He had to check. Screening the envelope from Freddie's prying eyes he opened it, but seeing there was nothing but the clue and further directions, he held it out for the others to see, because the directions were even more baffling than ever.

Clue 6

This is the genius who once dared

To say that $E = mc^2$

To find Clue 7:

First take a grey-brown horse

Then add some pink cured pork

Next take E, divide twice by c

Add mc^2 and then you'll find me

N.B Hand in your quiz

Wednesday 5th April 11:00

'Tomorrow,' he noticed sadly.

'At least that's the penultimate clue,' said Jess.

'Oh so there are eight clues in all?' Freddie asked.

'Yeah. But where is it?'

As Jess pondered aloud, Ben stopped listening. He needed Mum back now, not tomorrow. He had to find a way to her, and his best chance was the Mercedes. In case they came for him, he'd better shake off his cousins.

'I'm going back in. I need the loo.'

'We'll wait here,' Jess replied.

'No, go back to your mum. I'll see you there.'

'I can't leave you, Ben,' Jess insisted. 'Or else I'll have to tell Mum.'

'Tell her what?' asked Freddie.

'Never mind. Okay, let's go,' Ben said, deciding that he'd just have to push them aside if the Mercedes appeared. Jess was being a real pain with this threat. He should never have told her about the Einstein Code.

He looked round. The market was much quieter than Oxford Street. There wouldn't be so many people to interfere, if Jess started shrieking kidnap again.

'I thought you needed the loo?' Freddie said.

'I'll hang on. No, don't take the brew. We'll take the lift,' he said, prolonging their time in the market place as much as possible. Where were Goatee Man and his mate?

There was still no sign of the Mercedes by the time they reached the lift. An elderly lady was waiting there too. She smiled at Jess, and greeted her, as elderly Stopfordians tended to do to pleasant children. (Though Jess wasn't being so pleasant right now, Ben thought.)

'Hello,' Jess responded, then turned to Ben. 'What were the instructions? Can you read them out again?'

He did so, noticing their companion's interest.

'I'll bet grey-brown horses are called duns,' said Jess.

'They are, love,' the elderly lady assured her.

'Why dun?' Ben asked Jess.

'Because pink cured pork is ham, isn't it? So the first word's Dun-ham, Dunham. And E divided by c then divided by c again is mass. Then add mc^2, the clue says, so you just add E, because $E = mc^2$. So it's Dun-ham Mass-E, Dunham Massey.'

'That's brilliant Jess! Awesome!' Ben exclaimed. Jess beamed delightedly.

'You're all there with your lemon drops, aren't you?' the old lady told her, smiling.

'What a great expression.'

'I've plenty more where they came from,' the lady told her as the lift stopped. 'Look after your sister,' she told Ben as they emerged (presumably because they were both fair-haired). 'She's cute as a barrel full of monkeys.'

'What a nice lady,' Jess said, as they crossed towards the car park.

'Stockport's full of 'em. It's friendlier than Didsbury.'

'But much grubbier. It's very smart, using Einstein's equation to tell you where to find the next clue,' Freddie said. 'Whoever's writing these clues is very clever.'

'Our teachers aren't idiots, you know,' snapped Ben, whilst inwardly agreeing with Freddie. Yes, the kidnapper was clever all right, but Mum had always said that Ballantyne was one of the cleverest men she'd met.

Clever and evil. Ballantyne, it just had to be Ballantyne. If he could prove it, it might force him to release Mum. But how?

Chapter 15

Mysteriouser and Mysteriouser

When they reached the supermarket Jess spotted Aunt Miriam loading the shopping into the boot, so Ben hurried over to help her with the last few bags and returned the trolley for her.

'I wanted to buy you a piece of cake tomorrow to thank you for this,' he said as she started the car. She turned to him, smiling indulgently.

'Where do you need to be?'

'Dunham Massey. Eleven am.'

'Do you know where? With the deer park and house and gardens it would take weeks to find a clue there without some guidance.'

Ben checked the letter. 'It says to hand in your quiz.'

'The basket in the kitchen then, presuming it's a house quiz. Or at the entrance if it's in the gardens.'

'Huh?'

'If it's a garden quiz, your teacher would need the Dunham Massey staff to cooperate,' said Freddie from the front seat, which he had claimed on grounds of seniority. Jess would sometimes fight for it, but not today.

'It'll be a house quiz then,' said Jess, flashing Ben a meaningful look. He agreed. There was no way Ballantyne would risk enlisting National Trust staff.

'But the kitchen's right at the end of the house, unless they let you sneak through the courtyard. You're not meant to,' said Aunt Miriam. 'So we'd have to be there for ten o'clock really, if you're to hand in your quiz at the end. I don't think I can spare the time, sorry.'

Ben and Jess exchanged horrified looks.

'It's not fair to Ben to mess it up now, not after all the time and effort he's put into it,' Jess said. 'We could unload the shopping and cook tonight's dinner, so you can work when we're back.'

'You'll cook?' Aunt Miriam sounded surprised. 'And unload? Then it's well worth a drive to Dunham Massey tomorrow, particularly if this weather holds.' It was still gloriously sunny.

'If Ben and Freddie will help me,' said Jess.

'Sure,' Ben agreed. Since it was the only way he could get to the next clue, he'd have agreed to clean their enormous house from top to bottom if necessary – but thankfully Jess didn't offer that too.

'We've got to think of a way to find her,' Aunt Miriam fretted as they waited at the M60 roundabout on Didsbury Road. 'I don't know about going to Dunham Massey, Ben. We'll be out a few hours, away from the computer. I don't trust Henry and Robert to check online news whilst we're there.'

'Dad's off?' Freddie said.

'He wants to work on his paper. He can't at work.'

'Rob will be no use. He'll still be snoozing.'

'We've got to keep up with the missing persons' sites. It's not a quick trip like Stockport. I'll have to ask your father for his phone.' (Naturally the most expensive and only Winterburn phone with unlimited internet use.)

'You've more chance of converting him to Christianity.'

'Well, then, we'll have to stay at home.'

Ben cursed – silently of course. Their parents' fear of online dangers had blinded them to its many wonders. But as they exited the roundabout he had a fantastic idea. He texted Jonno, trying to ignore Jess's burning curiosity as they exchanged a flurry of messages.

Urgnt need tblt PLS

R u hm?

Cld be. Wrz yr mum?

Upstrs w A 5 mins?

C u in 5 thx

He didn't want to mention Jonno's tablet until it had appeared. If his mum came downstairs with baby Anna (whose night-time crying had earned Jonno the unusually lavish Christmas present) she would see him leaving. It would be easier to smuggle a catfish through Customs than for Jonno to get his precious tablet past his mum.

'Have you got our keys in your bag?' he asked Aunt Miriam.

'Yes, I have. Why? Need to nip home?'

'Yes, I forgot my shaver,' he said, hoping she didn't offer him Uncle Henry's – disgusting (though not as repulsive as his underpants). Ben had only recently started shaving and hadn't given it a thought this week, so far. Soon they were pulling to a halt alongside the kerb.

'Be as quick as you can. I'll wait in the car,' Aunt Miriam said, holding out his keys.

'Jonno might call.'

'Oh yes. How is he?' she asked on autopilot.

'Okay, thanks.'

'I'll come in with you to check it's safe,' Jess said.

'We'd see if it wasn't. We're just outside,' said Aunt Miriam, but she was not to be deterred.

As Ben unlocked the door, his phone buzzed again. This message wasn't from Jonno, but an unknown number. He opened it and saw a jumble of code, so exited quickly before Jess noticed. He double-checked, but no, it was from a different mobile than the last code, so if he was right about that being from the Chief, was this from Ballantyne? Ben swallowed nervously.

'What's up?'

'Nothing,' he lied, slipping the phone into his pocket. A ball of tension had formed in his throat. He coughed.

'Are you sure you're okay?'

'Sorry, Jess, yeah,' he said, unlocking the door. 'Jonno's supposed to be bringing his tablet round, if he can sneak it past his mum.'

'Why?'

'We've got to get to Dunham Massey tomorrow.' But did they? Had something changed? Ben deactivated the alarm.

'We're not missing it. I'll get Dad's mobile.'

'You can't pinch it, Jess. He'll kill you. Or blame me again.

'True. I'll persuade him somehow.'

'You may not need to. I'll get my shaver. Watch out for Jonno.' He ran upstairs to his bedroom, and there sent Debs a quick text to request Ballantyne's mobile number.

'He's here, Ben!'

'Great. Just a sec.' He grabbed his shaver and ran downstairs, where Jess was updating Jonno.

'… and missing persons' sites and hospitals.'

'Hi, Ben. Sorry about your mum.'

'Thanks.'

'It's so *weird*.'

'I know.'

'The police don't think so,' Jess said.

'What? But she's disappeared, hasn't she?'

'They've put her photo on a police website, where there'll all supposed to be looking for her, but no one's seen her so far.'

'Or nobody's looked.'

'Yeah,' Ben agreed absently, worrying about the new text. His phone buzzed again. He checked it. 'Debs,' he told Jess who had raised her eyebrows enquiringly.

'When are you coming home?' Jonno asked.

'When I get Mum back,' Ben replied. Jonno looked so forlorn that he added, 'But thanks for the tablet. It might help find her.'

Alarm flashed across Jonno's face. 'Oh shoot! I forgot the charger.'

'Can you get it?'

'No chance. It's in the kitchen. She'll be back there now. Can you hang on?'

Ben looked at the car where Aunt Miriam was pointing at her watch.

'Doesn't look like it. How long's it got?'

'Two hours tops.'

'That should do us. Thanks a lot.'

'No worries. But take care of it else I'm toast.'

'Sure.'

After waving Jonno off they locked up the house. The message in his pocket was gnawing at him. Whatever it said could change everything.

In the car he read Debs's text, which gave Ballantyne's mobile, and with Jess watching curiously, scrolled down his incoming messages. No match. Of course he could have a private mobile. He forwarded the two mystery numbers to Debs, asking if she recognised them.

But don't call them, he added.

Why not? D x

He didn't want Debs to get any hint of the connection to the kidnappers, else she'd follow it up herself, so he wondered what to say.

'What's up?' Jess asked.

'Just thinking.'

'That's a first!' sniped Freddie from the front seat.

'Freddie!' his mother warned, whilst Ben thought of a (hopefully) plausible answer.

Mum wrote them down. SPC I think. Who?

'What's Debs saying?' Jess probed.

'She can't find any information about the meeting on Friday. Top secret she thinks,' Ben lied.

'A heck of a lot of texts to say that. Were you communicating one letter at a time?' asked Freddie.

'No!' Ben replied, scathingly. 'She wanted to know how I am,' he added, hoping to end their incessant questions.

It didn't.

By the time they were back at Aunt Miriam's he was glad to unload the shopping to give him a minute's respite from the interrogation. They were so nosey, these Winterburns. They wanted to get inside his head, but it was the only private place Ben had left. It made him even more determined to keep the code to himself, though the way Jess was blackmailing him regarding the Einstein Code was reason enough.

As he carried the last bag in he said, 'I'll just take my razor upstairs, okay?'

He hurried to the spare room, got a clean sheet of paper and started copying out the text. But before he had finished the first line, Jess started yelling.

'FREDDIE, COME BACK!'

Ben heard him stomping up the stairs and quickly stuffed the code under the duvet.

'IF HE'S NOT HELPING, I'M NOT!'

Ben shot out of the spare room before the adults got involved.

'I'm coming, okay? What are we making?'

'I want spag bol but Jess wants chilli. So she can make it,' he grumped.

'I'll help, if you do. We'll make spag bol, how's that?' Ben offered, hoping Jess would agree.

'Depends what her ladyship wants.'

'Let's find out.'

Freddie was behind him as Ben hurried to the kitchen and asked Jess to cooperate.

'But I hate mushrooms!'

'Without mushrooms. Please Jess.'

'You'd both help?'

'Sure.'

'Okay then.' Jess took charge. Consulting a recipe book, she told Freddie to chop the onions and Ben to chop the carrots and garlic whilst she browned the mince. Freddie turned the cold tap on and left it running.

'Your dad would go mad at you wasting money like that.'

'Onions are hydrophilic.'

'Huh?'

'They love water. So they get it from the tap, not my eyes.'

'Mum peels them with wet fingers. Your dad would prefer her method to yours. That's a first.'

'What the eye doesn't see …' Freddie began, grinning mischievously.

'Come on! I want those onions,' Jess cut in.

'You can have them. Here,' said Freddie, carrying the chopping board over. Jess tipped them into the casserole. 'What now?'

'Find the herbs. Oregano, basil, bay leaves and pepper. Is the garlic ready?'

'Nearly,' said Ben, who was just finishing the carrots.

'Good. I'll have that next. Freddie, could you get the tomato purée from the fridge? And two tins of tomatoes from the cupboard?'

'Okay, Miss Bossy Boots.'

Jess turned and poked her tongue out at him, but Freddie didn't respond. Having delivered the garlic, Ben tried to escape, but she asked him to help Freddie to set the table before leaving.

'I'll do mats if you do cutlery,' he offered and to his surprise Freddie accepted. (Usually he would do the exact opposite of anything Ben suggested.) He was then asked to provide Jess with a glass of water, but eventually he had satisfied all of her demands and was free to get upstairs.

He continued to copy out the text, and soon had it transcribed.

OGFF B NJHU VP QYHPTE ?

JFCUQOU MKCTBTZ EBT QCSM UJVTTFBA TKY RN

Great. Now for the alphabet backwards sheet. He found it at the bottom of the pile of papers he'd hidden in the top drawer.

220

O was l, G was t and F was u. *Ltuu*? No it couldn't be. He tried again, but got the same incomprehensible result. Worrying, he tried a few more words, before being forced to acknowledge that the code had changed. Silently, but violently, he cursed. Punching the bed a few times helped, but Ben soon realised the best way to vent his frustration with them was to crack the code.

Vowels. Shortcuts. The single B must stand for a or i. VP and RN must contain a vowel or y. So must EBT – and he already knew B was a vowel. He also knew e was the most common vowel, so he counted how many times each of the possible vowels appeared.

B – 4   V – 2   P – 2   R – 1   N – 1

That couldn't be right, surely? So few vowels in so many words?

'Idiot!' he exclaimed as he realised that both V and P wouldn't be vowels; neither would both R and N. One of each must be a consonant, and P or N could easily be y.

He looked at the other letters. T occurred six times so was probably a vowel and was doubled in the longest word, so either o or e, he guessed.

'Hi Ben, what are you doing?' Jess asked, bursting in.

He turned the paper over quickly. 'You should have knocked!'

'Sorry, I just …' she began. 'What's that?' she asked, pointing to the transcript.

'Code,' he admitted. It was no use pretending otherwise.

'What code? Where from?'

Ben sighed. 'From Ballantyne, I think.'

'How do you know that?'

'I've had two.'

'*Two*?'

'If you hadn't been blackmailing me about the Einstein Code I'd have told you.'

'I haven't been!'

'Threatening to tell your mum unless I do what you say.'

'That is so not fair, Ben. I've been helping you! She's my only aunt and I want her back. I love her too, you know.' With tears in her eyes, red-faced and furious, Jess fled.

'Oh stuff!' Ben ran his hands down his face. She was so emotional nowadays. He didn't need all this upset, he needed to decode the message. But first he'd have to apologise. Clutching his phone and the paper, in case anyone else burst into his room, he hurried to Jess's room.

'It's me,' he said, knocking on the door. 'I've come to say sorry. Are you okay?'

The door flew open.

'No, I'm not! I am very angry indeed,' said a now dry-eyed but clearly furious Jess.

'Sorry.'

'*Why* would you hide it from me, Ben? *Why*?'

'Let me in and I'll tell you everything,' Ben said, looking from side to side, dreading any other Winterburn hearing this conversation.

'I'm your partner. Like Tommy and Tuppence or Peter and Harriet, you do not keep secrets from me. Right?'

'Right,' Ben agreed, but this was not a detective story, it was Mum's freedom.

'Okay. Since that's sorted you can come in.'

He went in, feeling Jess was being a bit unreasonable, but he hated her being angry with him, so was prepared to give ground. He showed her the first text.

'Have you decoded it?'

'Yeah. It says: Be reunited with your mum Oxford Friday.'

'*What*? That's amazing. That's awesome. Oh, Ben!' Looking as thrilled as he had been, she flew to him and enfolded him in a hug.

'But I need to know if that's changed,' he said, gently detaching himself. 'This code's from a different number. I reckon the first was from the Chief, because the Einstein Code's got Ballantyne all over it. So this could be from Ballantyne too.'

'And you haven't cracked it, so the coding method's changed?'

'Exactly. Yeah. The first one was easy. Well, once I saw it, it was. Just the alphabet backwards, you know. A is z and Z is a and B is y and so on.'

'But this one isn't so easy?'

'I was just trying to spot the vowels.'

He showed her what he'd just written.

B – a or i

T – e or o

V/P – vowel or y

R/N – vowel or y

'Why?' Jess asked, as she so often did, so Ben explained.

'Ah. So TBT in MKCTBTZ is useful. But eae, oao, eie, oio – none of them comes in the middle of a word does it? Unless it's an old-fashioned word like encyclopaedia, and even then there aren't three vowels together. It won't be alleluia. Sequoia's famous, but it can't be that,' she gabbled, brain evidently buzzing. 'So B or T is wrong I think.'

'B is definitely a or i unless you can think of a one letter word that's a consonant?'

'No. So T can't be a vowel. Good thinking, Ben. What else could?'

They ran through possibility after possibility, but each time they seemed to be making progress, they came up against a problem. Jess suggested they tried to guess a word.

'Maybe they're giving you Friday's venue. The six-letter word might be Oxford.'

'No,' Ben said, looking at it. 'The first and fourth letters are different.'

'Could the three-letter word be Mum? No, first and last letters are different. Maybe *and* then or *the*?' Jess suggested.

'EBT and TKY both have three letters. Neither of them can be Mum,' Ben realised, disappointed.

'So T or Y is e, if one of them is *the*.'

'But T can't be a vowel,' he reminded her.

'Let's say Y is e and TKY is *the* then.'

'It can't be. Sorry Jess,' Ben added, seeing her face fall. 'T can't stand for itself, else every letter would stand for itself and it wouldn't be in code.'

'Not necessarily. That's true if it's a simple code – add on a letter or take one off or something. But sometimes letters are just assigned randomly, say a is coded S and b is coded D and c is coded U, for example.'

'I know, but the other one was in a pattern, so this one will be, I think, Jess. It's more likely I'm right than you're right.'

Her eyes gleamed. She loved a challenge.

'They're different setters though, aren't they? So let's see,' she said. She took a piece of paper and wrote out:

OGFF B NJHU VP QeHPtE ?

'Could be, but I don't like that word,' said Ben, pointing to the one beginning M.

'It's chastity without an s,' said Jess.

'It won't be that.'

'No,' she agreed. 'I'm just trying to find the word shape.' She stared at it for a while then shook her head. 'No, I can't think of it. Sorry, Ben.' The door slammed downstairs. 'Dad's home! Oh flip!' she exclaimed, looking at her watch. 'The sauce will have dried up. We'll have to get the spaghetti cooked. I'll do that if you if you tell everyone dinner will be ready in fifteen minutes.'

'Okay,' he agreed, staring at the code.

'So you've got a few more minutes. Good luck.'

'Thanks. I'll need it.'

It was only a few seconds later, surely, when Freddie knocked on the door.

'Grub's up! Jess says if you don't come now she'll kill you.'

'Okay.' Ben abandoned his latest attempt to crack the baffling code and hid the papers in the top drawer. He was almost tempted to text the sender to ask for a clue, but he could imagine Ballantyne smiling his twisted smile, enjoying bamboozling him. He wouldn't get the chance.

But Uncle Henry did.

'What about the science quiz, Ben? How are you getting on with that?' he said as soon as they sat down (minus Robert, who was at a friend's). And for the rest of dinner he didn't let up.

He started with the Big Bang, when time began.

'So God couldn't have created the universe, not without exploding,' Freddie said.

'God is just fiction, and preposterous fiction at that, but the Big Bang isn't,' Uncle Henry said. It was the ultimate expression of $E = mc^2$, he continued. That initial blast around 13.8 billion years ago was packed with so much energy that everything (from planets and stars to the long blond hair Ben was attempting to pick out of his pasta without offending Jess) came from it. It could still be heard today; the crackling of interference on a TV set is the noise of the Big Bang, he said, not that Ben had ever heard a TV set crackle.

'They thought it was pigeon poo!' Freddie exclaimed.

'Freddie! Not whilst we're eating,' Aunt Miriam chided him.

'But they did!'

After that came inflation – probably (for reasons Ben couldn't hope to follow, they were flying out so thick amongst whirring arms and blobs of sauce) – but only for a microsecond. (How did they know? Ben didn't ask and fortunately Uncle Henry didn't pause to explain.) Sub-atomic particles called quarks had appeared as the dark universe cooled – mass out of energy, yes, he'd got that now, Ben confirmed – and a model had been constructed to explain the properties of these quarks, called the Standard Model.

'But it generated one quark that should theoretically exist, but had never been seen until recently. Do you know what it's called?'

'No.'

'The Higgs ...'

'Boson!' Ben realised. He recalled Mum's excitement when the Higgs boson's discovery was announced at CERN – she had probably realised why it was so important. He hadn't. And he still didn't, because apparently the Standard Model was defective.

'It explains the quantum world, where particles are so light that gravity doesn't matter. But not the classical world, the world we know, where, if you let you go of a spoon, it drops to the floor,' Uncle Henry said, releasing his Bolognese-coated spoon. It clattered to the floor.

'Henry!' Aunt Miriam remonstrated, getting up.

'It's science, Miriam.'

'I think Ben could have imagined a spoon falling to the floor without you actually doing it,' she said, bending to mop up the mess with a tissue.

'But particles wouldn't fall like that. They're whizzing all around us right now.' He windmilled his hands to demonstrate, clouting Aunt Miriam's shoulder.

'*Henry!*'

'Sorry.'

Freddie grinned at his dad. 'Particles are really interesting. The more closely you try to pin them down, the less accurately you can. That's Heisenberg's Uncertainty principle, it's worth remembering,' he claimed.

'Doubt I'll ever need it.'

'You might, Ben. In the Einstein Code,' Jess said.

'True.'

Uncle Henry continued, becoming more incomprehensible as he became more enthusiastic. Superstrings, dark matter and spin foam whizzed over Ben's head as he sucked in spaghetti without even trying to understand. If the Einstein Code got that difficult he'd just ask Freddie; it would be impossible to ask Uncle Henry. Stopping him in full flow was like trying to stop a tsunami with a twig.

But eventually dinner was finished, and coffees were declined – Aunt Miriam said she'd stick to water so she could sleep and volunteered to clear up since they had cooked. Ben looked at Uncle Henry, but there wasn't a twinge of guilt. Did it never even occur to him to offer to do it? His friends' dads helped out so much more. But as Mum often said, "Henry has a Stone Age mind in a modern man's body."

So Jess and he were able to return to the guest room and try again to crack the code.

'Shall we start with the question?' Jess suggested.

'You're the expert on questions.'

'The only question word finishing with a double letter is will, so that might be the first word.'

'Great idea. I'll try it.' As he was doing so, he noticed B must therefore be a, since it couldn't be i.

Will a NJHU VP QYHPTE ?

JlCUQwU MKCTaTZ EaT QCSM UJVTTlaA TKY RN

'Could be, Ben. Will a blank be blank? Will a thing do thing?'

'Yeah. So P is o or e.'

'You love the vowels don't you?'

'It's easier than finding consonants. There's only five of them.'

'So where are the others? J or H in the second word probably,' Jess mused. 'Y or H and maybe P or T in the last word of the question.'

'So H is probably a vowel.'

'There isn't an H in the second row,' Jess noticed. 'It's probably u, the least common vowel.'

'Okay.' Ben took a clean sheet and noted it and their other deductions down carefully.

As Jess watched him she said, 'I think s is U, or rather U in the code is really s.'

'Why?'

'The first word of the second row. Look at the ending.'

Ben did so and saw what she meant.

'Okay. Anything else?' he asked, adding it to the list.

'Not for now' Jess replied, looking at their list:

a: B

e: P or C

i: G

o: P or C

u: H

s: U

'Why don't you try e is P and o is C, and I'll try o is P and e is C,' he suggested. Jess agreed and a few minutes later they compared answers.

e is P, o is C

Will a NJus Ve QYueTE ?

JlosQws MKoTaTZ EaT QosM sJVTTlaA TKY RN

o is P, e is C

Will a NJus Vo QYuoTE ?

JlesQws MKeTaTZ EaT QeSM sJVTTlaA TKY RN

'But which six-letter word has ue or uo in the middle?' Jess asked, comparing them.

'And where's the vowel in the last two words?' Ben responded.

'This is impossible!'

'If Ballantyne's behind it, anything's possible.'

'But everything we try is wrong.'

'It must be a really cunning code. Typical Ballantyne.'

'But why would he text you when he's also writing the Einstein Code? No offence, Ben, but it doesn't make sense.'

'This code doesn't make sense. The more I look at it, the less I understand.'

'Mysteriouser and mysteriouser,' Jess said.

'It's mysterious all right. But mysteriouser?'

'Like Alice in Wonderland. Or was it curiouser and curiouser?' Jess wondered.

'It doesn't matter. Maybe he's just torturing us. Maybe it's impossible to solve.'

'Perhaps we should ask Freddie for help,' Jess suggested tentatively.

'No way! We've got all night to work on it. If we haven't cracked it by tomorrow then I will, okay?' Ben promised, making him even more determined to crack it.

But when Aunt Miriam disturbed them to tell them to get to bed (there was so much paper everywhere that she spotted nothing she shouldn't and assumed they'd been playing – *playing*? – code cracking together) not even Jess had managed to decode the message.

'It's a fiendish code!'

'It's so twisted it's just got to be from Ballantyne.'

Chapter 16

So Near ...

He had a terrible night, becoming increasingly frustrated by the convoluted code, which thwarted every attempt he made to crack it. Eventually he fell asleep, surrounded by paper. Mum was in great danger, and somewhere nearby but he couldn't find her. They were in school but he was hopelessly lost. Everything was out of place, corridors led to dead ends, staircases had moved. At the end of a corridor, through a bricked up door, he could hear her, tearfully pleading. He started tearing at the wall, pulling it apart brick by brick, but no matter how many he removed, other bricks shifted to fill the gap. He persisted until Mum's pleas died into a whimper, and then a horrifying silence. With a sickening sense that it was too late he woke, bathed in sweat, heart pounding and utterly terrified.

Seeing the pages of abandoned attempts at cracking the code returned him to reality. Still rattled, he scrabbled through the sheets until he could find the last one. He tried to focus and looked at the longest word, with B (a or i) as the penultimate letter. The last letter could be what? He swallowed, his mouth as dry as dust. His head felt full of wool. Last letter, try and think. It could end in n or t maybe – or s?

There was a rap on the door.

'Ben, are you awake?' Jess called.

'Sort of. Hang on, I need to get dressed,' he replied, reaching for his jeans. 'Okay,' he said, as he fastened them.

She entered, saw the mass of paper and asked, 'Any luck?'

'No. I thought I was getting somewhere last night but as usual came straight up against a brick wall. In fact I dreamed of walls.'

'Did you? Well if you haven't solved it, we'd better ask Freddie. After Dunham Massey.'

'Oh stuff it! I'd forgotten! What time is it? Have I time for a shower?' He badly needed to wake up.

'Just, then come and have breakfast.'

'I don't need breakfast.'

'Try telling Mum that. She'd never let you leave without it.'

'Okay.'

'I could show Freddie the code if you'd like.'

'Sure. Show him the texts if you like,' Ben added, handing her his phone. 'I can't do it.'

After a hasty revitalizing shower he joined the others for breakfast. Freddie gave him a significant look, but nothing more, so Aunt Miriam was still oblivious to everything they knew about finding Mum. Which was mightily unfair, because it looked as if she'd had an even rougher night than Ben.

'I can't believe we've still not heard,' she complained, running her hands through her hair. She had been mainlining coffee to wake her up, but of course it had also increased her agitation. He got up to give her a quick hug.

'Still up for that cake at Dunham Massey?'

'I've not forgotten, don't worry,' she said, returning the hug with interest. He looked down affectionately on her dark curly head. It was almost as if he was comforting her, a reversal of their roles (and Freddie also seemed to see it as such, because he didn't taunt Ben as a result). But he was hiding so much from her that he felt utterly wretched. Once he'd got Mum home he could tell Aunt Miriam everything and she'd understand – hopefully.

'Let's get going,' Jess said.

After a flurry of finding bags, phones and money they were ready and in the car by half-past nine, Jess clutching Jonno's tablet. She sat beside Ben, busily checking missing persons' sites, whilst he stared out of the window, worrying about the coded text. He should have enlisted Freddie last night. What if he was meant to do something, and the deadline had now passed? It was a beautifully sunny day, but the weather didn't cheer him – and neither did the roadworks they encountered on the motorway, so that they didn't arrive until twenty past ten.

'Do we really have to go right through the house to get to the kitchen?' he asked.

'Yes, we do, I'm afraid. Now they've built the new ticket office and café they're even keener on guarding the back way to slip into the house.'

'We could shoot on ahead.'

'Not without tickets you can't.'

'I hadn't thought of that,' said Ben, thinking guiltily of the paltry amount of cash he had left. 'Sorry about all you've been spending on me.' He knew Uncle Henry wouldn't approve.

'It's okay, you're free. We've got a family membership,' Aunt Miriam said (meaning of the National Trust, which kept many historic sites open for everyone's enjoyment in principle, though you had to pay the membership, or an entrance fee.) 'Just pretend you're Robert.'

'Slouch a bit. Grunt. Drag your knuckles on the ground,' quipped Freddie.

'That's not very nice,' Aunt Miriam rebuked him gently, but she was smiling.

They went to get their tickets (more delay) and headed up to the lake where young children were excitedly pointing at assorted ducks, mainly mallards and coots plus a few majestic swans. Though Jess and Aunt Miriam paused to watch them, Freddie went straight past with Ben.

'Do you know what it says? The code I mean,' Ben added.

'Give me chance! I only had about ten seconds with it before breakfast. You think it's from Ballantyne, Jess said. Why?'

'Later,' Ben said briefly, seeing Aunt Miriam and Jess approaching. They waited by the carved tree (which was nearly as fantastic as Rory's bench) for them to catch up.

Together they turned towards the house, as everyone called it, though on that scale, Mount Everest would be a molehill. They passed under an archway into the cobbled courtyard. Aunt Miriam pointed out the man on the chair blocking their entry through an opening on the left. 'He's a guard, so there are no shortcuts to the kitchen.'

'Even if we show our tickets?'

'No need. There's plenty of time,' Freddie claimed, but he thought it was a school quiz. Ben was jittery, but trying very hard to act natural.

Jess pointed to the deer grazing on the sculpted front lawns, four a mottled brown and one white.

'There's the albino! I've never seen it on the front lawn before.'

'A good omen, I hope,' said Aunt Miriam.

'Yes,' agreed Ben, his mouth dry with nervous excitement.

In the entrance hall of the grand house Freddie asked the ticket inspectors if there was a quiz.

'Yes, though it might be a bit young for you,' said the woman.

'Could we have one between us, please?' asked Jess.

'Certainly. It's more for your age,' she replied, evidently underestimating Jess's maturity as people often did, due to her height, until they got to know her. 'They're through here.' She led them into a passageway where there was a basket containing clipboards and pencils. 'When you've finished, return it to the basket in the kitchen.'

Jess smiled triumphantly at Ben.

'It could have changed. They're always changing things here, so it's a great house to visit because it's always interesting,' she enthused. The ticket inspectors beamed at her.

'Do you need any advertising? You could employ her,' Aunt Miriam said.

'We'll certainly bear you in mind,' the man responded, amused.

'Have you ever been inside the house?' asked Freddie.

'Not that I can remember,' Ben replied. Big mistake, he soon realised, for Freddie clearly considered the history of the two families who had owned the house – the Booths and the Greys – absolutely fascinating. They entered the first room, with an enormous fireplace that put even Uncle Henry's to shame and family portraits hanging on the walls.

'The Booths and the Greys were on opposite sides of the Civil War. Thomas Grey – that's Lord Grey of Groby – signed to have Charles I's head chopped off. See, on the execution warrant,' Freddie said, waving a copy of the gruesome document underneath his nose. 'But the Booths were given that in thanks for trying to arrange his escape.' He pointed to a black circlet of material in a frame beside the enormous stone fireplace.

'What is it?'

'The necklet Charles I wore for his execution.'

'He wore it round his neck to have his head chopped off? Where's the blood?'

'It's black. Maybe that's why.'

They turned right under a portrait of a bearded man proudly wearing a red robe.

'That's William, the 9th Earl of Stamford,' Freddie said, but Ben was already leaving the room. 'That's the chapel on your right.'

'Ben's in a hurry, it's like all chapels.'

Ben turned left, into a small room lined with dreary portraits. Freddie pointed out a table by the entrance with playing cards inlaid into its top.

'There are only three of them in the world. The Queen's got one at Windsor.'

'Good for her,' Ben said, continuing to what looked like the exit, but he emerged onto a balcony above a grand dining room. He wheeled round angrily.

'It's a dead end!'

'I know. But this is important. That's Elizabeth of York, the mother of the princes in the tower,' Freddie said pointing to one of the portraits.

'I don't give a stuff about Elizabeth of York. Where's the kitchen?'

'We have to retrace our steps, I'm afraid,' Aunt Miriam said, leading Ben back past the enormous stone fireplace and Charles I's execution necklet. (Ben couldn't resist checking for bloodstains as he hurried past, but couldn't spot any.)

'We have to go up then down, like in Manchester museum,' Jess said.

'Not again.' Typical Ballantyne, he thought. How amusing he must have found it, selecting the hiding places for the clues. Oh no! What if they met Goatee Man with Aunt Miriam? She'd shout the house down if he chased Ben, or even spoke to him.

As they went upstairs Freddie, unaware of Ben's trepidation, continued to act like a demented tour guide.

'See that girl with the long curly hair? It's actually a boy. That's a Van Dyck, that's Charles I's children,' he said as they passed several large portraits. He turned left at the top of the staircase.

'No, Freddie, Ben doesn't need to see her bedroom. This way,' said Aunt Miriam turning right. Freddie scurried back to catch up and joined them as they entered yet another room.

'That's Roger and Jane with their mother,' said Freddie of a full-length portrait on the far wall. (He persisted in calling the 10th Earl of Stamford Roger and his no doubt heavily titled sister Jane as if he knew them personally.) It was more natural than all the pompous posturing in the portraits downstairs. Two children were holding their mother's hands, the girl trailing a teddy from her other hand. They looked a nice family, Ben admitted. Freddie nodded, pleased.

They went through into a light, elegant room, which was longer than a cricket pitch. There was a grand piano by the entrance.

'You can play it – it's a Bechstein grand.' Freddie gazed at it longingly.

'No time, Freddie, I'm afraid,' said his mother firmly. 'Not if Ben wants to finish his homework. I expect some of these other families are from your school, are they? What do you get at the end, a prize?'

'I don't know,' Ben replied, tingling with nervous excitement. It all depended on Clue 7. It might direct him to Clue 8 later that afternoon, and then the Einstein Code would be finished, and he'd get Mum back today, not on

Friday. How delighted Aunt Miriam would be, he thought as he followed Freddie into a dark red bedroom containing a ridiculously ornate four-poster bed and a display case stuffed with silver (a real bedroom essential).

'This is another dead end!'

'Yes, but this is the *royal* bed. Just look at the tassels,' said Freddie, pointing up to some feathery embellishments atop the four posts.

'I don't give a *stuff* about tassels, I want to find Clue 7. Fast!'

'I want my coffee and cake. Come on,' said Aunt Miriam, turning back. 'We go down this corridor, Ben, to get to the stairs.'

Freddie tried to pull Ben into another room.

'It's the Dunham silver. Most of it was gambled away by a decadent ancestor but Roger bought it back,' he said.

'I don't give a toss! Where's the kitchen?'

'You should *see* the punch bowl!'

'I'll ram that punch bowl down your throat if you don't stop this mad tour guide act. You're driving *me* mad too.'

'Right. Find the kitchen yourself then! I try to teach you but you just don't care, do you? You're determined to be ignorant!' Seemingly enraged, he wheeled round and marched down the passage at the sort of speed Ben would have welcomed from the start. Jess raised her eyebrows at Aunt Miriam.

'Let him go,' Aunt Miriam said. 'He'll meet us in the kitchen.'

'He's trying to beat us to the clue. Come on, let's beat him,' Jess said. But Aunt Miriam couldn't race to save her life and it was a fair way to the top of the stairs. Ben watched for Goatee Man warily, but they didn't meet him. He was probably well ahead of them, Ben thought, checking his watch. Five minutes to go!

The kitchen was across a courtyard at the bottom of the stairs. Unable to bear another second's delay, Ben charged across the cobbles, but before he had reached the kitchen Freddie emerged from it, brandishing the cream envelope that Ben was so desperate to find.

'Is this what you're after?'

'You know it is.'

'Don't open it! That's Ben's!' Jess cried.

'I wouldn't.' As if, Ben thought, as he took it from his thoroughly exasperating cousin. 'You should see the kitchen. It's massive, with the original ranges and table – they had to rip them out at Lyme when it was a training college, so Dunham's kitchen is really special. It leads through to the dining room where King George and Queen Mary once dined, that's George VI you know.'

'I'll bet Ben's more interested in where we'll eat,' said Aunt Miriam, but she was wrong. Clue 8 was his big worry. Where and when would he find it?

He tore open the envelope, looking for one thing only.

Thursday 6ᵗʰ April 11:00

'Tomorrow!' In response to Jess's querying look he explained. 'Clue 8's not till tomorrow.'

'Bad luck,' she sympathised.

'Why?' Aunt Miriam said.

'I wanted to get it over with today.'

'What does it say?'

'It doesn't matter,' Ben said, deeply disappointed.

'Never mind, let's get that cake,' Aunt Miriam said, unaware the prospect of getting her sister back that afternoon had vanished.

He trudged to the restaurant behind them. It was based in the old stables, where Mum and he had enjoyed lunch with Debs on that sunny afternoon last summer. As he got a tray, he felt such a yearning for her, such a strong sense of her, that it was as if she was nearby. He looked round, but couldn't see her, then checked his Inbox, but there were just a few messages from friends.

'Come on, teenager, off your phone. You look as exhausted as me, so a cake will do you good.'

'I'm okay. I'm treating you.'

'I know and I appreciate that so very much. I'll have a piece of this delicious carrot cake, please.' Ben checked the price above the counter. He could just about afford it, so he put a piece on the tray. He couldn't afford a cake for anyone else though, but Aunt Miriam insisted on treating them all to a cake and what she called a proper drink (not tap water).

Ben chose apple juice and caramel shortbread, Aunt Miriam and Freddie had coffee and carrot cake, whilst Jess opted for dandelion and burdock and chocolate cake. Once Aunt Miriam had paid (accepting Ben's £3.25 graciously) they found a free table and sat down.

'You can read us the clue, can't you?' begged Jess.

Ben was thoroughly fed up with Ballantyne and the tortuous Einstein Code.

'I don't know if I can be bothered.'

'I understand that. It's hard to care about anything but finding your mum, isn't it?' Aunt Miriam said. 'Mm, this carrot cake is delicious. Thank you, darling, lovely of you.'

Aunt Miriam would love to know she'd helped get Mum back, he suddenly realised. He should therefore involve her in the Einstein Code as much as possible. So he read the clue out, carefully screening it from her.

Clue 7

An element, a tool, a man,
A lady, verb and noun I am.
You may seek me near, you make seek me far,
I'm the heaviest atom made in a star.

To find Clue 8:
In the market for a story?
Tells of things both good and gory,
Takes you back ten thousand years,
Tells of people's hopes and fears.

'Oh, they rhyme,' she said, sounding impressed.

'Yes, they're good for a state school aren't they?' agreed Freddie.

'Our teachers are all right, you know.'

'Bet you don't say that in school,' Aunt Miriam teased him.

'Solved it yet?' Freddie asked.

'No. Have you?'

'Naturally. But I'm waiting for you to get it,' he said, so smugly that it almost put Ben off his caramel shortbread. Almost. As he chewed, an idea struck him.

'Is it iron? Your dad says the heaviest atom made by stars is iron.'

'No. He says *all* atoms are made by stars, but most stars can only make elements no heavier than iron internally. By fusion, remember?' Ben nodded. 'Hydrogen and hydrogen make helium and so on?' Ben nodded again.

'Heavier atoms than iron need more energy than most stars can produce, so then they die out, forming a brown dwarf or suchlike.'

'Giant stars, though, explode into supernovae,' said Jess, 'making every element under the sun in a magical chemical shower.'

'It's not magic, it's science.'

'Magical means amazing, not supernatural. Of course I know there are no fairies involved.'

'But it's nice to think we're all made of stardust, isn't it, Ben?' Aunt Miriam said with a sad smile.

He so needed to find Clue 8 and bring Mum back.

'To iron's a tool, for ironing clothes. To iron is a verb, and you iron with an iron, so that's the noun. The Iron Man's from the films. Is there an Iron Lady?' he asked.

'There *was*, but she's dead now. Margaret Thatcher was known as the Iron Lady. She was Britain's first female Prime Minister,' said Aunt Miriam.

'So Clue 7 is iron,' Ben concluded. 'Great. But where will Clue 8 *be*, that's what I'm stuck on.'

'Read it again,' said Jess, so he did. There was silence except the clinking of coffee cups and glasses whilst they all considered.

'Could it be Stockport Story Museum, the one connected with Staircase House?' Jess asked. 'It's in Stockport market.'

'In the market for a story, oh yes!' Aunt Miriam agreed

'It does have prehistoric stuff there, so it could be,' Ben said.

'It must be. The rest is really vague, it could apply to any museum,' said Jess. 'But it must be local. All the other clues have been.'

'Well they couldn't ask parents to drive their children to Land's End,' Aunt Miriam said, under the impression a teacher had set it. Ballantyne was capable of anything, Ben thought.

What a sadist! The last clue, the most important clue, was so vague that it could almost be anywhere. Ballantyne would love to see the pain he was inflicting on Ben right now.

'It is Stockport Story isn't it? Or are there any museums like that in any other towns? Like Oxford?'

'Why Oxford?' Aunt Miriam asked.

'You know it so well.'

'Well yes, there are lots of museums in Oxford, but if you're going that far, what about the Tower of London? Many very gory things indeed happened there.'

Ben shook his head. The directions were uselessly vague. He had to get back to solve that text. Because if that didn't tell him how to find Mum, there was a very real chance he'd go to the wrong venue entirely.

He might never, ever find her.

And what would Ballantyne do to her then?

Chapter 17

Code Cracking

When they got back, it being Aunt Miriam's, they had to have lunch, but none of them wanted bread after the cake they'd recently eaten, so it was just meat, fruit and salad.

'Or would anyone prefer cheese?' Aunt Miriam asked, once they were all sat down.

'No, this is fine, thanks,' Jess said. They all ate fast, even Freddie, the slowest, pickiest eater, showing that he too was keen to get to the code. Aunt Miriam didn't mind them finishing early, because she was scanning the paper, hoping she'd see something about Mum. She hadn't much else to cling on to.

'Shall I make you a coffee before I go?' Ben offered, feeling guilty about the mountain of information he was withholding from her.

'No thanks, I'll stick to water for a while,' she replied, eyes fixed on the newspaper.

So Ben was able to hurry upstairs, passing Robert lumbering downstairs for breakfast.

'Morning.'

'You still here?'

'I'll be here until we find Mum.'

'The sooner you find her the better,' he grunted.

So you get your house back. You don't care about Mum, Ben thought, glaring at his retreating back.

He hid the clue in his bag, put his mobile on to charge and then found the others in Freddie's room. He was sitting at his vast desk, head bent over a notepad.

'He's just making a chart of letter distribution,' Jess explained.

'Why?'

'Morse's frequency table,' Freddie replied, as if any idiot would know that.

'What? Am I expected to know what he's talking about?'

'Samuel Morse, the inventor of Morse code, analysed printers' type. Look,' said Jess, handing him an encyclopaedia lying open on the bed. It showed a table, in which E was used most (12,000 times) and Z least (200 times).

'Oh so E's the most common letter and Z the least. Even I knew that.'

'Whereas in this code, we have this,' said Freddie, theatrically tearing off the top page. 'It'd be so much quicker with a computer, but Robert was awake, so I couldn't use his.'

'You mean you use it when he's asleep?' asked Ben, surprised.

'Of course,' replied Freddie with his cocky grin. 'Half the day he's out or asleep. It's a shame to waste it.'

'Doesn't he mind?'

'He doesn't know. If you tell him, I'll tell him about this,' he threatened.

'It's all right, I'm not going to talk to him unless I have to.'

'Does anyone? Look,' said Freddie, showing them his chart.

7	T
4	B, C, F, U
3	E, J, Q
2	H, K, M, N, O, P, V
1	A, R, S, Y, Z

'So T stands for e?' said Ben.

'Looks almost certain.'

Ben stared at the code Jess had obviously transcribed from his phone (her handwriting was neat, Freddie's terrible).

OGFF B NJHU VP QYHPTE ?

JFCUQOU MKCTBTZ EBT QCSM UJVTTFBA TKY RN

'I thought that T was e for the same reason, but we worked out it was wrong. Can't remember why though.'

'We need a fresh approach, so let's try it out. Can I borrow some paper?' Jess asked.

'You don't need paper. The last word of the first line ends e something, probably ed, er or es. There's a three-letter word ending e on the second line – probably the, that's the most common three-letter word, and there's a double e in the eight-letter word. All likely,' Freddie said.

'But complicated to work out whether B, C, F or U stands for t,' Ben said, looking at Morse's frequency table.

'It's not going to be easy. The first one was, so *you* could crack it,' Freddie added as condescendingly as possible. 'But this was written after Monday lunch.'

'Well yeah, I didn't get it till yesterday.'

'Yes, that's when you *got* it. But it doesn't mean it was composed then. Still the same logic applies. It's meant for us, not you.'

'So why did he send it to me then?'

'He knew you'd need our help. On Monday we advertised that we were helping you all round SPC. And you gave your mobile to the Board Secretaries, but not to Ballantyne.'

Ben considered. Though offensive, Freddie might also be right about the timing.

'The first text arrived when we checked the passports on Monday.'

'Your phone was switched off that morning. You showed it me, remember? To demonstrate 993?'

'Oh yeah. I didn't switch it on till I got back home.'

'So when exactly was the text sent? Maybe it's not from SPC at all.'

'It must be.' But, worried, Ben left to get his phone, which was charging in the spare room. Only Mum, Aunt Miriam, Jess, Debs and a few of his friends had his number, and most of them knew Ben liked cracking codes. But none of them would know they'd be reunited on Friday – that would imply Aunt Miriam or Jonno or someone was in cahoots with the kidnappers, which was ridiculous. No Way!

He sat scrolling down his Inbox. The first message had been sent at 12:01, just as they were leaving SPC. But the baffling code had been sent on Tuesday at 15:28.

He returned to his cousins, to tell them. Both could be from SPC, they agreed.

'But only if the first coder was very quick.'

'It's almost as if they were trying to tip you off,' Jess said. 'Which is totally different to the Einstein Code.'

'Yes, but that's a school quiz.'

'Just saying,' said Jess.

'But we've got to solve this,' Ben said.

'I don't think we'll get there through letter distribution,' Jess replied. Freddie glared at her. 'The sample's much too small to be statistically viable,' she explained in Winterburn-speak, but it seemed to convince him. Freddie gave a small, but perceptible nod, though he still looked grumpy. 'It's useful, but not the answer.'

'What is though?' Ben demanded, pacing the room. He couldn't believe Freddie hadn't come up with the answer, he'd expected so much from his great brain.

'We've all got to think again,' said Jess. 'It can't be impossible.'

'But it's like the hardest code ever!'

'Enigma was the hardest code ever,' said Freddie. 'But Alan Turing cracked it.'

'That's right, Freddie, what was it?' Jess said. 'The cogs moved on after every letter? So if A stood for b the first time, it would stand for h the next time, then z, then u, then …'

'Okay, I get it. What are you saying? The coding method changed from word to word?' Ben asked, frantic to solve it.

'From letter to letter.'

'Oh.'

'But that would be far too hard! It took Alan Turing months!' Freddie protested.

'Can we ask him then?' Ben asked.

'Haven't you even heard of him?' Freddie responded.

'No.'

'Haven't you seen Alan Turing Way near the university?'

'No!'

'Or *The Imitation Game*?'

'NO! What the hell are you saying?'

'We can't ask him, Ben. He's dead. Sorry,' Jess said, intervening before the urge to strangle Freddie had completely overtaken him.

'Blasted, blasted, blasted hell!'

'No point stamping, Ben,' Freddie said haughtily, making his imminent death even more likely. He turned to Jess. 'If the letters move on each time, we need to write a computer programme.'

'No, we need to find a key. They needed a key – wasn't it *Heil Hitler* or something? It came up in every message. And there was a commander who said *Alles ist gut hier* or something every time, which Gordon Welchman spotted,' Jess said.

Ben stopped and looked at the code, thinking. It wouldn't be that complicated. It would be something he could crack. It had been sent to him, it was meant for him.

Could *this one* be from Mum?

But Jess, unaware, started talking about secrets.

'The best keys are a secret only two people share. That's how Peter coded for Harriet, a poem they'd written together, or translated or something,' Jess added. 'So no one else could possibly solve it.'

Secret: Ben had a secret, a really big secret that might just impress Ciara at the Year 9 prom. Unbeknown to his mates, cousins or anyone except them, Mum had been teaching him to ballroom dance. (*Strictly* had a lot to answer for.)

'Hold me like this, yes, that's good. Is she tall? Great, it won't be a problem then. Now you go forward whilst I go back. It's always like that, men get to lead, haven't you

249

noticed?' (Said with a smile.) 'One step, two step, one step, two step, that's right.'

Could it be?

One step, two step, one forward, two forward? So FF could be from d e – or e d, from the other dancer's perspective.

'Brilliant!' Ben exclaimed. 'What looks like a double letter isn't, and what doesn't is.'

'Huh?'

'Can I borrow your desk for a minute, Freddie?'

'Be my guest,' Freddie said, standing up. 'You're making as much sense as the Quantum Paradox.'

'What? No, never mind. I didn't ask anything. Just leave me be for a bit. I might be wrong. You think of your way of solving it.'

Need a ... As Ben continued to decipher it, his excitement died away.

'It can't be from Mum, can it? Why would she say this?'

He showed his workings to his cousins.

NEED A LIFT TO OXFORD?

'She can't be offering you a lift if she's kidnapped. She wouldn't have a phone either. Why did you even think it was from her?' asked Freddie scornfully.

'Well done, Ben,' Jess said pointedly, glaring at her brother. 'How on earth did you work that out? Is that the entire message?'

'No there's loads more. Hang on,' Ben replied, sitting down at the desk again, and feeling increasingly uncomfortable as he continued to decode the message.

HEATONS LIBRARY CAR PARK THURSDAY SIX PM

'It's from them. Told you,' Freddie said.

'Mum knows I'd struggle to get to Oxford without a lift,' Ben said, desperate for the text to have been a communication from her.

'She can't be offering you a lift, can she? They're hardly going to let her go driving round the country, you idiot.'

'It's not from her. I'm sorry, Ben. It's from them. The kidnappers,' Jess said, more kindly.

'It's a way to get you in that Mercedes. They're going to kidnap you, too. Heaven knows why, but they are.'

Ben walked out of Freddie's bedroom and into the spare room, numb with dread. Getting Mum back was going to be so much harder than he'd anticipated. He sat on the bed, staring into space, trying to understand: the Einstein Code, the texts and the midnight conversation he'd overheard. How did they interlink?

There was a tap on the door.

'Ben, are you okay?' Jess asked timidly.

'Yeah.' He opened the door. 'Sorry Jess, I'm just …'

'Missing her. I know. Me too, but it's worse for you, far worse.'

'Even worse for her. I've got to get her back, Jess, Away from them.'

'It's getting too dangerous, Ben. Far too dangerous. Can we show Freddie the Einstein Code? I'd like to see what he thinks.'

'Okay.' Ben shrugged. It was worth a try. By the time his cousins returned he had the clues unfolded and spread out on the bed.

A lowly patent clerk once dared

To prove I equalled mc^2

As far as man can ever go,
The biggest concept you will know,
It's wonderful and yet so strange
For when it's squared, it doesn't change

One man switched a torch on
Thought: 'Light beams are not free,
They come from mass the torch has lost.'
Hence Fat Man finished me.

Though we call it a Dog
To us it's brightest of the bright,
You'll see it nearly nine years ago
If you look up tonight.

The higher you go,
The faster it goes,
The faster you go,
The slower it goes.

This is the genius who once dared
To say that $E = mc^2$

An element, a tool, a man,

A lady, verb and noun I am.

You may seek me near, you make seek me far,

I'm the heaviest atom made in a star.

'Do you know all the answers?' Freddie asked.

'I think so. Energy; infinity; Nagasaki; Sirius; time; Einstein; iron.'

'Is there anything we've missed?' asked Jess. 'Anything you can spot that we haven't?'

'Of course. I know what it will start with.'

'Huh?'

'Look at the first letters. That's why it's called the Einstein Code, isn't it? The first letters of the answers spell out his name.'

'Oh yes! So it should start with an N,' Jess said.

'But that doesn't tell us anything! He knows where Mum is and he isn't telling me. He's playing with me like he's a cat and I'm a mouse. He's evil! I hate him!'

'Calm down,' said Freddie, which had the opposite effect to that intended. 'Think back to the first clue. Where did you find that?'

'At home on the doormat. So he knows where we live. I already knew that from his thugs breaking in last Friday.'

'And when did it arrive?'

'Last Saturday.'

'On what date?'

'I dunno, what the hell does that matter?'

'Today's the fifth, it's Wednesday, so Saturday would have been – the first,' said Jess. 'The first of April. Oh!'

'What?'

'April Fool's Day.'

'You're idiots, the pair of you! You're saying this was an April Fool's joke, that some nutter's had me chasing round Manchester – being *chased* round Manchester – desperate to find Mum and it's all a great big joke?'

'I'm not an idiot! Take that back!' Freddie demanded.

'You are if you think it's a joke.'

Wheeling round, Freddie stormed out.

'I see why you're angry, Ben, but we're only trying to help,' Jess said quietly.

'I'm sorry, I'm just … it's a nightmare, you know?'

'I know,' Jess sympathised as a door downstairs banged. 'I think that's Dad coming home.

'Thought he *was* home?'

'He'll have popped into work. He can't stay away.'

A couple of minutes later Aunt Miriam called them all to dinner, except Robert, who was at a friend's again. Either he'd become immensely popular suddenly (as likely as County winning the FA Cup) or he had moved on very quickly from Bianca.

'Sweetheart, I hope you don't mind, but I've rung Miranda and Sunitra's mums and cancelled tomorrow,' Aunt Miriam told Jess.

'But we've been planning it ages!' Poor Jess looked really upset.

'I know, but with all that's happening …'

'I'm sorry, is it because of me being here?' Ben asked.

'No, it's because your mum isn't, darling. I'm struggling to look after this family at the moment, never mind guests.'

'Okay, Mum, sorry,' Jess said.

'We'll have them over soon. Promise. As soon as we've got Aunt Sue safely home.'

'Thanks Jess,' Ben said, seeing her disappointment. He was making life difficult for all of them.

But so was Uncle Henry, for him. When they sat down to dinner he again asked how the science quiz was going.

'It was iron today. The heaviest atom made in a star,' Ben added hoping that would prompt the Fred Hoyle anecdote. Thankfully it did, so Ben tuned out, worrying. Unless the Einstein Code told him exactly where to find Mum he'd have to accept that lift. But the Einstein Code would – it was going to reunite him with Mum, it promised. So he'd have to persuade Aunt Miriam to drive him to Oxford. He resolved to talk to her after dinner but didn't get the chance, because just as they finished clearing up, Marcus arrived.

Aunt Miriam offered him tea, coffee, or wine.

'A glass of wine would be lovely,' he said, smiling. 'Only a small one though. I'm driving.'

'White or red? Either would be cellar cold.'

'How cold's that?'

'In our house? Very.'

'Lovely. White then, please.'

There was further discussion about the grape variety, which Ben found incredibly frustrating, but eventually they were sitting down, with olives and cashew nuts to snack on, and everyone with a drink of wine or sparkling grape juice. (Ben didn't want it, but there was no point arguing when Aunt Miriam was entertaining.)

Serious discussions finally began.

'We fear Sue's been kidnapped,' said Aunt Miriam. Ben's stomach lurched with alarm. Had Freddie talked?

'Really?' Marcus looked shocked too.

'She's not been found, her body's not been found and even more suspiciously, her car's not been found.' Ben exhaled with relief. 'With all the surveillance cameras in this country it's hard to believe someone could completely disappear. Unless someone's keeping her.'

Marcus nodded. 'I see what you mean, but why?'

'We know something you may not want us to know,' Aunt Miriam began carefully. 'We know Sue was at St Saviour's last Friday evening.'

'How?' asked Ben, startled.

'Oh sorry, I thought I'd told you, Ben. Her old tutor called. She saw Sue there last Friday.'

'*Really*?'

'Yes. Not to talk to, she saw her through the window, hurrying across Front Quad. It was teatime, she said, which in Oxford is about four-thirty. She assumed she was involved in the SPC meeting.'

Had she been in Oxford ever since? But before Ben could ask, Uncle Henry strode into the room.

'You didn't tell me we had visitors,' he complained, glaring at the wine.

'I thought the doorbell might have been a clue,' Aunt Miriam bit back. 'But I suppose you were so engrossed in your work you didn't hear it.'

'Exactly.' Her criticism had as little impact on him as a snowflake. 'So to what do we owe the pleasure of this visit?' he asked, extending a hand towards Marcus, who stood up and shook it.

'I was just explaining that we think Sue's been kidnapped and that we know she was at St Saviour's last Friday,' said Aunt Miriam. 'Help yourself to wine. Jess, will you get a glass for your dad? Please?' she added in response to Jess's mutinous glance.

'Okay.' Jess shot out of the room for an extra glass, desperate not to miss anything. Ben sympathised.

'Do you think Mum could still be there?'

'She's not in St Saviour's, you've checked.'

'Have you? You're moving mountains to find her, aren't you?' Marcus said, looking impressed.

'Trying to. But I've not moved the right one yet.'

'I've not found her overseas yet either. Sorry.'

'It's kind of you to spare the time to look.'

'I want Sue back. We all do,' said Marcus as Jess returned with the glass, which she handed to her father. He poured himself a glass and offered Marcus a top-up.

'No thanks, I'm driving.'

'I'm not,' said Aunt Miriam, proffering hers.

'Who could Pete and the Chief be?' asked Freddie. 'That's what we want to know. Assuming they're SPC, Pete can only be Ballantyne, Swarbreck or Nixon.'

'Hold on. It's a giant leap to assume they're from SPC. They could be from a rival company, trying to induce Sue to share industrial secrets,' Marcus said.

Ben hadn't thought of that.

'Do you think that's likely?' Aunt Miriam asked, leaning towards Marcus.

'It's possible. We deal with some pretty dodgy companies in even dodgier countries.'

'So wouldn't they approach you for a ransom then?' said Aunt Miriam. 'Not us, but you?'

'*Ransom*?' Uncle Henry sat bolt upright.

'It's all right, Henry, we haven't been asked for any money. The question is, has SPC?'

'If so, it hasn't been shared with me.'

'But it would be, wouldn't it? You're number three in the organisation, aren't you, after Sir John Knox and Lord Hanbury?' said Freddie.

Marcus laughed. 'I don't think my colleagues would see it like that.'

'But you really think that's possible, Marcus?' Aunt Miriam asked, leaning forward, looking as frightened as Ben felt.

'Possible, yes. Probable, no. It's never happened before, as far as I'm aware. But I wouldn't necessarily know about it. It would be handled right at the top, by Sir John or Lord Charles.'

'And whoever received the ransom demand presumably?' said Uncle Henry.

'Yes, that's true. So who would kidnappers contact?' mused Marcus.

'Probably Sue's manager. Who's that?' said Uncle Henry. Jess brought him up to speed with what everyone who cared about Mum had known for the last five years.

'And he's called Peter. Could he be mixed up with kidnappers?' Aunt Miriam asked.

'I doubt it very much,' said Marcus. 'But I'll talk to him tomorrow if you like.'

'He's got leave booked,' Ben blurted out, before realising Debs might have told him that in confidence. 'I think he mentioned it the other day.'

'Well I'll give him a call then.'

'He's going to Oxford tomorrow.'

'Is he? Then I'll try and see him tonight.' Marcus stood up. 'I'd better get going if I'm going to get over to him.'

'Why?' asked Jess.

'He lives out in the sticks beyond Bollington. It's a fair drive in the dark.'

Aunt Miriam stood too. 'It's so kind of you to put yourself out so much on our behalf, Marcus. I'll never forget it. I'll cook you a thank you meal when Sue's back.'

Marcus smiled. 'I'll hold you to that one day. But when Sue's back I'll take you out to dinner, all of you, because no one will be more thrilled than me.'

'I think Ben will,' Aunt Miriam said, smiling at him fondly.

'I've never wanted anything more. It would be like a miracle,' he replied.

'There's no such things as miracles,' Uncle Henry said.

'She'll be equally desperate to get to you,' Aunt Miriam told Ben, smiling at him.

'I know. I hate it.'

After Marcus left Ben begged to ring Dr Ashcroft, Mum's old tutor, but Aunt Miriam said that she'd told them everything she could.

'But I would like a word with you, Ben, if I could please?'

'Sure,' he said, wondering if he was in trouble.

They returned to the now deserted lounge. Aunt Miriam poured herself another glass of wine.

'If there is a ransom to pay, we'll pay it.'

'You can't. Uncle Henry won't allow it.'

'He won't have a choice. This house is half mine, our savings are half mine. If I have to sell up and move to a hovel, I'll do it to get Sue back.'

'That's so kind of you,' Ben said, knowing Uncle Henry would no more agree to that than he would to wear a mankini for work.

'It's not kind, it's love. I love her, just as you do. So I'd do anything to get her back. You know. You would too.'

'Of course. I'm sure she's still in Oxford. Would you drive me there on Friday morning? Please?'

'I can't, sorry. I've got some American visitors on Friday that I've got to persuade to part with a wodge of cash.'

'Can't someone else do it?'

'No. Sorry. Maybe tomorrow?'

'No I can't. Not in the morning,' Ben said, thinking of the Einstein Code. He may not need to get to Oxford after all. But what Aunt Miriam think if he put a school quiz before finding Mum?

'Oh neither can I,' she exclaimed, relieving him of his quandary. 'I've just remembered. But it's only work and if I knew for sure she was there I'd tell them to shove their job if they didn't let me go to bring her home. But I don't.'

'No. Neither do I,' Ben agreed sadly.

She yawned. So did Ben.

'Right, bedtime I think.'

It might have been, but Ben's brain refused to let him sleep. He worried about rogue companies, the Chief and Ballantyne, he puzzled over the first text, the second text and the Einstein Code, but the more exhausted he became the more confused he became. Nothing made sense and nothing felt right. Something was wrong. He couldn't put his finger on it, but something felt horribly wrong.

Chapter 18

The Last Clue – At Last

'I owe you a cake, remember?' said Aunt Miriam at breakfast. Ben, Jess, Freddie and she were all sitting at the kitchen table, Uncle Henry was closeted in his study or at work, and Robert slumbering in bed.

'Yes, last day of the quest,' said Ben, finding it hard to act cool when inside he was bubbling with excitement.

'What time was it we had to be there?'

'Eleven. But ten-thirty would be better. It's really important I'm not late.'

Aunt Miriam checked her watch. 'I've got a telecon with work at ten. We'll leave as soon as that's finished. Don't worry,' she added, catching sight of Ben's dismayed expression. 'If they're rattling on too long, I'll interrupt. We won't be late, I promise.'

'Could we just get the bus, so you don't have to worry?' asked Ben, unconvinced.

'With those men running round after you? Sorry, Ben, no. Your mother would never forgive me if I let anything happen to you.'

She'll never know unless I get that clue, Ben thought. But all he could do was give a resigned smile, whilst resolving that, if she wasn't on the doormat by ten-thirty, he would leave without her.

'Can I borrow your bike?' he asked Freddie after breakfast. 'In case your mum's late?'

'She'll kill you if you go without her.'

'I know. But can I?'

'It's too small for you. You'd wreck it.' Typical of Freddie not to share.

'You *know* why I have to be there,' Ben hissed.

'We need Mum. You need me. You won't crack the code without me and Jess.'

'I'll phone you if I need you,' Ben said, but there was no shifting Freddie, no matter how he tried. Nor Jess. She stuck to him like discarded chewing gum, worrying about all the things he'd been worrying about all night. He hoped that her sharp brain would spot what he couldn't, but it had no effect apart from winding him up even further.

At 09:55 he knocked on Aunt Miriam's study door.

'Do you want a coffee to help your telecon along?'

'That's very nice of you, Ben, but no thanks, I'm fine. I'll do my best to wrap it up fast.'

'Thanks. I'd *hate* to miss the last clue.'

'I know.' She smiled and turned back to her desk picking up the handset, Ben's signal to go. Should he tell her?

No adults, no police.

He was so near to the end, he mustn't mess up now.

If she knew, she'd forget the call and get him there.

Should he just push past the still talking Jess and go? Oblivious to her words, Ben waited in an agony of indecision.

'Sorry, I'll have to go now. See you soon,' ended his torment at twenty-past ten. Aunt Miriam emerged from her study. 'Give me two minutes. I'll meet you at the door.'

He hurried to the guest room, grabbed his phone and jacket and looked around; was there anything else he might need? This was the most important test of his life. He mustn't blow it. Would he have to go with Goatee Man to find Mum? As far as Oxford? Aunt Miriam would try to stop him. He must make sure she stayed well away. It was critical that he didn't mess up, but he had a strong suspicion he'd missed something. *What*?

'BEN! WE'RE READY!' Jess yelled from downstairs, prompting him to shoot downstairs as if escaping an inferno.

They set off at twenty-five past, and mercifully traffic was light so that they arrived at the supermarket car park with twenty minutes to spare. To speed things up even further, Ben shepherded them all to the glass lift. He was jangling with nerves, his mouth was dry and he was far too hot in his jacket. He took it off and turned to Aunt Miriam.

'You don't need to come in the lift with us. You can see those men aren't in it,' he said as it slowly descended the last few feet.

'I've got some birthday cards and presents to get,' Aunt Miriam said with a meaningful smile. Oh yes, fourteen next week, he had completely forgotten, it seemed completely irrelevant now. 'So I'll stay down here, but you must stick together. How much do you need?'

'It's free, I checked online,' Freddie said. Noticing Ben's surprise he added, 'It hadn't even occurred to you that it might be shut? When you've worked out where you need to be, I check it's open in case you've got it wrong.'

'Thanks. That's really nice of you,' Ben said, ashamed. Freddie was trying so hard to help him. He must be nicer to him. They would never be alike, but that didn't mean that he shouldn't try harder. He must stop dissing Freddie so much to his friends. He couldn't help being intelligent, no wonder he was proud of it. Ben would be proud too if he was as brainy as Freddie – though not as rude. He'd never be as offensive as him – or he'd have no friends.

The lift arrived.

'How long will you be?'

'I'll text you when we've finished,' Ben promised Aunt Miriam with a thrill. What a text! No, he'd call her. Even better, he'd get Mum to call her. She'd be so happy. Was she waiting in Stockport Story Museum for him?

'Stick together,' she ordered as the doors started to shut. Ben nodded and waved to her, feeling like his stomach contained an entire butterfly farm. Slowly the lift ascended.

'I think we need to be really careful,' murmured Jess as they hurried through the now bustling market. 'This is his last stab at you, Ben. If they're using the clues to try and trap you, they'll have to do it here.'

Yes, Stockport marketplace was the perfect place to pick him up to take him to Mum. She wouldn't be in the museum, he was being daft, she would be somewhere safe nearby.

'They won't want to trap me.'

'They might. Maybe that's what they've been after all along.'

'Then I should go alone.'

'No way! We're coming with you.'

'It's dangerous, Jess.'

'Less dangerous for all three of us,' said Freddie, again surprising Ben. Usually, at the first whiff of trouble, he scarpered.

'So we're all going in?'

'Definitely.'

They entered the reception together. They told the receptionist that they were going to Stockport Story and he directed them straight in.

'I need the loo. I'll see you in there,' said Freddie.

'We'll wait for you,' his sister offered.

'No, don't. You can't be late,' he told Ben, with unexpected consideration.

Jess shrugged. 'Okay, we'll go. See you later.'

Ben and Jess entered the dark museum together. It wasn't as menacing as the Egyptian section at Manchester Museum, because it was spacious and far less thronged – Ben could see a couple of children with their mum, but no men. There were few possible hiding places, so it was easy to rule out the first floor. Ben kept checking over his shoulder, half-expecting Goatee Man to tap him on the shoulder and hand him Clue 8 with his wolfish grin.

'How big is the museum?' Jess asked.

'Quite big. There are a few floors.'

'Should we wait for Freddie downstairs?'

'No, he could be ages, and there are loads of different sections. We need to carry on,' Ben insisted.

They ran upstairs to the business section showing Stockport market's history, the Victorian boom of the cotton and silk mills and, in the entrance passage, the Stopfordian king killer John Bradshaw, the judge who tried and convicted Charles I.

'Freddie will love this,' said Jess, pausing to read the information about him.

'Come on, Jess, we've a clue to find.'

'I know.'

They went through to the display room. It was empty, apart from a mum and two daughters playing shop: one was offering plastic food on her trestle table "market stall", the other was negotiating hard for shiny plastic bread.

'Hi. Is there a letter for me in that food basket?' The girls looked uncertain, so he turned to their mum. 'It's a school quiz. A letter for me is hidden somewhere in this museum. I'm Ben Bradshaw.'

'What fun!' she declared, looking at her daughters. 'Shall we help him?'

'We're looking for a cream envelope,' Jess told them, smiling.

'Okay!' they agreed and enthusiastically rummaged through the basket for him (supervised by their mum) but didn't find the clue. Ben checked a jigsaw puzzle, but there was nothing underneath it, whilst Jess searched through the dressing up clothes the girls had already raided.

'It's not here. Come on, Jess.'

'Where?'

'Upstairs.'

'Freddie should be here.'

'He'll find us.'

'He's been ages. Can we go back and check he's okay? *Please*?' All eyes on him, Ben felt compelled to agree, but he was inwardly cursing his cousin for his weak bladder control as he hurried back down the stairs. He marched into the ancient history section, with Jess close behind. Freddie wasn't in the open display area, so Ben continued towards the alcove on the right, the only place his cousin could be, unless he was still in the gents' – in which case he'd miss the end of Einstein Code, Ben would tell him they were going on without him.

But Freddie was in the alcove, oblivious of their urgency, completely absorbed in a display. As Ben approached he noticed Freddie was holding the cream envelope. But they'd searched this section. He hesitated, confused, as Freddie bent forwards, carefully secreted the envelope behind the display, and then straightened up. Entirely empty handed.

It couldn't be true. It couldn't possibly be how it looked. But, as if sensing his cousin's presence, Freddie turned and saw Ben watching. His eyes opened wide and his mouth gaped, proclaiming his guilt more clearly than if he'd yelled it out loud.

'YOU LIAR!' Jess flew at Freddie and started pummelling him furiously, whilst ugly feelings boiled up in Ben, a mixture of rage, revulsion and bitter disappointment.

An attendant hurried towards them, calling, 'No fighting!'

Jess stepped back. Freddie had tears in his eyes, whether from pain or humiliation Ben neither knew nor cared. He was finished with Freddie.

He stormed out of the exit, out of the museum and down the market brew. He could hear Jess calling after him to stop and wait, but he ignored her, the passers-by and the pigeons. He wasn't aware of anything until Aunt Miriam grabbed hold of him, her hands on his arms, her face full of such concern that he nearly broke down.

'What's up?'

'Freddie,' Ben said. 'It was all a con of Freddie's.' Feeling hot tears burning his eyes, he wiped them away.

'The science quiz?' Ben nodded, too choked to speak. 'Why on earth would he do that?' He shook his head, unable to understand, helpless to explain. How Freddie could have been so callous, so unfeeling, so deeply and terribly cruel, was utterly beyond him.

And Aunt Miriam too, apparently, though she didn't know the half of it.

'Where is he?' she demanded, tight-lipped with anger.

'Dunno,' said Ben. He didn't care. He never wanted to see his cheating cousin again.

'We've got to wait for him and Jess. Oh, look, here she is!' Aunt Miriam looked towards the lift. Jess was emerging from it, alone. Aunt Miriam started moving towards her, accelerating as the distance between them closed. Ben trudged behind, devastated.

'Where's the scoundrel gone?' Aunt Miriam demanded.

'To the bus station. He didn't want to face Ben.'

'I'll bet he didn't,' said Aunt Miriam grimly, reaching into her bag for her phone. She retrieved a number, called it and waited.

'Freddie, I am appalled,' she said when he finally answered. 'To have Ben running around Manchester when it's so dangerous and he's so worried – I am not interested in pitiful excuses, it's Ben you need to apologise to, not me. Come back to the car. You'll have to face him sooner or later. It's not safe! There are dangerous men. Yes, that's probably true, but still. Well then, go straight home and be careful.' She rang off. 'He says the bus is there, waiting. I imagine you'd prefer a Freddie-free journey home, wouldn't you, Ben?'

Ben nodded. He would prefer a Freddie-free forever.

'I don't suppose you fancy a cake?'

'No thanks.' He felt nauseous and numb. He hadn't yet begun to process the enormous ramifications of the morning's events, all he could think of was Mum. He should have been seeing her smile. He should have been reuniting the sisters. He should have been taking her home.

'We've wasted all week on a wicked hoax,' Jess complained. True. What a fool he'd been. What an *idiot*. He'd wasted so much time and let Mum down so badly when she needed him most.

'Ben thinks Aunt Sue's in Oxford,' Aunt Miriam told Jess. 'He wants to go and look, but unfortunately tomorrow's the one day I've *got* to be in work.'

'We could go to Oxford anyway, me and Ben.'

'At twelve and thirteen? No, you can't.' Aunt Miriam unlocked the car and they got in.

'What if Freddie comes with us?'

'No!' Ben protested, from the back seat.

'Definitely no. It's far too dangerous. You heard what Marcus said. If she's been kidnapped, it's by a desperate rival. We don't even know how to get her back yet, you can't put me through that with you three as well.'

'But we must try and find her.'

'Darling, they'll be guarding her. The best thing we can do is let Marcus sort it out for us.'

'What if Dad takes us?'

'You could try him, I suppose.' But Ben knew it would be useless. He'd wouldn't cross the road to help Mum, let alone drive to Oxford and rescue her.

He had been so confident he'd be going to meet her and bring her safely home. Now he didn't know when he'd see her – *if* he'd see her ever again.

Tears trickled down his cheeks and, whilst Jess took her mum through the depths of Freddie's deception, he sat staring out of the window, desperately missing his mum.

'Poor Ben,' Aunt Miriam murmured. She opened his door when they got back. He got out mechanically, went inside, took off his coat and shoes and allowed himself to be led to the kitchen. Aunt Miriam sat him down and told Jess he needed sweet tea for shock.

He needed Mum. Only she could make him feel better, there was no one else in the world that had that power. He needed her so much but someone else had her. Someone cruel and powerful and deadly dangerous.

Those codes were real, weren't they? The texts?

As Aunt Miriam deposited a steaming mug before him, the front door slammed, making him jump.

'Who is it?' she called, but there was no response.

Jess sprang up. 'I'll go and see.' She went into the hall and said in such a stern voice that Ben knew she was addressing Freddie, 'Mum wants to see you.'

'Where is she?'

'In the kitchen.'

Ben got up.

'No, Ben. Wait. You deserve an explanation. Sit down, *please*,' Aunt Miriam said. Out of respect for his aunt, Ben waited, burning with anger. 'Come and sit down,' she ordered her son when he sulkily slouched in. She waited until he was seated, as far away as possible from Ben, arms folded defensively across his chest. 'What were you *thinking* of, pretending to be a kidnapper?'

'I wanted to give Ben some hope.'

Ben stared at him, astounded.

'*Hope*? *Hope* that his mother had been *kidnapped*?'

'It's better than her being dead!'

'She's not dead! Someone's got her!' cried Ben, because her being alive was all he could cling to. If she wasn't, then the life he'd loved had vanished forever. He would never see her again, he could never go home again, he'd have to live here.

With him.

He was passionately defending himself, blathering on about Ben having needed something to do to stop him worrying.

'How the *hell* do you think it stopped me worrying?'

'It occupied your mind elsewhere.'

'You haven't got a *clue* of what I'm going through. You can't have. Or you wouldn't have done it!'

'I was taking you to her.'

'*What*?'

'I was leading you to Oxford. That's where today's clue leads you.'

'I know she's in Oxford!'

'You *think* she is. Ben. We can't be sure,' Aunt Miriam intervened – inaccurately, Ben hoped.

'I taught you science!'

'You wasted my time! Time I should have spent looking for Mum.'

'No! I've *helped* you. I got you into SPC, remember? I gave you nothing for Monday so we could investigate.'

'You expect him to be grateful for that? Aren't you even going to apologise?' Jess said.

'For what?'

'For lying and cheating and swindling. For promising Ben you'd give Aunt Sue back to him, then letting him down with a horrible bump. You had him chasing rainbows, Freddie. It's the worst thing you've ever done.'

'No it's not!'

'You owe Ben an apology,' insisted Aunt Miriam.

Freddie stared at Ben mutinously.

'Sorry,' he said eventually, as if it was being torn from him.

'You're not.'

'No, I'm not. I've *helped* you. I've *distracted* you from moping.'

'You've betrayed me. That's what you've done. I trusted you and you've betrayed me,' Ben said slowly. He would never, ever, trust Freddie again.

Chapter 19

The Threat

During lunch (which Ben sat through, to placate his aunt, but only managed to pick at) he was hit by an even more sickening realisation. Freddie had been suspiciously bad at cracking the texted code. What if he'd been faking that too? What if he'd sent the codes?

Did he have two phones? Possibly. He could easily afford a few cheap handsets out of the huge allowance his grandma gave him.

Was he clever enough to write them? Definitely. Ben could have composed them without much difficulty (although he'd probably have made a careless slip, a frustrating feature of his schoolwork). But Freddie wouldn't. Yes, he was definitely clever enough.

Would he be that cruel? Undoubtedly. The Einstein Code proved that.

If he *had* sent them, then there had been no word from Mum, or about Mum, for a week, except for his lies. Nothing except a resounding silence.

He wanted to confer with Jess, so waited until Aunt Miriam was deep in conversation with Oxford police, then asked her to join him in the spare room. He shut the door behind them before voicing his fears to his cousin.

'I wondered too, but I don't think he did,' she replied. 'He's clever enough and cruel enough, yes, but he's so vain that he'd never have sat letting you crack it, if he could.'

'Yeah, he kept trying to get me to ask him how to solve the Einstein Code, didn't he?'

'Yes, he loves showing off his mighty brain.'

'It's an evil twisted brain.'

'I don't think he's evil, I think he's got zero empathy. He hasn't a clue what you're going through and how much the Einstein Code would upset you. He just thought it would be a fun diversion during the holidays. No, Ben, don't get angry with me,' she added quickly as Ben's face contorted with rage. 'I'm not defending him, I think it was absolutely awful of him. A horrid, cruel thing to do. I'm furious with him. But I think it was crass and stupid, not intentionally heart-breaking. But it clearly was.'

Hearing a tap on the door, Ben nodded his acceptance of Jess's explanation.

'Who is it?' he asked, ready to fight if it was Freddie. But it was Aunt Miriam, asking if she could come in.

'Sure.'

She joined them.

'At last they're taking me seriously,' she said regarding the police. 'Now that she's been missing for a week, they finally get that she hasn't just nipped off for a few nights' fun. Everyone's on the lookout now for her and her car.'

'Great,' Ben replied. His text alert sounded. Warily he checked the number, but it was just Jonno, needing his tablet back. He told Aunt Miriam.

'I'll run you home as soon as I've dropped an email to the police.' Aunt Miriam left whilst Ben tapped in a text to Jonno. Whilst it was sending he retrieved the previous coded text.

'This means I'll have to take that lift. If they turn up.'

'You can't, Ben. We'll take you.'

'Where? I don't know where I'm supposed to be.'

But Jess wasn't listening. 'Mum can't. We'll have to ask Dad. Or Robert?'

'No way would he give me a lift to the end of the road, never mind Oxford. But it's like meeting up anywhere, Jess. You have to say where, don't you?'

'Oxford.'

'No. It's like saying meet in Manchester. You could go to Piccadilly when you should be in Deansgate. Be on the wrong side of town,' he added, to ensure she understood.

'They might send you another text.'

'Let's hope so. Because if not I have to take that lift.'

'You can't, Ben. It'll be them.'

Before Ben could respond Aunt Miriam returned.

On the way home Ben kept checking his phone for incoming messages, but nothing arrived. He texted Jonno to tell him they were on their way. The reply came straight back.

Grt c u at yrs

The house looked so empty.

'I need to get straight back, so I'll just sit in the car if that's all right,' Aunt Miriam said.

'I'll go in with Ben,' Jess said.

'If there's anything strange, come straight out, won't you?'

'Sure.'

Everything was strange. The unoccupied house was strange. The silence was strange. The texts were strange. He couldn't share Jess's confidence that Freddie hadn't sent them. He walked slowly up the path and unlocked the door wondering if Mum would ever see their house again.

Or if he would ever see her again. Last Thursday, a week ago, might have been their last night ever together. Yet he'd wasted it online. They could have played a game, gone for a run, or even, given the recent good weather, enjoyed their first tennis match of the year. Would his increased power now beat Mum's skill? Perhaps he'd never know. How we wished he'd appreciated her more – and asked more questions, like Jess. Maybe she'd have told him about the meeting. Maybe he could have stopped her going. She'd been happy during dinner, as excited as him about their forthcoming holiday together – the one they should be enjoying now. He stepped over the mail and deactivated the alarm, more aware of the silence within than ever before.

'Oh, here's Jonno,' Jess said.

He greeted his friend whilst Jess went to check round inside. 'Thanks a lot,' he added, returning Jonno's precious Christmas present. 'Sorry if it's given you grief.'

'No worries. You okay?'

Terrible. Awful. Heartbroken. What could he say?

'Not bad. You?'

'Okay. You've not found her?'

'Not yet.'

'But *why*?'

'Mainly Freddie.'

'What?'

'You'll never believe what he's gone and done now.'

'Tell me later. I've got to get back with this or Mum'll kill me.'

'Sure. Thanks again.'

'Your birthday party's off I guess?'

'Yeah. Until Mum's back everything's off.'

'Yeah.' Jonno sighed. 'Sorry. Better get home.'

'Sure. See ya.' As Ben watched his friend down the path his text alert sounded. It was from the same number as the previous code and was a very long sequence of code.

He went into the lounge and told Jess, whilst dialling Aunt Miriam's number.

'Who are you phoning?'

'Your brother. If it's from him I'll *kill* him.'

'So will I. It better hadn't be.'

Uncle Henry answered.

'Sorry, is Freddie there? It's Ben.'

'You're with him every day, why do you need to call him?' he replied testily.

'It's just a question I've got to ask him. Is he there?'

'I don't know where he is. I'll check.' He put the handset down, doubtless in his study and then yelled for his son. After more yelling, Ben heard him stomping back to the phone. 'He's picking up upstairs, so I'll hang up when he has. Are you there yet?'

'Yes, Dad,' Freddie said.

Ben waited for Uncle Henry to disconnect before speaking.

'Have you just texted me?'

'No. Why?'

'You swear on your life?'

'I don't even know your number. You've never given it to me.'

'You'd better not be lying. Freddie, Mum's life depends on it,' Ben said, his eyes filling with angry tears. He wiped them away. 'Got that? If you're messing with me, you could kill Mum.'

'Kill her? I wouldn't kill her.'

'Someone might if we don't find her soon. You swear you didn't write those texts. Or the new one?'

'I swear I didn't. On my dad's life. New one?'

'Ben, we've got to go. Mum says,' Jess said, entering the lounge from the hall. Such had been the intensity of his conversation, he hadn't even noticed her leave.

'Have you got another code?' Freddie asked.

'Yeah.'

'It's nearly time for you to get that lift, isn't it?'

Ben checked. 'It's ten past three. Hell!' he added. The lift deadline loomed and he knew Jess was right. It would be suicidally stupid to take it. This code gave him a glimmer of hope, but he had no chance of cracking it in such a short time alone.

'Is there anywhere cheap that opens early for dinner near the car park?'

'There's the Thai place, yeah.'

'Thai's okay. What time does it open?'

'Four.' Why it was Ben's favourite takeaway.

'Right. I'll meet you there at half four, say.'

'I can't afford to buy us dinner.'

'I'll buy it for you. Because I upset you, apparently.'

'You did!'

'*Ben, come on*!' Jess hissed.

'Right. I'll book it,' Ben said. He rang off and told Jess.

'*Freddie*? *Paying*?'

'I know. He must feel bad.'

'Or Mum told him to. She's mad at him too.'

As if she'd heard Aunt Miriam burst into the lounge.

'Come *on*, you two,' she said. 'I've got work to do.'

'Sorry, Mum. But we might not come with you. Freddie's buying us dinner here at half four.'

'Well, I can't drive you back and forth all afternoon. But you can't stay here.'

'Why not?' Ben asked, deeply offended. It was his home, after all. It was daytime. He was practically fourteen.

'Because they have a key. Until your mum's back I don't want to change the locks. It's her house, and her decision, not mine. But I cannot leave you both at risk of being attacked by those thugs.'

Ben cursed himself inwardly. Why hadn't he thought of changing the locks?

'What about the library?' Jess suggested. 'We could wait in there, couldn't we? Those men wouldn't come looking for us in a library, Mum.'

'No. I doubt they know what a library is. All right then. As long as you promise to stay there until Freddie arrives? I'll tell him to meet you there. He can get on his bike. Both literally and metaphorically.'

'Okay,' said Ben, understanding nothing except that she was still angry with her son.

'Right, come on then. Out of here and on our way.' Ben followed her out, wishing he'd had the chance to transcribe the code. He set the alarm and locked up, watched by Aunt Miriam, who said, 'My taxi duties are over for the day, I hope. I've got to prepare for tomorrow.'

And so had he. Ben's mouth felt dry and his stomach rumbled, possibly through tension, but probably because he'd hardly eaten at lunch.

Worried about Goatee Man, she trailed them to the library, which was *mightily* embarrassing, but thankfully drove off as they went up the path – and fortunately, it transpired, because the library was shut.

'Stuff it. We need paper and pens!'

'Coffee shop?'

'I'm skint, sorry. The park?'

'There's no paper in the park.'

'It's probably the last method. One two, one two, remember? I can do that in my head. I'll bet you can too. Don't worry. We'll get it,' Jess said.

He breathed deeply, trying to calm down. Jess was right, and super smart. Panicking gets you nowhere, as Mum had so often told him. They hurried up Thornfield Road and entered through the gates that had been bolted last Friday night, but which were now wide open. The park was busy due to the Easter holiday sunshine. They found a deserted spot of grass under a tree and sat there. Ben opened the text and scrolled down the screen.

TVUSMN IVPO WLF JLKI VR XIG EVJFJI PH VMHJV HPYQ RFY FSMNHKF NDRF VRQPTUSX HUMECB XFP DQ.

BNRRF. PR TPNLGF. PR JSKHREU. RV OQ IENKOC SGXRJQQ

'Flipping heck, it's long!' Jess exclaimed.

'Easier to solve. Right, one back, two back. That makes it s-t-t-q… No, that can't be right. What do you make it?'

'S-t-t-q-l-l,' Jess slowly confirmed. 'Sorry Ben, the code's changed. I was afraid it would.'

On his home territory Ben could swear freely – so he did.

'Come on Ben, think!'

Recognising the wisdom of her words he sat down and shut up. They tried lots of different methods.

'It's not back to front like the first one,' Ben realised.

'It's not just one back, something simple like that.'

'It's not one forward either.'

After they'd tried many other combinations – some very convoluted indeed, but not one of which was correct –

279

Jess took his phone, scrolled up and down the message and suggested a different approach.

'Look at the two PRs near the end.'

'Yeah, there's PH further up. Bet P's a vowel.'

'Yes. But it can't be e, it's not er or em. It's probably a or i.'

'I can't find mum,' Ben said, meaning the word, not the woman he was missing so desperately. 'No three-letter words start and end the same, unless it's like the last message where one letter can stand for different letters.'

Jess gave Ben a worried look.

'If it's really hard like that last one we might be sunk.'

'I might have to take that lift.'

'You can't! Come on, let's try again,' she urged. They examined the text again, sharing Ben's phone.

'Q is doubled at the end of a word, so probably l or s.'

'Good. So P's a or i, and Q is l or s. Any pattern there?'

He scrolled through the entire message again.

'I reckon R and H are vowels,' he said.

'There aren't many vowels that start and end two-letter words are there? Are there any?'

'O. Of, on, do go.'

'Oh yes! Well done, Ben. So R is o. That's three back. We're getting somewhere.'

'But not if P is a vowel too. There's no two-letter word with two vowels, is there?' Ben asked.

'Apart from ai, no and that's a three-toed sloth of South America, so it won't be that.'

'How do you know that?' Ben asked. Even for a Winterburn, this was impressive.

'Scrabble. Oh and aa and ae and oo …'

'Jess, we need to crack this code!'

'It's hard to tell whether R or P is a vowel.'

'We'd better get to the restaurant,' Ben said, checking his watch yet again. They stood up and brushed the grass off their jeans. 'The other gate's better,' he added as Jess started back towards the Thornfield Road gate. He led her past the children's play area – not so long ago he'd been playing there, happy and carefree; now he was fighting against time to save the woman who used to watch over him while he played. Ben gulped. Was he up to it?

They went past the tennis and basketball courts to the Balmoral Road exit. Freddie was locking his bike to the park railings further along.

'What does it say?' he asked, when they greeted him.

'We don't know yet. Here,' Ben said, handing over his phone. 'You swear again you didn't sent it?'

'Of course I didn't. I've told you I didn't.'

'You told me you didn't write the Einstein Code!'

'No I didn't! I never said that!'

Before Ben hit his cousin – and the urge was stronger than ever before – Jess intervened.

'Boys, stop fighting! We need to work together, not against each other.'

'Solve that code then,' Ben challenged him. Freddie again regarded the screen.

'No wonder you couldn't solve the code, looking at it like this. You should have written it out.'

'We didn't have the chance to get paper and pens.'

'Good job I did,' he said, pulling a sheaf of paper from his bag. 'Right, where's this restaurant?'

'Heaton Moor Road,' Ben replied, trying to resist the urge to tell his patronising cousin to get lost. They walked towards the crossroads with Freddie staring at the code, muttering. 'We cross here. It's there.' He pointed across the road. Freddie looked up and his eyes widened in alarm.

'Looks expensive. What about that Italian?'

'Twice the price, and shut. We could try the posh one over there if you like. It's open now but way more expensive.'

'No. Here's fine,' Freddie said, as Ben had expected. He led them over the crossing, pushed open the restaurant door and led them in. He was pleased to see they were the only customers.

'It's strange without adults. Do we have to show our money or anything?' Jess whispered.

'No. They trust us to pay,' Ben bluffed, hoping he was right. A waitress approached, so he asked if she had a table for three. She nodded and led them to a table by the window without asking for wallets or ID. Ben and Jess sat on one side of the table and Freddie sat opposite Jess.

'Have you really got the money?' Jess whispered when the waitress left to get menus.

'Yes. Now shut up whilst I write it out,' her brother charmingly snapped. It was a wonder Jess put up with him.

'Put it in the middle, so Ben and I can see,' Jess told him, but he ignored her.

The waitress returned with menus and asked about drinks. Ben went for tap water, because even though he loathed him presently, it wasn't right to punish Freddie financially. He quickly scanned the menu, checking how much his various favourites cost, and decided on a relatively cheap curry.

'Let us look, Freddie,' he said when Freddie bent over the transcribed code.

'It's my paper.'

'It's my phone. And to me.'

282

'Shut up! I'm nearly there, I think. Hang on. Let me write it out. That's it! Got it! Look,' he declared, pushing a paper across the table.

Ben turned it round so he and Jess could see.

WLF 341

XIG 412

RFY 412 - can't be

PR TPNLGF. PR – 6 letters, hence 23 412341 23 – YES!

'What the hell does this mean?'

'Three-letter words are probably the. That's where I started. The first the is letters eleven, twelve and thirteen of the code. W is three after t, L is four after h and f is one after e, hence pretty easy,' Freddie said, just as the waitress returned with their drinks.

'Was he speaking English?' Ben asked Jess. She rolled her eyes.

'Ready to order?' the waitress asked.

'Yes, please. Have you solved it or not?' Ben asked Freddie.

'Yes, definitely. PR is no.'

'Oh I get it!' Jess declared.

Ben looked at her, hope surging through him.

'What would you like?' the waitress asked.

'Oh, er … Malaysian chicken satay with jasmine rice, please,' Ben responded

'Do you have to have rice?' Freddie asked, from behind a menu.

'Yes, I'm starving. If not I'd have aromatic crispy duck and that'd be a lot more.'

'A quarter wouldn't.'

'I need more than that.'

'Does it have to be jasmine rice?'

'If you want me to have coconut, I love that too.'

'That's even dearer!'

'So I'll have jasmine.' The cheapest variety on offer.

'And for you?' the waitress asked Jess. She chose Thai green chicken with jasmine rice and again Freddie quibbled.

'Or you could have a soup, followed by chicken buns – they're yummy,' Ben told her.

'That's even more!' Freddie protested, turning the menu back and forth to check all the prices.

'I'll stick to the curry with rice then,' she said, grinning at Ben.

Freddie selected a Massaman curry, telling them he'd share their rice and the waitress departed.

'It's not one two three four forward, it's one two three four back, isn't it?' Jess said.

'It's plus one to codify it.'

'Yes but minus one to decode it.'

'Can you two stop squabbling and tell me what the hell it says?'

'Shall I do it?' Jess asked.

'Yeah, let Jess do it,' Ben said. 'I can read her writing. Don't worry, you get all the kudos for cracking it.'

'I know what it says anyway,' Freddie huffed, pushing across the pen and a blank sheet of paper.

'I need the code.'

'Use Ben's phone.'

'It's low on charge. Oh stuff!' Ben added, as he attempted to switch his phone on and got no response. 'It's dead already. Useless!'

'Give me the code, Freddie.'

'Give her the code or I'll rip your guts out and stamp on them.'

Giving Ben a death stare, Freddie pushed across the transcribed code. It was even worse than his usual handwriting.

'I can't read that,' Ben said.

'I can. I think. It starts at one?' Jess asked her brother, who nodded. She got busy writing. 'It's in Oxford!' she declared a short time later. Ben looked across and read what she'd written. Above the letters were numbers, 1,2,3,4,1,2... Below were letters in Jess's neat writing.

'Stroll from the High to ...' he read out. 'How do you know it's Oxford?'

'The High's what people call the High Street there,' Freddie replied.

'Yes, Bridge of Sighs,' Jess muttered.

'Definitely Oxford,' Freddie said. 'That's the bridge across New College Lane. How are you going to get there?'

'Well if we know where to go, I don't need to take that lift. We'll tell your dad all this science has made me want to go to Oxford. He'll take us. He'll be off, it's Good Friday.'

'Not necessarily. Mum isn't.'

'Could you phone him to ask? He loves Oxford. You two can keep him busy whilst I go – what's up Jess?'

'It's bad, Ben.' She looked so frightened that it scared him. She pushed her decryption across.

Stroll from the High to the Bridge of Sighs down New College Lane tomorrow Friday ten am.

Alone. No police. No friends.

Or no family reunion.

'Well that's okay isn't it? Your dad takes us, I go to this lane and meet them there alone.'

'It's not one lane, it's more like three or four,' Freddie said. 'There are lots of corners to get round the colleges. You could be at one end and they could be at the other and you'd never see each other.'

'It's like you being at the park and me being at your house,' Jess explained.

'Like separate roads then?'

'Exactly. And you can't see round them because of the high college walls.'

'So I could miss them?'

'Easily.'

Two waiters arrived with the food. Ben watched them lay it out, thinking. And suddenly he realised what the kidnappers were threatening.

If he missed the meeting, they'd kill her. It was a threat now. Not only a fear, his greatest fear, but a direct threat.

'What's up Ben? You've gone pale.' Jess said.

'I've got to take that lift.'

'No, Ben don't!' Jess protested.

'If not, they'll kill Aunt Sue. That's what they're saying, Jess. He has to.' Freddie said.

'Please don't, Ben.'

'I've got no choice, Jess. To get Mum back, I've got to trust them.' But how could he trust murderers? He checked his phone, feeling sick. Seventy minutes to go.

Chapter 20

The Last Goodbye

The food Ben usually relished now seemed as unappetising as gravel. He watched his cousins eat, rebutting Jess's protests and pleas and when Freddie complained he was paying an arm and a leg for this, he even managed to force a couple of forkfuls down, but it made him too nauseous, so he stopped.

All he could think about was the danger Mum was in.

When the waitress returned she asked if he'd like the food he hadn't touched packing up for later.

'No thanks. Could we just have the bill?'

'Are you paying?' Freddie asked hopefully.

'Sorry, no. I'm skint.'

'It's your apology to Ben, remember, Freddie.'

'Not an apology. Just an olive branch. I've got nothing to apologise for.'

'You deceived Ben, you raised his hopes and it was all one big lie!'

'I didn't lie!'

'Yes you did! Every time you pretended you thought it was a school science quiz you were lying. Every time you pretended not to know where it would be hidden you were lying. And every time you pretended not to know what it said you were lying. It was one big lie!'

'I was acting, not lying! *He* was lying.'

'He was not!'

Ben had sat watching them squabble over trivialities for long enough.

'It doesn't matter one little bit. Don't you get it? If that lift goes wrong, they're going to murder Mum.'

'Ben, we've *got* to tell the police.'

'No police,' Freddie pointed out.

'That's what you said! And you solved this really quickly. Did *you* write it?' Jess said.

'Of course I didn't!'

'Freddie, if you did, tell me now,' Ben said. 'I won't get angry. I don't want to take that lift, believe me.'

'I didn't write it,' Freddie assured him solemnly. Truthfully? Or not?

The waitress returned with the bill. Freddie accepted it and looked pleasantly surprised. He handed her three notes.

'I want change, please.'

'Yes, of course.'

Ben stood up. Jess looked alarmed.

'Don't go! We'll get Mum to take you. Or Dad. We'll get someone. Freddie and I will go down New College Lane too. We know the SPC men and Goatee Man. We won't miss them between the three of us.'

'I'm not going *near* New College Lane!' Freddie protested.

'Neither of you can go. Look what it says! Alone. No police. No friends. So don't tell the police – or anyone. *Else Mum will die*,' he added slowly, packing as much emphasis as he could into each dreadful word. 'You can't risk it, Jess.'

'But they might kill you too!' she said, eyes brimming with tears.

'Don't be stupid!' her bother rebuked her. 'Why take him to Oxford to do that? There's plenty of hit men in Moss Side.'

'He's right. They won't kill me,' Ben told Jess. But his little cousin looked so distraught that he added, 'Don't be sad. I'm bringing Mum back.'

'Ben, I'm so scared I'll lose you too.' Tears trickling down her cheeks, she stood and stretched her arms out, so he hugged her. It made it worse. She started sobbing.

'I'll be fine. Promise,' he said, gently rubbing her back. The waiters were staring at them. 'Don't cry, be happy. I'm going to get Mum back!'

'Yes,' she snuffled.

'By this time tomorrow we'll be home. I'll call you the minute we are.'

'Call us the minute you get her. Then we can tell the police who the kidnappers are and they can arrest them whilst you come back home. Here,' Freddie said, pushing a wad of notes across the table. 'It's for your train fare back.'

'I can't take that.' Ben pushed it back.

'Take it!' Freddie hissed, so vehemently that Jess turned to watch.

'I don't need it!'

'How the hell are you going to get anywhere without money?'

Ben didn't want to fight, not now. He took a deep breath and thanked him calmly. 'We're fine, thanks. Mum has money and cards. But it's very kind of you,' he added.

The waitress returned with Freddie's change. He handed back a fiver as if it were a fortune.

'Your tip,' he said loftily. She smiled and thanked him.

'If she'd known him, she might have fainted,' Ben quipped, trying to make Jess smile. Unhappiness wasn't the last memory he wanted of her, if it was the last time he'd see her. He feared it might be.

For he knew he was running a terrible risk. Ballantyne and Goatee Man hated him and he was walking straight into their trap, if Jess was right. But it was the only chance he had of bringing Mum safely home. So there was no choice at all. He had to go. Unless …

'Right, Freddie,' he said, looking him square in the eye. 'For the very last time. You swear on your mum's, no, your dad's life, you didn't send that text?'

'Of course I didn't, dimwit. Didn't you notice? It's from the same number as last time. It's from them, not me.'

'Oh no, it is!' Jess realised. 'You mustn't go Ben, it's far too dangerous.'

'I've no choice. I've got to go for Mum. And if you tell the police, we'll both die. You've got to let me go alone.'

'But that's playing right into their hands!'

'Of course it is. They wrote it, remember?' Freddie said.

'Let me go alone, like they said. See you soon.' With a quick smile at Jess, he turned and headed for the door, walking as fast as possible.

'Come *on*!' Jess urged fiercely, behind him.

He darted out onto the pavement, needing to cross the road. On the near side a bus was approaching – close, but just beatable. The other lane was temporarily traffic-free. Ben hurtled across, knowing Jess and Freddie would have no chance of following.

'Ben! Wait!' Jess yelled from the far side of the road, as traffic streamed past in the bus's wake, but he ignored her. It was a short race to the library car park, which he easily won. As he got there the hope that Freddie had sent the menacing text vanished, because the white Mercedes was waiting for him, engine purring, ready to leave. As he approached the dark passenger window opened, revealing Goatee Man wearing shades.

'I knew you'd come.'

'Take me to Mum.'

'Gerrin then,' he said with a jerk of his shaven head.

Ben opened the rear door revealing a cool dark interior, a contrast to the bright sunshine outside. As he climbed in he tried to see the other man, Goatee Man's mate, but the high-backed seat obscured him entirely (so he wasn't tall). He was wearing a distinctive aftershave smelling of Christmas spice; cloves, cinnamon and orange, Ben recognised in the pungent scent.

The car pulled out of the car park and was accelerating up Balmoral Road before they passed his cousins. You could see out of the car surprisingly well, given the impenetrable darkness from outside. Jess stood aghast, gaping at the car. But Freddie was talking on his mobile.

'That's my cousin. He'll be telling the police. Your car will be traced.'

But there was no response from the front, increasing Ben's agitation even further. Had he made a really stupid mistake? Jess had thought so. And she was smarter than him and more intuitive about people. She was probably right, then.

Ben closed his eyes, sick with dread.

The car stopped.

He opened them. Mauldeth Road lights, at the junction with Didsbury Road. But the driver was in the right hand lane.

'It's *left* for the M60. The blue pyramid, you know?' The blue pyramid had seemed ridiculous at first, Mum said, but had become a useful landmark for the Stockport exit on the motorway.

They ignored him again.

'Oxford's left,' Ben repeated. But as the lights changed the car turned right. What the hell were they doing? Ben's agitation increased even further. He was in the hands of maniacs.

But before he could develop an escape plan the car veered left into the small car park opposite the shops.

'Out!' ordered Goatee Man.

Confused, Ben obeyed. There was another Mercedes facing them, a black version of the same model, also with tinted windows. Goatee Man shoved him towards it. Ben stumbled but managed to remain upright.

Oh, they were switching cars, to stop the police finding them, Ben realised. Goatee Man pulled open the rear door for him. As Ben bent to climb in he felt a sharp jab in the back of his thigh, like a bee sting. He climbed onto the back seat whilst feeling to see if the sting had remained in him, but it hadn't. Rubbing the back of his leg he sat down. As he reached to strap himself in, a wave of tiredness rolled over him. He lolled back, absolutely exhausted and sank into sleep.

'Is this strictly necessary?' someone was saying, from very far away.

'The Chief said so, so yes. Regrettable as I personally find it,' someone replied.

His head was pounding, he felt groggy and nauseous, and there was an uncomfortably tight band around his chest.

'And they're the perfect victims,' an American said.

'That's what the Chief said.'

'And this, gentlemen, is 993,' a northerner announced.

Ben just managed to stop his head jerking up in recognition. He cautiously opened his eyes a little. The floor was dark-stained wood; on his right there was a huge stone fireplace; on his left there was a cluster of shoes and trouser-clad legs, far too many to take on. A thick rope bound him to the chair on which they'd placed him. He clamped his eyes shut and listened.

'It looks like water,' commented an Asian man.

'And smells like water,' the northerner said. 'But you wouldn't want to drink it, gents, I assure you of that. Even spilling it on your hands could kill you, dependent on the dosage.'

'So it gets through skin, does it? That sure is interesting,' the American added thoughtfully. *Why?*

'How long does it take?' asked the Asian.

'That depends on the dosage. Days, hours or seconds, why is why it's so perfect for our plans,' said a seemingly pleasant voice with a little laugh, causing Ben to jolt so suddenly that he feared the men would notice. He forced himself to relax, slowing his breathing down, but inside he was raging

Marcus! How *could* he? What a lying piece of scum!

Fully awake now, Ben was determined to remember every single detail of their conversation to relay to the police as soon as possible. He'd listen, he'd escape and he'd nail them.

'Careful, one drop of that and you're dead,' Marcus said.

'It's so concentrated?' an Arabian man asked.

'Pure product. Not diluted at all. That's right, isn't it, Pete?'

'Certainly is. I made it myself,' northern Pete answered – surely Nixon? Ben was less sure of his voice. He'd try and sneak another peek soon, he resolved, straining at the ropes, and feeling a surprising amount of give.

'So they should take just seconds to die?'

'Yes. Seconds.'

'Good. A humane way to reshape the world,' the Asian said.

'As humane as possible, yes,' Marcus agreed. But they shouldn't believe a word he said, Ben thought, he had obviously suckered them in with his grandiose claims, just like he'd suckered Ben and the Winterburns.

'It's time to demonstrate how well it works on our guinea pigs,' Pete said.

Sick, Ben thought, as his forefinger crept upwards towards the knot around his wrists. He had loved his guinea pig, Pickle, and he found the prospect of murdering such docile pets disgusting. Apparently one was young but big and they were debating whether he'd die first, or the lighter adult.

The knot was loose. It was starting to give.

'Much lighter after her week without food,' Nixon said.

They'd *starved* her then would *murder* her? *Creeps*!

'He's the size of many adults. Assuming he's a child would give us a false result. If he dies too fast, the female will be a true guide. She's definitely a fully-fledged adult.'

'A nosey interfering menace,' Nixon said bitterly – and weirdly, as if he hated the guinea pig.

'Which is why you've got her son?' the Asian asked.

'Exactly,' Pete said. 'We want her to watch.'

'But she's still asleep. They both are.'

Pickle often slept in the daytime.

'We'll wake them up.' Footsteps approached him. The guinea pigs must be nearby. Ben kept his eyes tight shut, trying to breathe slowly and naturally, giving nothing away.

A slap rang out.

'Susan Busybody Baxter. Wake up!'

Stunned, Ben opened his eyes. He couldn't see her. He threw off the ropes, sprang up and span round.

'*Mum*!' She was bound to a chair behind his, her face reddened by Nixon's slap – for which Ben would never forgive him – her arms bruised, her head slumped. He ran towards her. '*Mum*!'

But before he could reach her, both Nixon and Marcus lunged at him. Marcus, fitter, younger and stronger, got to him first, trapping him in a tight bear hug.

'Quick, get the syringes,' he urged. 'He's strong and he's fighting.'

But he wasn't as strong as Marcus. Ben struggled with all his might, but Marcus was built like a bull.

'Ouch!' Marcus exclaimed as a heel connected with his shin, but he held on. Ben kicked again, and strained with all his might, but his arms remained pinned to his sides by a hug as strong as steel.

'*Let me go*!'

Nixon was approaching, holding two syringes at arm's length. Each was loaded with a clear liquid.

Ben froze.

'That's not 993, is it?'

'You bet it's 993,' Nixon responded, leering. 'For you and your meddlesome mother.'

'*No*! Not Mum! She doesn't know a thing. She's been asleep.'

'She knows far too much.'

'Stop gloating and get on with it,' Marcus urged. 'He's strong, Pete, I'm telling you.'

'No! *Please*. Not Mum!'

'Stop fighting. It's okay, Ben. You won't feel a thing. Cool it. It'll be better for both of you,' Marcus murmured.

'Why would I believe you?' Ben demanded through gritted teeth, struggling with all his might.

'Trust me.'

'Never!'

Suddenly Marcus let go. Ben shot forwards into Nixon, who plunged a syringe into his left arm. The lethal liquid started creeping upwards, inexorable and cold as death.

Ben gulped. There was no antidote. He would die – but there still might be time to save Mum.

So whilst Nixon concentrated on depressing the plunger, pumping yet more poison into Ben's unresisting body, he grabbed the other syringe, which Nixon held in his weaker left hand.

The coward released it immediately, pulling his hand back as if from searing heat, looking horrified. Determined not to be a murderer too, Ben carefully directed the syringe towards the dark floorboards before discharging the deadly contents. Nevertheless Nixon jumped back.

'You little *swine*!' he cursed.

'Why isn't he dead yet?' the American asked.

'He's strong. Just a few seconds more,' Marcus said.

No time at all then.

Ben threw himself down in front of the mother he'd missed so much, the mother he'd longed to be reunited with, knowing he had just seconds to wake her.

'Mum! It's me, Ben.' He gently cupped her bruised face. 'Mum! *Wake up*!'

Her eyelids flickered.

'STOP! POLICE! NOBODY MOVE!'

Ben ignored the panic around him, intent on his beloved mother, determined to wake her before it was too late.

'*Mum*! It's *Ben*! Wake *up*!'

296

Her eyes opened. Her face broke into the most beautiful smile he had ever seen.

'I love you, Mum. I'm so sorry, they've …'

'BEN!' she screamed, as he slumped into darkness.

Chapter 21

Friday afternoon

She arrived at the hospital with her husband and younger children in her wake. She hurried to her sister's ward.

'Sue Baxter?' she enquired of a nurse at the reception area.

'She's in the first room on the right.'

She bustled in, ahead of her family for once.

'Sue, darling, it's so wonderful to have you back,' she cried, embracing her beloved sister, carefully avoiding the tubes trailing from the backs of her hands to the bags suspended above the bed. 'You look terrible. Beautiful as always, but in shocking condition. Those bruises! You're so thin!'

'They're evil. I will never forgive them. Not for me so much as for Ben.'

'Me neither.' Jess embraced her. 'Hello, Aunt Sue. I'm so glad to have you back.'

'It's thanks to you and Freddie, and Ben of course, that I am,' she said, smiling at them both. Freddie raised a hand in greeting, standing well back. 'You rang the police, didn't you?'

'Yes. Ben didn't want us to. He thought if we did they'd kill you both,' Jess replied.

'They very nearly did. Hello, Henry. Thanks for driving down.'

'Miriam couldn't. She was incapable.'

'I'm afraid I was in a terrible state when Jess and Freddie told us what was happening. I'm only sorry the police didn't find you sooner.'

'So am I. Poor Ben,' his mum said.

'Yes, how –' began Jess, but she was shouted down by her father.

'Miriam's been very upset and it's all your fault. Why on earth did you stick your nose in?'

'*Henry*! It's their fault, not Sue's. And if Sue and Ben hadn't got involved, they wouldn't be safely behind bars!'

'Marcus isn't, the swine.'

'They'll catch him soon.'

'It's typical of you, self-indulgently causing disasters that Miriam and I have to mop up.'

'*Henry*!'

'It's okay, Miriam. You're right, Henry. If I hadn't stuck my nose in, all this wouldn't have happened.' She broke off, coughing. 'Excuse me.' She took a sip of water and continued. 'But I didn't have anything to give the police until I heard what they were saying at that meeting. Then they kidnapped me, so I couldn't,' she added angrily.

'How did you find out about it?' Jess asked.

'My 993 files had disappeared and since Nixon had been spotted skulking round my office, I shot straight up to the gods to confront him. He wasn't there, but had the weirdest jottings on his rough pad, which gave me a clue where they were.'

'How?' Jess asked as her aunt broke off, coughing.

'Give her time to recover,' her mum said. 'And rehydrate. That's right, Sue. Plenty of small sips. You can tell us more when you're better. So you drove to Oxford?'

'Not before I made sure. Becky confirmed where they were. Don't tell anyone, especially Marcus.'

'We won't be talking to him again. But SPC won't have him back, will they? He's a criminal. Such an evil man. When I think how he pretended to help!'

'Did he?'

'He did. Many times.'

'He was trying to stop us finding you,' Freddie said. 'I told them it was about 993, but they wouldn't listen.'

'Yes. I thought Ben would spot the xxf straight away, that he'd go to Debs, that she'd know Nixon must be involved –' She broke off in another fit of coughing. Her sister refilled her beaker from a jug alongside her bed and passed it to her. She took a sip.

'Aren't you thirsty, Aunt Sue?' Jess asked.

'They haven't given me a thing since they caught me, so I have to take it slowly.' She took another sip – whilst her sister called the 993 gang the worst swear words Jess had ever heard her mother utter.

'Were you hiding in a priest hole?' Jess asked.

'I was, listening to a meeting that should never ever have happened.'

'But they caught you?'

'Marcus caught me. He's very fast, sadly. But if I hadn't been in work heels, I'd have stood a fighting chance.'

'Bad luck, Aunt Sue,' Jess sympathised.

'That's how he escaped this morning, I'll bet. But I didn't see. I only had eyes for Ben.'

'Poor Ben. Wasn't he brave?' his aunt said.

'Amazing.'

'He's as foolish as his mother, it seems to me. Criminals are best left to the police!'

'They wouldn't be in the hands of the police were it not for Sue, Henry.'

'And Ben. And Jess and Freddie, who helped him so much. I'm so annoyed about Marcus though. I left Debs a clue about him on my desk. Didn't you go in there?'

'No, Ballantyne kept us out,' Freddie said.

'What clue?' Jess asked.

'A message to contact SPC Brazil. To us it means Golden Boy.'

'Why?'

'A golden statue they have in their reception. We nearly cracked up the first time we saw it. It's exactly like a little naked Marcus. He's been Golden Boy ever since. Until now.'

'Now he's Traitor.'

'Yes, shame Debs didn't see it, or she'd have had them behind bars days ago.'

'I told her it was 993,' Freddie said, 'but she didn't believe me.'

'You thought Nixon was Pete, didn't you, Jess, you clever girl?' her mum said.

'Well done, Jess. And Freddie too,' their aunt congratulated them.

'Where's Ben?' Jess asked.

'In the next room along, fast asleep. They knocked him out with their disgusting drugs. As soon as they let me off these blasted drips I'll be in there myself.'

Jess and Freddie left the adults to it and went to see their cousin.

His eyes were closed, his blond hair ruffled, his face pale against the pillow.

'He looks so peaceful, doesn't he?' Jess said.

'He won't be in a minute,' replied her brother. He strode forward and shook his cousin's shoulder. 'Come on, Pain In the Backside, wake up! We've come to rescue you!'

Ben gasped and sat up. Eyes wide, he asked, 'Where's Mum?'

'Next door. She's with Mum and Dad,' Freddie added, deterring Ben from his initial impulse of joining her. He didn't need a lecture on quarks and quasars right now. He'd wait until Uncle Henry had left.

'How's she doing?'

'She's okay, Ben. Not so good yet, but quickly getting better. And you saved her!'

'Well not really. It wasn't 993, it was knock-out drops.'

'In both syringes?'

'I don't know. In mine it was.'

'But probably not in hers. So you saved her.'

'Nixon or Marcus must have mixed up the syringes,' Freddie said.

'Or I'd be dead.'

'Well, we're very glad you're not,' Jess said. 'Sit up so I can hug you.'

Ben did so, holding his arms out. Jess hesitated, perhaps because he had no top on. 'Come on! It's thanks to you and Freddie that they rescued Mum.' Poor Jess was blushing. 'You've been amazing this past week,' he said, cuddling her. 'A total star.'

'You're a hero.'

'Oooooh he's your hero, is he, Jess?'

'Not just mine, everybody's,' Jess bit back, detaching herself quickly. 'Greater love hath no man than this, that a man lay down his life for his friends.'

'Jess! That's from the Bible!' Freddie said, horrified.

'It's from school. It's our Doxology.'

'A what? Oh never mind,' Ben quickly added.

'If Dad knew they were teaching you the Bible he'd have you out quicker than a rotten tooth.'

'I don't believe it. It's just a collection of fantasies and fables.'

'What about Marcus?' Ben asked, to divert Freddie from trying to get Jess pulled out of the school she so adored.

'I know, the Judas,' Jess said.

'Really? I think he's more like Ben than a Judas. Or rather Ben's like him,' said Freddie.

'*What*?' Ben exclaimed, offended to the core.

'He's tall and muscly. So are you. He's blond. So are you. He has blue eyes. So have you.'

'So do loads of people.'

'Yes, but loads of people weren't dating your mum fourteen years ago, were they?'

'Don't you dare say he's my dad!'

'I'm just amused. You set out to find one parent, but I think you've found two.'

'Shut your stupid mouth!'

'Ben, Freddie, stop it. You're alive, your mum's alive and we're all going to have a lovely night. We're staying in Oxford's finest hotel, Ben.'

'How come?' It would be way too expensive for Mum, but as for Uncle Henry – he might die of shock. 'Your dad doesn't know, does he?'

'He's not paying. Ballantyne is.'

'*Ballantyne*?'

'It's on SPC. He's not paying himself,' Freddie said.

'*Why*?'

'He feels it's SPC's fault we got involved. And it was. It was through your mum finding out about 993 at work. Told you it was 993,' Freddie gloated.

'Yes, but it was Jess who thought Pete was Nixon. You were right.'

'Female intuition,' she said, smiling. 'You were so *brave*. You sacrificed your life to save your mum.'

'Anyone would have done it.'

'Not anyone. Only very, very brave altruists.'

'What are −? Oh, never mind. Anyway I don't want to stay in a hotel tonight. I want to go home.'

'Home is where the heart is.'

'Family's where the heart is, not home. I know that now. I'd live anywhere with Mum, She's what makes it home.'

'I'm just glad you're both alive.'

'So am I,' Ben agreed. Alive had never felt so good.

THE END